A SUPERIOR MYSTERY

A SUPERIOR MYSTERY

by

Carl Brookins

DEDICATION

Jeanie, editor, wife, friend.

Author's Notes and Acknowledgments

None of the people in this story are people you know, or think you know. This is a work of fiction. There may, however, appear to be similarities to people you do know. That is inevitable. I have tried to represent relevant parts of the region around Chequamegon Bay accurately, particularly the physical setting of the bay, and the towns of Ashland, Bayfield and Washburn. That includes the museums, the galleries, streets and buildings, and the marinas and restaurants.

Everyone in this part of Northern Wisconsin in the various agencies, including the National Park Service and U.S. Coast Guard, were unfailingly cooperative. Scott Mitchen and the people of Timeless Timber were most generous and open with their time and information, for which I thank them. Many others' research and writing about the region were of great help. I want to particularly note the work of Mary T. Bell, *Cutting Across Time* and *Cutting The White Pine*; Guy Burnham, *The Lake Superior Country*; Tom Hollatz, *Gangster Holiday*; Agnes Larson, *History of the White Pine*; J. E. Nelligan, *White Pine Empire;* M. Swanholm, *Lumbering in Minnesota;* Tony Woiak, *B BOOK I, Beer Bottles, Brawls, Boards, Brothels, Bibles, Battles and Brownstone;* and Walker Wyman, *The Lumberjack Tales from Louie Blanchard.*

One could not ask for a finer publisher in Bill Manchee, nor a more patient, good-humored editor than Lisa Korth.

I also offer heartfelt thanks to Julie Faschiana, Scott Haartman, Michael Kac, Kent Krueger, Jean Paul, Charlie Rethwisch, Susan Runholt, Tim Springfield, Monica Ferris, and Anne Webb, members of Creme de la Crime for their persistent careful input.

Lastly, I owe more than I can express to the finest gang of touring authors one could possibly fall in with: Deborah Woodworth, Kent Krueger, and Ellen Hart, the Minnesota Crime Wave.

A SUPERIOR MYSTERY

A Top Publications Paperback

First Edition
12221 Merit Drive, Suite 750
Dallas, Texas 75251

ISBN#: 1-929976-17-8
Library of Congress 2002112847

The characters and events in this novel are fictional and created out of the imagination of the author. Certain real locations and institutions are mentioned, but the characters and events depicted are entirely fictional.

Printed in the United States of America

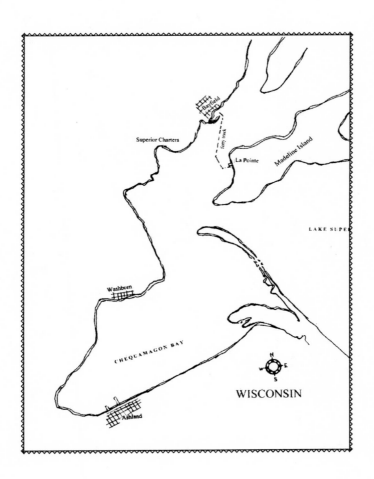

PROLOGUE

Sparks flew into the dark sky from the fat black stack and died in the night, as an unseen hand shoveled more coal into the firebox. The thrashing propeller and the chuffing of the steam engine concealed the increasing sounds of the lake, of waves sloshing higher against the low-riding sides of the cumbersome raft. The wind had come up, just a little more, as they passed Houghton Point. Jarl "call me Jack" Rylston didn't like the uncertain feel of it, but it didn't mean a whole lot, far as he knew. The wind had shifted and now blew more strongly out of the northeast, he knew. It blew directly into the open mouth of the long bay called Chaquamegon, pronounced Shwamagun. *In his three winters late in the 1890s working in the big woods of northern Wisconsin, Rylston had learned little about the weather on the big lake. True, he'd frequently heard men in camp talking about it, about the sudden storms the big lake brewed up. There were stories about boats that foundered in the steep waves, about the men lost, their bodies gone forever in the deep cold lake. Superior, the biggest lake in the country, they said. The fishermen who told those tales wrestled out a different sort of living in the summer months and only went into the woods when the heavy snow came and the big lake froze.*

This wind out of the northeast had that raw, reckless feel of a coming storm. If it had been full winter, he'd expect snow by morning. If it was still full winter, this way of getting out of the woods would not have been possible. The water would have been frozen as far as one could see and no boats would have been on the move. Even so, the cold dark waters made him uneasy. But hiding in Bayfield was no longer something he could abide. Some of the men in the bars where he had been spending too much time after he slipped out of the Wisconsin woods early were giving him the evil eye.

Rylston shifted on the log. He was not used to the surging, moving platform under him. He had never been a river pig, riding the roaring spring drives of winter-cut timber down the snow-melt-swollen streams to the gathering places, the mills farther south in Wisconsin, or to the shore of the lake to wait for the rafting tugs. He was a teamster. His job was to drive the team of big Belgians with their towering loads of heavy logs down the icy trails and back-country roads to the river banks. What he knew about the lake was almost nothing. It was too cold to swim in, too far to see across, and dangerous, regardless of the time of year. He set his boots more firmly on the big oak log and hunched over, cold, horny, hands gripping the long pike pole to steady himself. Somewhere he had lost his heavy mitts, probably in the saloon he'd left so precipitously. When he clenched his left fist, the back of his hand tingled and he could feel the scab from the knife wound grab at the skin. The wound had opened again and there was a warm wetness on his skin. He adjusted his balance on the restless logs under his feet. A single slip in the dark would be his last. He could suffer a smashed leg or worse between the big rough timbers. There was a bite to the air and Rylston used one hand to pull his sheepskin coat more tightly around his wiry body.

Loggers did not ride the big rafts across the lake, although tugboat captains sometimes hired a man to ride at the back of the boat and keep a weather eye on the timber they were dragging through the water. Fortunately for Rylston, this one had no boom watcher. Normally, they did not haul logs into the bay at night, either. But spring had been long in coming this year. The ice went out late and then storms on Lake Superior had kept the boats in their slips while the winter cut waited in the bays and at the stream mouths along the lake. Now, the Ashland mills that lined the shore at the foot of the bay were getting low on timber. If hauling logs across Lake Superior was risky, riding a boom at night was more so, even during the calmest of times. Rylston knew he had to get away, out of Bayfield, out of timber country. An acquaintance in town was found to ferry him out to the boom as it eased on by the little harbor at Bayfield. It had cost him and he had tipped the boy one of his last quarters. He could never risk slipping back to the camp to collect the wages owed him; nor dared he try to make it on foot the thirty miles to the railhead at Ashland. The last snowfall had made overland travel near impossible. That preacher, Ames was his name, had told how tough it was to travel from camp to camp when the heavy spring snows fell. The few roads around the lake were no better. A ride across the bay was the quickest and the best way to slip town, long as the ice was out. He would grab a freight train and be heading south to lose himself in Milwaukee or Chicago before they knew he was gone.

The wind freshened and the white and yellow pine and hemlock moved even more restlessly under their heavy load of hardwoods. The huge chained logs that formed the outside floating fences smacked together and began to surge against the insistent pull of the steamer. It would take little for the whole thing to come apart. Rylston had heard of it—timber loose and washing up days and weeks later on the shore of the bay to be scavenged by settlers. He thought about moving farther back so if anything happened he would be closer to open water. Then he remembered how cold the water was and shrugged. There was no place to go now except down the bay. Above him, the featureless black sky, full of thick clouds, looked down uncaringly.

The waves and the wind rose quickly after that and the logs began to bound through the water, struggling against the confinement of the perimeter chains. The noise grew louder. Rylston thought he heard the sound of timbers sundering, and glanced over his left shoulder. He did not hear the snapping sound of a faulty link in the tow chain that parted somewhere toward the back when the boom started to break apart and logs to pile up. Nor did he hear the explosion that sent a .44 caliber lead slug into the back of his head and blew away his life.

Chapter 1

The royal-blue hulled Tartan, its colorful red and yellow striped spinnaker in full bloom, charged through the water. Billowing curls of white foam creamed away from her bow. The noise of wind and water was terrific, exhilarating. The big lightweight sail sagged slightly then filled again with a crack as Mary Whitney tugged at the wheel and trimmed the Tartan's course.

"Downwind mark in two minutes," called Phillipa Trent, one of the three teenaged crew members aboard the sloop captained by Mary Whitney. She shifted her feet at the wheel to a wider stance and glanced around. She'd just confirmed in her own mind that her sloop, *Sea Queen* was in a favored position among their group to take a direct line to the mark. What worried her were the slightly smaller boats they were overhauling at this critical time in the race. There were only two larger boats with a chance to catch them before they made the upwind mark. Unlike America's Cup racing, where two almost perfectly matched sailing machines duked it out in a series of races, club racing pitted boats of various sizes, carrying crews with widely differing experience, against each other in what sometimes looked like a free-for-all, especially when rounding the floating buoys that marked the end of each leg of their triangular course on the choppy waters of Puget Sound.

Mary knew they would have to drop their spinnaker, raise the genoa and make a 70-degree course change, all while keeping an eye on the boats around them where similar activities were happening. Mary and her crew would try to make the turn as neatly as possible and as close to the mark as they could safely manage, attempting to save even a few seconds. Races were often won or lost at the turns. She had to take every possible advantage, since most of the boats in this race were faster and her crew of three teenagers was not experienced in handling a sailboat in race competition. The *Sea Queen* was not designed nor fitted out as a racing boat. She was an elegant, comfortable, cruising sloop, but Mary and her husband, Michael Tanner, enjoyed the occasional visceral charge of competitive sailing on Puget Sound. Tanner would have been aboard today had not a last-minute emergency at the office called him away.

Mary's crew this windy Saturday afternoon was made up of young but avid sailors happy to gain racing experience. Watching them scramble over the deck and enthusiastically bend to their duties, a wistful expression sometimes flitted over Mary's face, remembering years past when she was that young and that agile.

Lacking competitive speed, Tanner and Mary Whitney had to rely on their sailing skills and careful analysis of the course and the interplay of wind and current, along with the occasional happy guess, to gain whatever advantage they could. Once again, Mary's reading of the conditions of the course, and the agility of the three monkeys crewing for her had kept them just barely ahead of most of the pack. Mary felt the Tartan slow just slightly. At that moment, Dale Barstowe, the gangly sixteen-year-old son of one of Tanner's partners, pointed astern and called a heads-up to Mary. The overtaking boat was supposed to stay well clear, but sometimes in their enthusiasm to get round the mark as smartly as possible, enthusiasm overruled prudence. Perceived violations of rules usually occurred at the marker buoys.

The larger Hunter stole some of the Tartan's wind as it thrashed by on the right and Mary glanced across. The Hunter's crew was poised and ready for the coming course change. She could almost feel the tension radiating from their deck. The graceful sloop's mast seemed to vibrate in the rising wind.

"Carrying a lot of sail, isn't she?" said Dale, turning and bending to the winch and line he would use to control the jib when they came about.

"Get ready," called Mary to Phillipa and her cousin Jerilynn. The two girls crouched on the foredeck, ready to spring into action.

"Hey!" shouted Phil. The Hunter had altered course to run directly ahead and was crossing *Sea Queen's* bow too closely. A warning horn sounded from the nearby race committee boat and a violation flag went up.

Mary luffed up to be sure they'd clear the stern of the Hunter, collapsing the lightweight spinnaker early, and made her turn a little wider of the mark than she'd intended. While the two girls hauled in the spinnaker and smartly raised the genoa, Mary spared a glance for the scene; spread before them shining jewel in the afternoon, the city of Seattle. Its skyscrapers and spires stood bright against the muted green foothills of the magnificent Wenatchee Mountains that rose in the background. The sun flashed off the shiny top of the tall, slender Space Needle. Her blood sang. She loved her home, Seattle, and on days like this, the surge of the waves and the tang of the salt air with the sun warm on her cheek were the nearest things to paradise she knew she'd ever have. If only

Michael were here now with her on the deck.

Ahead and to their right, the Hunter that had just passed them at the mark tacked to avoid another boat. The Hunter's new course again brought the boat directly across *Sea Queen's* bow, again too close for Mary's peace of mind.

"Hang on," she called. She glanced left and right to be sure the way was clear. Winning wasn't so important to her that she wouldn't luff again to clear the danger ahead. At that instant there was a report like a gunshot. The four aboard *Spindrift* looked up in consternation to see the Hunter's genoa disintegrating and her main sail beginning to stall. Mary slammed the wheel hard to the right, desperately trying to avoid a collision, but it was too late. Closed in by a smaller boat on her port side, she had no choice but to attempt a hard right turn. The stern of the Hunter, now almost dead in the water, was far too close.

Mary felt the contact through the soles of her feet. The abrupt collision jammed Mary none too gently against the big destroyer-style wheel. Her stomach knotted and she felt the pain of her beloved Tartan. Chunks of wooden toerail and jagged pieces of white fiberglass exploded into the air as the *Spindrift* slammed her bow into the stern of the Hunter. Had the disintegration of the Hunter's genoa not slowed her, the leading boat might just have made its crossing of *Spindrift's* bow. As it was, even Mary's lightning reaction couldn't steer *Sea Queen* out of danger. Technically, she was in error, since the rules call for the following boat to stay clear, but that was a problem she'd deal with later.

"Are you guys all right?" Mary called.

Dale Barstowe, still clinging to the winch drum in a white-knuckled death grip, said in a shaky voice, "It looks like they just fell down on deck. Nobody went overboard. Are we gonna sink?"

"Not likely. Those fools aboard the Hunter are probably in more trouble than we are. Drat! Go forward and help the girls if they need it. And let's get those sails down."

While Mary loosed rattling lines and secured the boom, Dale scrambled forward and the three teens dropped the sails and began to tidy up, amid awed glances at the damage to the two boats. Motor launches carrying spectators and the race committee boat clustered around. With a glance at the people on the Hunter, none of whom she recognized, Mary dropped down the hatch and went forward. There was a jagged hole in the deck that let in a lot of light but only a little sea water when waves slapped against the hull. The immediate problem, she saw, was that the anchor block holding the forestay to the hull might be in danger of tearing free. That could instantly transform the steel cable into a lethal weapon. She hurried back to the cockpit where she fitted the specially designed wrench to the backstay turnbuckle and quickly slacked off the tension on the mast and then on the rest of the standing rigging.

While she showed her crew how to rig a towing bridle, Mary heard in the distance the boom of the cannon signaling the end of the last race of the day.

* * *

The finely tuned engine of the silver Porsche whined up the scale as Tanner shifted down, rounding a tight corner. His feet danced on the pedals.

The telephone call that had sent him flying out of his office at Tanner & Associates had been frustratingly cryptic. There'd been an accident on the race course and

Spindrift was damaged. The captain, Mary Whitney, and her three crew members, had all been taken to Harborview Hospital's emergency room. Sharply questioned, the caller was unable to supply any additional information.

Tanner, his stomach churning and his pulse elevated, had dropped the telephone and run out of the office. As he neared the hospital, a looming sense of dread rose choking in his throat. He'd lost his beloved first wife, Elizabeth, in a deadly and murderous boating collision. Now this. It was too much to bear. He pounded the steering wheel in impatient frustration and snarled silently at a slow-moving truck that briefly barred his path. Then he was parked and out of the car, racing across the hospital lot to the emergency room entrance.

Tanner banged through the double swinging doors to the ER as if they weren't there and headed for the pretty woman at the reception desk. As he crossed the polished tiled space between the doors and the desk, a tall, auburn-haired woman in white shorts, blue tennies, and a tan windbreaker with a dark-gray sling cradling her right arm, appeared coming from the ward.

"Mary! My God, are you all right?" Tanner skidded to a stop in front of her. He drew two deep, calming breaths. Then he gently placed his arms around her and drew her close. "I was so frightened when I got the call."

"I'm okay, sweetie, I'm fine." She bussed Tanner on the cheek and patted his shoulder. In spite of her irritation at the incident that had brought her to the hospital, she was comforted by Tanner's presence.

"What about Phil and Jerilynn? Dale? I didn't get any details, just that there'd been an accident during the race. What happened?"

"They've been checked out by the doctor and gone home already. Aside from a few bumps and bruises, we're all okay. This sling is just a comfort thing for a day or two. Can we get out of here?"

While Tanner drove them home to their northside apartment overlooking Seattle and Puget Sound, Mary described the collision.

Tanner listened without asking any questions.

Mary concluded with, "It was terrible, Michael. The feeling in the pit of my stomach, hearing those crunching sounds and seeing pieces of fiberglass and teak flying around. Well, you know what I mean."

Tanner knew all too well. He'd narrowly escaped death from the ramming of his chartered sailboat almost three years earlier, the incident in which his first wife and her friend, Alice, had drowned.

"The wheel knocked some of the breath out of me and when I looked around, both of the girls were out of sight. One minute they were there on the foredeck, dealing with the spinnaker, but when I looked for them after we hit that Hunter they were just gone." She shook her head slowly. "They'd just fallen down on the deck and got some killer bruises, but that's about all. Jerilynn banged her knee, but there's nothing broken, thankfully. The doctor said they'll both be sore for a few days and black and blue for a while longer."

Tanner smiled. "Probably the last time either of those girls will be allowed to race with us again. How's the *Spindrift?*"

Mary's smile disappeared. "Not good. Looks like there's major structural damage at the bow. We took on a lot of water when they towed us in. At least we didn't lose the mast."

"How's the other boat?"

Mary turned her face to Tanner and there was an icy look in her eyes. Her voice was a little south of cool when she responded, "I never asked."

Tanner sighed. "It looks like we're not going to get much sailing in this year. Well, I'm sure we'll find some way to pass the time."

Chapter 2

"What's the verdict on *Spindrift?*" Mary Whitney turned to watch her husband, one of Seattle's most successful public relations and advertising executives, come through the door of their spacious apartment. He seems to be running a lot these days, she thought.

"Not so good," Tanner said, coming across the living room and dropping his briefcase and jacket on the couch. Without breaking stride, he swept her into a tight embrace that carried them across the big living room and onto another couch that faced the panoramic windows. Their view of Puget Sound from their sixteenth floor apartment on the north side of Seattle was magnificent on this rare sunny afternoon. But neither Michael nor Mary, dubbed the M & Ms by some of their close friends, was paying attention. They were too engaged in kissing and caressing each other.

"C'mon, Michael, tell me," breathed Mary, pulling her head back a few millimeters. One hand was crawling north on Tanner's thigh while her elbows briskly fended off Tanner's probing fingers that had already found their way under her sweater and were reaching for her breasts.

"Who cares about some old piece of fiberglass? This is much more interesting."

"Listen, buster! The *Spindrift* is not some old piece of fiberglass, as you inelegantly put it." She moved her head aside, avoiding his questing lips.

Tanner dropped his face to Mary's bosom when he couldn't reach her mouth. "Hey!" He flinched. Her fingers had reached their goal and squeezed him hard enough to get his full attention. "Okay, okay. I give." Tanner laughed and slid his hands out from under Mary's sweater. He leaned back against the pillows.

"Stay on the point," she said, squeezing him again but more gently. "What's the verdict on *Sea Queen?*"

A week after the damaging mid-course collision, Mary Whitney had decided her boat yard should do a complete survey, not just repair the jagged hole ripped into the yacht's starboard hull. They were going to have to replace the damaged railings around the bow and a bent forestay collar as well. She figured they might as well do a complete job and repair or replace other worn and damaged gear since the insurance carried by the Hunter's owner would cover the most serious expenses. But even if all went smoothly the repairs would take several weeks. If replacement parts were difficult to obtain, the Tartan could be laid up for months. Mary frequently consulted with Tanner on affairs of the *Sea Queen*. Tanner always deferred to her decisions in matters concerning the sloop. Mary had talked several times with the yard people regarding repairs to her beloved Tartan, but Tanner had been in the neighborhood this time when the preliminary analysis was ready so he brought home the survey.

He reached for his soft leather carrying case and from it drew a thick sheaf of papers. "There appear to be stress fractures in several places on the hull and it looks like there's some deck delamination in a few spots. Also, the deck could stand stripping and refinishing. Stefan thinks some of the hull plates where the standing rigging is attached should be replaced as well. He's already been on the phone with Tartan and they're sending an engineer out to take a look."

"Sounds like a complete refit, doesn't it? That's going to cost a small fortune. How long before we can put her back in the water?"

"Stefan thinks it'll be several months. Winter, maybe, before we can even do some trial runs and retune the rigging. One of Stefan's people wondered if you'd like to sell her and buy a new boat."

"And you said . . ." frowned Mary.

Tanner smiled and gave her nose a quick tongue-kiss. "I said the only way Mary Whitney would ever buy a boat to replace the *Sea Queen* was if she sank in forty fathoms and no one was willing to even attempt to raise her."

"Exactly right. Uncle Matt and Gramps picked out that boat for me and even if it is out of style, I want to sail her as long as possible." What Tanner also knew was that Mary had made an almost mystical connection with the *Sea Queen* the instant she first saw her.

"It does raise the question of what do we do for a sailboat this year. Stefan knows about a big ketch that we could look at. He heard it's up for lease or sale. Of course, we could just stay ashore this summer." Tanner grinned when he said the words, predicting his wife's reaction.

"Pooh, I don't think we want a ketch, but I'll find something we can use while *Sea Queen* is laid up. Right now, dinner awaits." Mary scrambled away after another kiss and tugged Tanner to the dining room.

After dinner, Tanner and Mary Whitney relaxed, each with a small balloon of brandy in hand, and watched the evening darkness gather in the hollows and valleys of Seattle. Behind them, a Mozart symphony played softly on the stereo. Lights appeared in the communities across Puget Sound and below them in Seattle proper. Running lights on seagoing ships slid by as marine traffic approached or departed the busy port. Some shipping would continue up the coast, through the San Juan Islands. It might follow the Inside Passage all the way to Alaskan ports. Other freighters would turn west, through the strait of Juan de Fuca and into the Pacific Ocean.

"Mary, doesn't your family have some ties in the Upper Midwest?"

"Yes, my Great-Great-Grandpa was a contemporary of that railroad builder James Hill, and of course he dealt with the Weyerhaeusers and other logging companies. What's up?"

"We've had an inquiry from a lumber company somewhere in Wisconsin, and I just wondered if there might be a Whitney connection."

"Where in Wisconsin?"

"Ashland, I think. Do you know where that is?"

"Nope, can't say that I do. Don't your people at the agency look up such things for you?"

"I didn't ask them to. I didn't get around to reading the mail until late and anyway, it probably isn't something we'll be interested in doing. I didn't recognize the company name, so I doubt they're very big. I can't imagine why they'd want a firm like ours way out here in Seattle to represent them."

"What do they want you to do?" Mary rose and went to a small bookcase in the corner of the living room. She pulled a world atlas off the shelf and began to page through it.

"Put together a promotional and advertising campaign. Maybe they're an old company starting a new venture."

"What's the company name?"

"Hmm. It starts with 'C', I think. I really don't

recall."

"Could it be a Ch?"

"I don't—what's your interest? We'll probably turn 'em down anyway."   Tanner sat up straight. "Actually, I think you're right. C-H, maybe it sounds like Chuck something. I remember thinking it might be an Indian word."

Mary looked up at him off the page and smiled sweetly. "Chequamegon. Native American word."

Mary went to where Tanner was sitting, carrying the big atlas in her arms.

"That's it, Chaquamegon."   Tanner nodded and pronounced the word.

"Here," said Mary, placing the atlas on Tanner's lap and pointing. "Here's the city of Ashland, Wisconsin. See this bay?   It's part of Lake Superior.   It's called Chaquamegon Bay and here's a national forest in northern Wisconsin with the same name."

"I'll be darned. How'd you find it so fast?"

Mary smiled at her husband, and tapped her temple. "Lots of lumbering around that bay a hundred years ago. The Whitneys had some interests out there."

"I get it.   What I don't get is why this little lumbering concern in Wisconsin wrote to me."

"Well, sailor, I don't read minds, so I haven't a clue. But I bet you'll find out before too long."

Chapter 3

The next day Tanner sat at his big polished wooden desk gazing with something less than fondness on several untidy piles of folders and documents. His telephone buzzed discreetly and when he picked up the receiver, his private secretary and assistant, Marie Clark, said, "There's a call for you on three. I think you'll want to take this one."

"Why?"

"Trust me, boss."

Tanner grinned at the telephone and pressed the appropriate button. The connection wasn't a good one and the line crackled. "Michael Tanner here," he said in a neutral voice.

"Mr. Tanner, good of you to take my call. I guess you're pretty busy out there and I won't take up much of your time right now. We've never laid eyes on each other, sir, but I feel as if I know you pretty good. Yessir, I do, I do. And I'm looking forward to seeing you in the flesh one day real soon."

"Are you, indeed? Perhaps you'd better start at the beginning, Mr. . . . ."

"Oh, sure, sorry about that. You're a busy man, no doubt, no doubt. I shouldn't have assumed you'd recognize my name. It's Anderson, George Charles Anderson, Mr. Tanner. I'm the one wrote you that letter about a little recovery project we've got going up here in Wisconsin?"

"Excuse me, I don't..."

Anderson rolled cheerfully along. "Well, I wrote that letter, but I figured, there's always the chance you'll be too busy to really take much notice, my company being all the way out here in Wisconsin. So I decided to follow up with a call after you'd had a chance to consider my offer."

"Mr. Anderson, I'm afraid I haven't seen your letter. If you'll tell me what this is all about, perhaps we can come to some understanding here." Tanner was beginning to feel as if he and Anderson were speaking separate languages.

"Yep. Sure. Like I explained in my letter, I'm the president of Chequamegon Resource Recovery Company, and we're taking a real careful look at Lake Superior up here. 'Specially around Ashland and some other places along the shore of the big lake. Naturally, I'm not at liberty to disclose exactly where those places are, you understand, I'm sure. Business confidentiality and all that," he said.

Tanner took a breath and started to say something, but it was like trying to interrupt the tide. Anderson went right on talking.

"We know there's a huge volume of sunken logs up here, sitting on the bottom of Superior. And with the concerns the Sierra Club and some of those other environmentalists have about cutting old growth timber, well, we just thought what if we could recover some of the lumber from the lake bottom? Why, a whole lot of the stuff they cut back in my great granddaddy's day never made it to the mills, you know? They lost it to the lake. And because the lake's so cold and all, that timber is just sittin' down there pretty well preserved. Why, d'you have any idea what some of those old timbers here are like? Sixty, seventy-foot hardwoods trunks, straight as an arrow? Hardly a knot in 'em. And tight? Real tight growth rings 'cause they grew so slow. That's old growth timber down there Mr. Tanner, and it's worth a lot of money. See, Mr. Tanner, one of the mills, I think it was the Schroeder mill, here in Ashland, recovered a bunch of logs back in the twenties, so we know it's feasible. And with today's market, and ecological concerns, and all, I think we got a pretty good thing here."

Tanner looked up to see one of his partners, Perry Barstowe, and Marie Clark standing side by side in the doorway, smiling at him. After her dose of Mr. George Charles Anderson, she must have mentioned him to Perry. Now they were both watching to see how Tanner was handling the flood of words. He crossed his eyes at them and waved them away. Anderson ran out of steam at that moment, or maybe just breath, Tanner thought, and he jumped in. "Let me ask you something, Mr. Anderson."

"Oh, sure, but call me George. I figure we're going to be on a first name basis right quick."

"One of the first things that occurs to me is this. Won't all that wood be rotten after so many years in the water?"

Anderson laughed. "That's what everybody thinks, but they're wrong. If the wood is always immersed in water, it's actually preserved. Why, we've made some incredible finds. And let me tell you, some of this stuff is rarer than hens' teeth. You'll get the answers you want when you get here to Ashland."

"This is all fascinating information, about the timber I mean, but I don't quite see what it has to do with us. With Tanner and Associates. Perhaps you can be a bit more specific."

There was a pause, as if George Anderson was changing direction. Tanner had a vision of a big locomotive on a turntable ponderously shifting to a new track, steam and smoke billowing out in several directions. The engine chuffed and Anderson started to speak again.

"Well, Mr. Tanner, it's like this. We think we've got the state and the locals pretty well behind this operation, finally. Ashland could sure use some new industry, new jobs up here. I figure to harvest a whole lot of old growth lumber from the bottom of that big puddle and turn it into high grade veneers and furniture and such-like. We're getting some good press, but I want to avoid delays and I don't want to run afoul of the historians and some splinter save-the-snail-darter-group, you take my meaning? Plus, we need to generate some serious interest in the products we're starting to turn out. So I figure we need a cracker-jack PR firm like yours, Mr. Tanner, to help us out. I figure at least a five year contract ought to be about right. Why, shoot, Mr. Tanner, you come out here, you'll see some beautiful country, and we've got this great big lake you can sail on."

"Sail on. What are you..." Tanner opened his mouth to interrupt the flow of words. Alarm bells were ringing. This Anderson knew entirely too much about him. Then Tanner had another thought and closed his mouth. He'd learn more by keeping his mouth shut.

"Why sure, I know you and that pretty wife of yours like to sail. We have a lot of sailboats not twenty miles up the shore from Ashland, and I'm sure we can find some nice accommodations. Fact is, if I lean over right now and look out my window, I can see several sails out there on the bay. Pretty as a picture, you bet. The two of you come out here, you could have kind of a sailing vacation at the same time you make this business trip. Have you and the missus ever been on this lake?"

Tanner was smiling at the man's outpouring, somewhat, but not entirely, disarmed. Anderson rolled on. "After that we'll either be in business or outta business."

"No, Mr. Anderson, we've never sailed on Lake Superior. Look, I'm sure there are some very good public relations firms in the Twin Cities. Tanner and Associates just doesn't do much business outside the West Coast."

"Always a first time, you know?" Anderson responded.

"And I'm not sure we're entirely on the same side. My partners and I—"

"Barstowe and Christian, right?" Anderson interrupted.

Tanner looked at the phone in surprise, then said, "We have problems with some of the clear-cutting policies being used here in Washington and in Canada, sir, and ..."

"I don't see that as a problem. We're not in the logging business, you understand? In fact this recovery project is a way to alleviate some of that stuff. Besides, since you're married to the Whitneys, I expect if you ask your wife, you'll learn they're more than casually interested in our little project here."

"Excuse me?"

"Why sure. I didn't just pick your name out of a hat, you know. What kinda operation do you think I'm running here?" Tanner heard a chuckle over the line. "I checked you out pretty good before I wrote. Now listen, Mr. Tanner, I can tell you're interested and I know this'll be a good fit. But I understand you need to check some things before you make a commitment. You do that, check us out an' all. But don't be too long. I need you on board before the summer gets much older. I'll expect to hear from you very soon, Mr. Tanner. You have a nice day now." The connection clicked in Tanner's ear and Anderson hung up.

Tanner was left with an odd mixture of feelings. He gently placed the receiver in its cradle, thinking hard.

George Anderson was either more or less than he appeared. But which was it?

* * *

By the middle of the afternoon a slim file marked CRR appeared on his desk from Research. The first page was a brief biography of the principal founder of the company, George Charles Anderson. He had a board, one of whom, Theodore Schroeder, was identified as the attorney of the company. The company had several investors, all of whom were identified as board members. They had filed incorporation papers in Madison, Wisconsin, three years earlier. CRR was incorporated at five million dollars as a privately held corporation located in Ashland, Wisconsin. The vice president and corporate secretary was a woman named Jeri Reif with a Bayfield, Wisconsin, address. Tanner knew from his examination of the map that Bayfield was a small town across Chaquamegon Bay from Ashland.

Additional research revealed that Anderson had a short history of company startups which had then been sold to larger, wealthier companies. Neither Anderson, Schroeder, nor Ms. Reif appeared to have sufficient funds to bankroll CRR to the tune of five million. A scribbled marginal note suggested that the other investors, all together, couldn't raise that much capital. There must be other investors who were not board members. Since no public solicitation of funds or sale of stock was indicated, Tanner knew there was a lot of financial information which did not have to be revealed.

Tanner thought about what he had learned. On the face of it, he could see no compelling reason to take on CRR, except for the intriguing phone call from Anderson. He called in Marie, who smiled and said, "After I talked with Perry, he started an office pool about whether we take the job or not."

Tanner said, "You won't find out today. But let's start a file on this company and keep Research running down any remaining leads they may have." Then he sat back to think about his conversation with the CEO of CRR, a man who came on like an unsophisticated country boy, but one who used words like "alleviate" and spoke mostly in complete sentences. Maybe it was just his way, but maybe it was some kind of act. Either way there was definitely something out of the ordinary there. And then there was all that personal detail Anderson had.

Chapter 4

"I do not like it, *Mister* Tanner. I didn't like it when you first told me about your conversation with this George Anderson, and the longer I think about him and about that Ashland project, the less I like it."

It was Sunday morning, two days after George Anderson's locomotive-like conversation with Tanner.

"I don't disagree, but face it, neither of us is exactly a low-profile nonentity." Tanner and Mary Whitney were indulging one of their favorite weekly activities, spending Sunday morning in bed with the *Seattle Post-Intelligencer* and the *New York Sunday Times*. Across the room, a thirty-inch television muttered along, displaying a segment of CBS's *Sunday Morning*, the sound turned to a low background level.

"Now what are you frowning at?"

"Hmmm?" said Mary and raised her eyes over the edge of the *Times* to regard her husband. When she did so, the frown lines between her eyes smoothed out. "Oh, just a mention of my ex here."

"Edwin Tobias III made the papers?"

"Yes. The SEC is looking into one of ET's stock sales." She folded the business section and looked at her husband, who was gazing calmly at her.

"I've never told you much about my ex-husband, have I?"

"No, other than to point out that while he is your

first husband, giving him, and me, a number could imply there might be a string of others." Tanner smiled when Mary stuck out her tongue.

"One day, my love, I'll tell you the sad and bitter story of my failed marriage. To get back to the subject at hand, it still seems strange that this Anderson would know so much about me. Why does he care? I don't have anything to do with your agency business. Gives me the creeps."

Tanner nodded and rubbed one bare foot against Mary's equally bare calf beside him under the duvet. "I agree with that. This George Anderson had an odd habit of sliding between country cousin speech patterns and fairly precise language. His presentation wavered between sloppy and hard-edged."

"Presentation. You did say presentation."

Tanner nodded and continued his calf rubbing. "Or performance if you like. A perfectly adequate, clear and concise business letter. But on the telephone, he was sort of a hale fellow, at least some of the time. He rattled on a good deal. Maybe he was nervous, although why that would be I haven't a clue."

"Performance, presentation. Good choices, I bet, even though I haven't heard this Anderson person. Stop for a moment, you're distracting me." Mary slid her leg out of reach of Tanner's foot. "So you think this Anderson was giving a creepy performance on the telephone in order to— to what?"

"Another good question. I've been running that call through my mind ever since we spoke. I'm beginning to think the whole thing is a calculated effort to interest me in going out to Ashland and meeting with their principals."

"It sounds like this George Anderson has succeeded." Mary smiled and picked up the book review section of the paper.

"You think so?"

"Yep."

"If you're right, here's why. Anderson has gone to some effort to learn about us. And he's hustling the agency, using the information he's picked up from wherever. Now, apart from your feelings about him, I have to wonder how and why he's doing whatever he's doing. So, I think Chequamegon Resource Recovery bears some investigation. A *quid pro quo*. They investigate us, we investigate them."

"I think we should go out there."

"We?"

Mary nodded and smiled. "I'd like to meet this Wisconsinite who has so much interest in me and in our affairs. Didn't your Mr. Anderson suggest that we could combine business with vacation and try out a new sailing venue if we take CRR into the agency's fold? Sounds like a good deal to me."

"He did."

"All my life I've heard about how the Whitneys and others got started in those big forests along the Canadian border. Let's go see 'em. I can also watch you in action."

Tanner arched his eyebrows. In their year of marriage, Mary Whitney had never before suggested she might be actively interested in his agency's business. She had her own wide array of activities in the Whitney corporation and a variety of civic and charitable organizations of which she was an active board member.

"You just want to go sailing on Lake Superior."

"That too."

* * *

The Northwest Airlines MD-320 touched gently onto the concrete at Twin Cities International Airport and taxied to its assigned gate. Eager passengers already clogged the aisles, hauling belongings from the overhead bins and waiting impatiently to get off as soon as the door was opened. It seemed as if they were trying to flee an unseen presence that had been trapped with them for three hours at 35,000 feet.

The early morning flight had been only partially filled. When Tanner and Mary Whitney exited the plane, they were among the last passengers off the flight. Due to heightened security around the country, no one met them and the concourse was almost empty. There was heavy foot traffic in the baggage claim area. Tanner's glance slid over a man leaning casually on the counter at one of the auto rental booths.

"It's brisk out," said Mary, lowering the window of the white Lexus Tanner had rented.

"May in the Upper Midwest. You want the heater on?"

"Nope. Let's enjoy some untreated Minnesota air for a while."

Tanner piloted the Lexus away from the airport and followed the well-marked highway east toward Interstate 35E. "We have about five hours driving time to get to Bayfield. I've booked us into a lakeside condo there. Bayfield by the Lake."

Mary was looking at the information they'd brought along which included large-scale maps and charts of Bayfield County, Ashland and the Apostle Islands in Wisconsin. "I'm sure the countryside is lovely, but five hours in a car? Tell me again why we didn't fly to Duluth, which is a lot closer. I even bet we could have chartered a private plane to get us to Ashland. There's a small airport marked on the map just south of town."

Tanner glanced over and smiled at her profile. "I guess it's just my suspicious nature. Or maybe your creepy feelings have infected me. With all the background we have on CRR, I still don't have as good a handle on the people there as I'd like, or on the situation. As a private corporation, they don't have to reveal a whole lot. So I thought we'd go in quietly a few days ahead of our scheduled meeting with Anderson and try to pick up some additional background."

"Assess the scene, as it were. Determine who the good guys and the bad guys are."

Tanner nodded. "Assuming there are such distinctions."

* * *

The sun rested atop the forested hills on their left several hours later when Mary swung the Lexus north on Wisconsin Highway 13. After hours of freeway concrete and wide open fields, this two lane macadam road that wound through close-in forests of pine, interspersed with scattered farm buildings and home sites, was a welcome change.

"Ow," commented Mary as the car bounded over another concrete edge on the south side of Washburn. "This city street needs some work. Look how wide this main street is."

"Seems like a waste of real estate."

"Well, when the town was created, one of the principal means of transportation was wagons drawn by teams of horses. Turning them around required sizable open space, hence, wide streets."

Tanner smiled. "Do you know that or is this just

speculation?"

Mary laughed and glanced across her companion toward the lake which was now in view down a long slope between the buildings. "I went to the library. I can do research too, you know. Oh, just look at that water!"

Tanner gazed down at one of many bays along the south shore of Lake Superior, the largest inland lake on the continent. The water was a calm, intense blue. "Turn right somewhere and let's go down to the shore."

Mary's only comment was to raise her eyebrows and make a right turn at the next intersection. Shortly they nosed down the steep shore line until they reached the small marina. Wooden docks and fingers stood mostly empty. A few cradled small sailboats. There was nobody around and no sign of activity in the yard or sheds. Tanner got out of the passenger seat and stretched, eyes fixed on the blue lake that ran all the way to the horizon.

"So that's Lake Superior." He took a small pair of binoculars from the glove box of the Lexus. He scanned the water and what he could see looking southeast. "Ashland must be that smudge on the horizon," he commented.

"Wow," said Mary. "This is Chequamegon Bay you see before us, source of the logs that the recovery company is harvesting."

"Lot of water."

"And this is only a small part of it."

"You want me to drive now?" asked Tanner, replacing the binocs in the glove box.

There was no answer.

Tanner glanced around to see Mary moving slowly away from the car, down the shore. Where they were parked there were no docks, just a gently sloping, coarse sand beach that disappeared under lapping water. She walked toward the lake, head high, eyes apparently fixed on the place where the water met the horizon. Tanner saw her toes touch the water.

"It's very cold." Mary's low voice was almost lost in the space that separated them.

Tanner watched for a moment in silence and then said, "Mary? Are you all right?"

She turned then and gave him her brilliant smile. "Of course, sweetie. I was just listening to the lake." She turned and retraced her footsteps to the car.

"Would you like me to drive?" Tanner asked again.

"Nope. I'm fine. Bayfield is just a few miles up the road."

They swept around a long curve that outlined another small bay and saw through the trees a large marina filled with a forest of bare masts. "Port Superior," said Tanner, checking the road map, and soon the marked entrance appeared beside a branching road into the forest. The outskirts of Bayfield appeared a mile later.

"Fresh lake trout. Yum," said Mary reading the sign on a small store nestled beside the highway.

"Turn right down the hill when you get to Manypenny Lane," said Tanner. "The condo will be a block or two to the right next to the lake. Just go a block past Maggie's, according to my notes."

"Seriously?"

"Seriously."

"Manypenny Lane. I like this town already. What's Maggie's?"

"A popular watering hole and restaurant, I understand."

"Didn't I read about some elegant place called the Rittenhouse, also?"

"Yep. Very upscale, much to my lady's taste, I

suspect. We'll check it out," Tanner smiled.

Moments later, the gray and white-trimmed buildings of the Bayfield by the Lake condo and time-share came into view. Mary parked the car in the lot and she and Tanner went into the office.

When the couple returned to their car, both were smiling.

"How do you like them apples?" said Mary. "Not only is our suite non-smoking as we requested, but it's on the east side with a great view of the harbor and the lake."

"And the islands."

Their suite consisted of a large bedroom in pale blue and gray, equipped with a comfortable king-sized bed, a living room, with a wet bar in one corner and a big picture window that looked northeast over the lake, a big sofa, a desk, some chairs and a fireplace. The bath had a commodious shower and his and her basins.

"Gorgeous view. Now what?" asked Mary.

"I vote we take a walking tour to orient ourselves to Bayfield while there's still some daylight. Tomorrow morning I'd like to drive around Ashland before our 11 o'clock at CRR."

"Michael, I've been thinking. How do you feel about my joining you at that initial meeting with Mr. Anderson?"

Tanner nodded. "Sure. It isn't strictly kosher, but then, neither is George Anderson."

"Good. Thanks. This way, I'll be able to form an independent judgment of the man."

"Plus, my beauty," said Tanner leaning over and kissing Mary's cheek, "I'll be able to draw on that judgment for my own uses. Let's go for a walk."

The sun was still hot, hanging low in an almost clear blue sky, but the air off the big lake cooled things considerably. Mary and Tanner strolled toward the municipal marina, passing two commercial fishing operations perched at the edge of the lake.

"They process lake trout and whitefish," Mary said, consulting her guidebook.

"Here's the Coast Guard station," said Tanner. "I wonder if they get much business?"

A young man in a sharply pressed, deep blue uniform stepped through the door. He nodded and said pleasantly, "Good afternoon." He squinted at the sky and remarked, "I guess I should say good evening."

Tanner introduced Mary and himself, explaining their presence as tourists. "We're from Seattle. We've never sailed in the Apostle Islands. Looking at all the sailboats, it just occurred to me to ask how busy your station is?"

"Summers are our busiest time," Ralph said. "But there aren't many major emergencies. We've had to call in a helicopter to take a heart attack victim off one of the islands, and occasionally a couple of powerboats will collide. But even during the sailboat races, like the Trans-Superior Race, we don't get a lot of action. In the winter we're called on for ice rescues once or twice a year. A good deal of our work involves cooperating with the Park Service. The Apostles are all a federal preserve, you know."

Tanner nodded. He pointed toward the long wood-sided slip just in front of them. "I see you've got just the one inflatable here."

The Coastie nodded. "Ordinarily there'll be one or two others and our forty-one. It's in dry-dock at Duluth right now for a refit. We expect it back any day now."

"What about smugglers?" asked Mary suddenly. "With all that water and the long Canadian coastline, isn't that a problem?"

The man nodded. "I guess I wouldn't call it a big problem, but yeah we see some drug smuggling, and marijuana. On account of it's legal in some parts of Canada, you know."

Tanner and Mary left the Coast Guardsman and crossed the wide paved street. They saw on their right a tree-shaded city park reaching to the water's edge with picnic facilities, a swing and other play areas for children. Straight ahead along the wide pavement were parked cars and trucks, plus a few big motor and sailing boats on cradles and stilts. Some of the boats were still covered with their winter coats of blue plastic sheets. A couple had ladders leaning against their transoms. Yellow or orange power cables hung over the sides and snaked across the pavement to electrical junction boxes. A large man with a gray beard and smudges of gunk on his forearms and nose ambled by, nodded pleasantly, and disappeared around the nearest cradled sloop.

Tanner turned his attention to the Bayfield Marina, alive with activity. While many slips were empty, more boats were in their assigned places, awaiting crews or patiently suffering late spring ministrations of their owners.

Mary squinted into the near distance and pointed toward the scattering of islands. "Those must be some of the Apostles. Except for Madeline over there, they're all part of the national park."

"You're well-informed, toots."

Mary smiled. "While you were immersed in travel arrangements and finding out about Chequamegon Resource Recovery, I found out about this part of the country. Look at this marina. It's certainly not like our Shilsole Bay back home."

"Nice. No fence, no gate. Anyone can walk out on

the docks and look at the boats. Same gulls all around, same noises."

"From the rigging," Mary finished. She sniffed the air. "Doesn't smell the same, though. No salt. People seem very relaxed out here. I like that." She hooked her arm in Tanner's and grinned into his face. "I also like this lake. I insist we find a boat to charter. At least do a day on the water. Look at all that water!"

"I'm sure we can arrange something. Let's walk over to the other side of town. That must be where the ferry docks."

They turned around and surprised a man walking twenty yards behind them at the junction of the main dock to the shore. He froze in mid-stride, flicked a cigarette into the water then turned down one of the branching docks. Tanner nodded and smiled at the man, who didn't respond.

"Look, Mary said, pointing down at the water beside the dock, "is that a teal swimming there?"

When Tanner once again glanced around, he and Mary were the only people on the dock.

Chapter 5

Chequamegon Resource Recovery was headquartered on Pierce Street in an unprepossessing four story building, two blocks off Lakeshore Drive. It was a solid building of massive brownstone blocks, undoubtedly quarried from the Apostle Islands. It had the look of an early twentieth century commercial building. Once inside, Tanner and Mary discovered that renovations had brought the building closer to modern times, including a new-looking self-service elevator.

"Up, madam?" murmured Tanner pointing to the elevator. He shook the sleeve of his lightweight tailored jacket down over the gold watch on his wrist.

"I'd rather walk, thank you. It's only one flight up, correct?" The couple took the stairs to the second floor. The stairs opened on a wide lobby area with wood-paneled corridors leading off in two directions. Directly ahead of them was a glass paneled door with an elaborate CRR in bold black script centered on the glass. None of the other doors they could see had signs on them. Tanner twisted the big brass knob and ushered Mary into an outer reception area. The hum and click of computer terminals, a lone typewriter, and the sounds of machines copying or shredding or faxing made a common and reassuring blend of business office noise. Tall windows along the western wall let summer sunlight in. A pleasant looking woman with long, very dark, straight hair at a central desk looked up from her terminal, smiled and said, "Good morning. How can I help you?"

"Good morning. I'm Michael Tanner and this is Mary Whitney. I believe George Anderson is expecting us."

The woman's smile widened and laugh lines appeared at the corners of her carefully made-up eyes. "Oh, yes of course. She held out a hand and gave Tanner a firm handshake. "I'm Jeri Reif, Mr. Anderson's executive assistant. Welcome to Ashland. We're very excited that you've come. They're all assembled in the conference room. Won't you follow me, please."

Mary glanced at Tanner with a question on her face. They knew it was irregular for a preliminary meeting to include more than just key principals. They justified Mary's presence because of the unusual depth of knowledge Anderson had revealed in his conversation with Tanner. Since Anderson had gone to extra lengths to learn about Mary Whitney, she would return the favor, in person.

Ms. Reif ushered them down a hallway to a solid door of richly polished, gleaming oak. She rapped twice on the door and then stepped forward to open it.

"Excellent. Excellent," boomed the voice Tanner remembered from the telephone. It came from the far end of what sounded like a large empty room.

"Anderson," Tanner murmured, then stepped to one side so when the door opened, Mary preceded Tanner into the conference room. She straightened her jacket and altered her carriage as an actor sometimes does, taking the last steps inside the character just as she makes her entrance.

"Right on time," Anderson boomed. "Good, good. I like that in a—"

Just inside the door Mary and Tanner stopped to

survey the room. Grouped around the far end of an enormous polished conference table stood six men. George Anderson had his hands on his ample hips, a black stogie in his mouth. Mary noted with relief that it was unlit and there were no ashtrays on the table. Sun streamed through the tall windows that lined the far wall, highlighting the heads and shoulders of the men in the room. Mary took in the fact that she and Tanner would sit facing the sun, while the faces of the men from Chequamegon Resource would be shadowed.

As she walked further into the room, she straightened perceptibly, tilted her head up ever so slightly. She even walked differently, Tanner realized, projecting a subtle aura of self-possession and assurance. It was her boardroom persona coming to the fore.

George Anderson smiled hugely and came around the table on the visiting couple's right to reach Tanner first. His eyes flickered appreciatively across Mary Whitney. He took Tanner's hand in a smothering grasp and pumped it once. Anderson was built on a big scale, from his sturdy legs, hips, and protruding belly, to arms that strained the fabric of his white, short-sleeved, shirt. Only one of the other five men in the room was wearing a jacket.

"Mr. Tanner, I can't tell you how pleased I am to see you here in our board room. And this must be the little lady. Ms. Whitney. It is a distinct pleasure to meet you."

Tanner thought he saw a flicker of something like distaste cross the face of one of the men behind Anderson.

"Now," Anderson swung away and waved a big paw at those behind him, "lemme introduce my team. This here's Arne Anderson. He's our vice president for sales." The second Anderson, a smaller, younger, version of his brother George, smiled and leaned forward to grasp Tanner's outstretched hand. He ignored Mary.

"An' this here's Charlie Eddington. He's my advertising manager. You and he'll be working pretty close once this deal gets going." Eddington nodded at Mary and shook Tanner's hand with a damp, firm grasp.

"Meet Richard Kemperer, vice president for manufacturing, another one you'll no doubt be seeing a lot of." Kemperer produced what appeared to be the first unaffected smile since they'd entered the room. Kemperer was slim and blond, about Tanner's height and build. He met Tanner's eyes in a long direct look and then smoothly turned to smile warmly at Mary.

Anderson clapped a big hand on the thin shoulder of a dark, stooped man who stood quietly to one side. He was the only man wearing a suit and a neatly knotted tie. "This here's Stan Krizyinsky. He's VP for marketing. He's a Polack, but we don't hold that against him, do we?" He grinned in Krizyinsky's face. Krizyinsky didn't return the favor. He turned from under Anderson's arm and took Mary's hand. He raised it to his lips in a theatrical gesture and murmured, "Enchanted. Welcome to Ashland and Chequamegon Resource Recovery. I am sure we will have a most fruitful association." His voice was pure American with no trace of accent. Dropping her hand, he bowed slightly to Tanner who nodded in acknowledgment, wondering how much of Krizyinsky was performance and how much was the man's ingrained sense of *politesse*.

"And here's Teddy Schroeder, our vice president of administration."

Schroeder, a slim sandy-haired man who looked younger than the others, winced at the diminutive use of his name.

"All right, gentlemen, and ma'am. Let's sit down and see where we are." He gestured to the chairs and they all settled. "I don't have a formal agenda. We're just going to get acquainted and listen to a few ideas. Mr. Tanner, whyn't you tell us what you have."

Mary crossed her legs and smoothed her skirt over her knees, watched by Arne and Krizyinsky. She relaxed into the comfortable chair and composed her features into a serene and contemplative look. Tanner glanced at her, signaling recognition of her board-member posture.

Tanner briefly sketched his company, the kinds of services they offered and mentioned a few of their clients. Then he pointed out some of the possible options available to CRR. After that he stopped and sat back. The whole thing had taken only a little more than ten minutes. The CRR executives looked as if they expected more.

"We're very anxious to examine your ideas," said Eddington, with a sidelong glance at George Anderson.

"I consider this a very preliminary exploration," Tanner responded. "My associates and I will have to learn a good deal more about your company before we'll be ready to make a formal presentation. Because you are a privately held company, there are gaps in our knowledge. Remember too, we don't yet know the scope of what the company does and just exactly what kind of association we're planning here. T and A—" six pairs of eyes blinked and Mary Whitney smothered a smile— "has, through long and successful practice, discovered that we do our best work when we and the client are open and detailed with each other. If we are going to be working together, it will be very much a collaboration, one that both firms are comfortable with."

The six CRR executives looked as if they'd been accused of something faintly underhanded. George Anderson frowned and drummed his big fingers on the table. "Well, I sorta thought we were past the preliminaries," he said, "after you decided to come all the way out here."

"I'm sorry, George," Tanner said, "but if you recall, we never really discussed what you want from my firm. We're qualified to create and manage marketing, public relations, or advertising campaigns. We've done integrated planning and we can handle international as well as national campaigns. We can ratchet up from almost any point to a combined large-scale operation. It's always better to know where you're going before you start, even if CRR decides to delay or even use a different firm for a later part of your marketing and publicity efforts. I'm sure that once we nail down your primary expectations, as well as preliminary financial considerations, I'll be in a much better position to determine whether Tanner and Associates is right for this job."

Tanner sat back and smiled across the table. He wasn't going to reveal much more without additional information from the CRR side of the table.

Kemperer frowned and said, "Well, somebody was misinformed. Do you make a habit of traveling two thousand miles on your own funds for a kind of site inspection before you decide to accept a client? I take it you didn't even bring us samples of your work?"

Tanner shook his head and leaned forward. "No, Mr. Kemperer we don't make a habit of the kind of travel you describe, but we do it more often than one might suppose. There are other reasons we came this distance." He glanced at George Anderson. "Your CEO was most persuasive, and my wife," he nodded and smiled at Mary, "wanted to visit the area. As you are aware, we are both avid sailors, but have never sailed on Lake Superior. This seemed to be a good chance to combine business with pleasure."

Mary smiled and joined the discussion. "As

Michael said, I was interested in this trip, partly because at one time my family had some interests in this region of the world and I've never been here before. Based on what Michael told me about your conversation on the telephone, Mr. Anderson, I gather you already have a considerable amount of information about Tanner and Associates. And even about me. I wanted to return the favor." The expression on her face took the sting out of the words. All the men in the room looked at her. Krizyinsky frowned. Kemperer nodded once, as if confirming some privately held thought.

After a moment of silence, George Anderson shrugged and began to detail the recovery operations of CRR. When the discussion turned to questions of markets for the wood, detailed responses, already hard to come by, disappeared altogether. Fundamental questions rose in Tanner's mind. What kind of help did CRR really want? Did they have the financial muscle to go full-bore into the market? How big was their potential resource?

After a seemingly off-hand remark about environmental questions brought a sharp look from Krizyinsky, Kemperer seemed to take himself out of the discussion altogether.

Mary Whitney was becoming increasingly impatient. Twice she'd started to raise financial questions, only to be cut off. She knew Tanner was irritated by the chauvinistic and patronizing manner in which the men of CRR had dismissed her and she knew from the tenor of Tanner's remarks he was getting ready to walk away from the table. It was sounding less and less as though CRR would become a client of Tanner and Associates. Tanner's earlier use of the initials of the firm, a deliberately provocative remark, was a signal of his unhappiness with the situation.

Mary sat up straighter into a moment of silence and said quietly, "Given the niche market prospects of the company, and the long-term outlook for the market, the stock market that is, I should think you are in a strong leveraging position." Eddington looked down at the table. George frowned. Only Stanley Krizyinsky looked directly at her and Tanner could almost see the thoughts speeding through his brain. It looked like he was going to respond and then thought better of it.

"Are you saying you think CRR is in a position to entertain or perhaps even solicit buyout offers?" said Kemperer. It was his first contribution to the discussion in several minutes.

"That was my thought," she nodded. "It looks as though you may not have the financial resources to mount the kind of advertising and marketing campaign you've been discussing. A larger parent could be one answer."

Anderson scowled. "We'll never sell," he said forcefully. "And we'd have to make a lot of progress here before significant investment income could be realized." His brother, Arne, nodded.

Krizyinsky continued to stare thoughtfully at Mary Whitney and then Tanner said, "financial considerations are important, gentlemen. After all if we do a deal with all the implications of an extensive, perhaps international nature, we need certain assurances. We have never been interested in planning such campaigns merely as an exercise. We've made it a rule to assure ourselves that the clients whom we work with have sufficient funds to sustain the programs we create."

"I can assure you," George started to sputter, "that we..."

"Excuse me, gentlemen." Mary's voice cut George Anderson and the others into abrupt silence. "I, of course, do not speak for Tanner and Associates. I do not represent them at this table. Mr. Tanner does that quite ably and he will make whatever decision he comes to for T and A." Again, six pairs of eyes blinked as Mary went blithely on. "While I am interested in his decision, since it may affect mine, my interest has changed. Some of those logs you propose to raise once belonged to my family. Whitney Enterprises, although no longer active in the logging business, is still involved in many other aspects of the timber industry. We are also an active investment player in the market, particularly with respect to emerging small and mid-cap companies. Active members of Whitney's board, of which I am one, are always on the lookout for investment opportunities. You might wish to remember that." She sat back in the stunned and gaping silence, the merest trace of a smile playing about her lips.

Arne Anderson was the first to react, "Wait a minute, Tanner," he roared. "I think you've sandbagged us here. There was no talk about financial dealings ..."

"Oh, shut up, Arne," snapped his brother. "We don't need that right now."

Krizyinsky had raised slightly in his chair and his voice floated through the silence. "Of course! I should have realized. Whitney. That name is almost as well known here in Ashland as that of the Schroeder Mills. Whitney Lumbering was one of the biggest in the territory at one time."

"Exactly," Mary responded. "But I reject the idea that we've arrived here under false pretenses. You will recall that Mr. Anderson introduced me, not as Mrs. Tanner, as he could have done, but as Miz Whitney. I was a bit surprised. Most people, meeting us for the first time, assume I use my husband's name, which is not the case. Had any of you taken the trouble to ask, I would readily have admitted my ancestry. Frankly, given the detail of some of your research, I'm surprised you didn't already know of my connection to logging in this area." The last Mary said looking directly into George Anderson's eyes.

"I didn't come here looking for an investment opportunity" she continued, "but you have revealed some intriguing possibilities. I think you would do well to explore in some depth what the infusion of a large amount of cash might do for you."

What Mary Whitney didn't say, because it would have only added to the embarrassment some of the CRR executives must have been feeling, was that it had apparently never occurred to them that a woman might have more than a passing interest in the subject of the meeting.

She dropped another small bomb. "Depending on how your discussions with Tanner and Associates proceed, and what I learn from examining your financials, should you make them available, I could consider making an investment in CRR, something on a scale that would help protect you from a hostile takeover and make marketing your products and raw materials more realistic. Depending on how our discussions continue, I suggest you consider this possibility a friendly investment." Mary slid her chair back, signaling Tanner that she too was ready to leave.

He stood. "We've taken enough of your time today and you have the broad outlines of the capabilities of our firm. You will doubtless want some time to assemble a financial presentation for Ms. Whitney. You also may require some time to discuss how this affects your plans and whether we should continue negotiations. Time is not a problem for us, so we'll be at your disposal. I'll leave our number with your secretary, George."

Only Arne Anderson rose to escort them to the

door. He grinned briefly and whispered, "Well, you've made the whole day a lot more interesting than I expected. We'll definitely be in touch."

Tanner wheeled the Lexus down the street toward Highway 13 and smiled at Mary. "Now that was interesting. Maybe we should team up for all my initial presentations."

"No, I don't think so." She shook her head. "I really should apologize. It wasn't my place to inject my own," she hesitated, looking for the right word, "self into your meeting. But they were so self-righteous, so chauvinistic, and I could see you were getting ready to tell them you didn't want their business with that T & A crack." She grinned.

"You were dead on. Don't you think it's odd they didn't tumble to your name right away?"

"George Anderson knew, but it looks like either he didn't share that information or he assumed that I, as a woman, wouldn't care about such things."

"Any other impressions you want to share?"

"There's something going on behind the scenes. I don't know what it is, but at times the tension was so thick it crackled."

Tanner grinned, nodding. "There seemed to be more agendas in that room than usual."

"I wonder if all those executives are in favor of hiring you."

"Frequently there is some disagreement. Sometimes it hangs on even after we've won a competitive bidding process. That's often the case, that not everyone wants to do a deal with us, but I agree, something's going on and it might not have much to do with Tanner and Associates. Can you do that? Decide to act as the family point person on investment opportunities?"

"You bet. Most of us don't, but occasionally something comes up that one of us thinks should be checked out. I couldn't make a deal by myself, but I can get our investment people to look at CRR and then take recommendations to the board as an advocate." She shrugged. "We do the same thing when one of the family comes along with a new charity somebody wants to support. Let's continue this over lunch." Tanner wheeled into the parking lot of their rented condo.

Chapter 6

"What are your other impressions of the men in that room?"

Tanner and Mary were sitting down to a cold lunch at a small restaurant south of Bayfield.

"I think George Anderson is a nice guy who's involved in something he's overly passionate about. At times it seems to get in the way of logic. He's also angry about something. His passion for the company's mission and the timber itself, and that anger may be interfering with his business judgments. I do think the company has potential, but I'm going to need more information about their present customer base and expansion possibilities."

Tanner nodded and hummed a snatch of an old sailing tune, "A Capital Ship for an Ocean Trip was the Walloping Window Blind."

Mary smiled. "If this turns into something worthwhile, you may be glad I'm along. It just might be my money CRR ends up paying you with."

Tanner broke open a hard roll and aimed his knife at the butter dish. "Regardless of how it turns out, I'm very much glad you're here. Now, what about Arne?"

"George's brother? I think he's just along for the ride. He was probably one of the sources of their original stake. But I got the impression he's not really interested in the recovery of sunken logs, or what they can do with them."

"Agreed. What about Kemperer?"

"Ah, he really wants to get his hands on the wood. I think he sees this as an artistic opportunity, perhaps more than as a business deal. There was almost an ambivalence there. He seems to have a very penetrating gaze, but at other times I had the feeling he was drifting, not really paying attention. He reminds me of some of the artists I've known at Udub and the museum. But I think there's something else in play with Kemperer. He seemed to be a watcher. Did you notice? A couple of times he seemed about to say something and then held back. The others seem to be the kind of managerial types you find in all these companies, competent but don't expect any brilliance or extreme dedication. If any of them have money invested in CRR it's only small amounts." Mary paused to take a bite of her sandwich and a sip of water. "The guy you have to watch is Krizyinsky. In spite of his theatrical act, I think he's dangerous."

"Interesting that you say that. He was the only man in the room, excepting yours truly, of course, who treated you with respect and paid attention."

Mary smiled. "That's partly why I feel that way. Did you see those hand gestures? A couple of times I thought he was going to burst out with something totally outrageous. He may even have realized who I was before the others did. I think he's an angle player. He was much too attentive. It was almost as if he was trying to jostle our boat. He's the kind of guy who'd make a play for me if he thought it would work."

"I may have to challenge him to a duel."

Mary laughed softly. "You better be careful what weapons you choose. That scar on his bristly cheek could be from a dueling sword."

* * *

Back at their condo, Mary called Arne Anderson at CRR to suggest she would be pleased to see their financial information if they were interested in considering a capital investment from Whitney Enterprises and that she was particularly interested in their assessment of potential markets for the recovered timber. When she hung up, Mary related his reaction. "He said they have most of the information already assembled, he just needs to update a few figures. Apparently they are looking for additional capital."

Tanner smiled at the expression on Mary's face. "You're kind of getting into this, aren't you?"

"There's no denying I get a kick out of finding a happy fit for some of the corporation's money. There's satisfaction at being able to help a group of dedicated individuals begin to realize their dream. I wouldn't ever want to be a stock broker, though.

"The investment world can be a funny place. I've watched my uncles go through full dress rehearsals with very elaborate charts and graphs, then discuss options for hours, fine tuning things when they were looking for expansion funds. At the other extreme, I've seen a man who controlled hundreds of thousands on his signature alone, make a decision to invest a ton of money after twenty minutes with a stranger who had a hand-written two-page business plan and no corporate charter. There are still people who make deals worth millions on a handshake. And it's a scene where the swashbucklers and the pirates still operate almost at will."

"What do you think it will take to get an investment from Whitney to CRR?"

"Depending on how much, and assuming the company is in good order, stock and a seat on the board,"

Mary responded promptly. "Whitney is a pretty benign investment partner, but there are certain basic guidelines we have to follow."

The telephone rang. George Anderson owned a big motor launch, and he was calling to say he'd be delighted to take Mary and Tanner for an introductory trip along the coast and around some of the Apostles. His wife would pack a nice supper and they could stay out as long as they pleased. It would be a way for them to get to know each other outside the context of the company, George had said.

Tanner reported to Mary and then remarked, "You know this will be a lot more pleasant than if he'd suggested eighteen holes of golf."

When they arrived at the gas dock that served the Bayfield municipal marina, Anderson's big cabin cruiser, *Merry Kay*, was taking up a good share of the space. George was on the flying bridge while a petite woman with very dark hair, cut short just at her ears, was directing a muscular, tanned young man who was holding a fuel nozzle attached to the end of a black hose trailing along the dock.

As they approached, George caught sight of them and waved enthusiastically. He wore a big bright grin.

"Sort of shark-like," muttered Mary with an answering wave.

The woman merely glanced at them and said, "Young man, do be careful with that thing. You don't want to scratch the deck." Once he had the fuel nozzle properly inserted, she raised her head and offered a welcoming smile to Mary and Tanner.

"You must be the Tanners. Welcome aboard. We'll be finished here in just a few minutes." Tanner handed Mary aboard through the boarding ladder opening in the railing that ran around the perimeter of the open rear deck.

Good to her word, a few minutes later the engines

rumbled into life and Anderson expertly steered the 40-foot cruiser away from the dock and along the wide lane toward the gap in the rocky breakwater that marked the harbor entrance. Without asking for help, the dark woman who had identified herself as Kay Anderson, skipped about the deck hauling in and tying down several big white fenders which had protected the hull from the dock.

Once they entered the wide blue expanse of Lake Superior, Kay Anderson visibly relaxed and invited Tanner and Mary to join her below in the main salon where she offered the visitors tea, coffee, or something stronger. Tanner opted for a beer while Mary and Kay shared a pot of strong tea.

"George will call us up to the bridge in a few minutes," she said. "He likes to get clear of the marina and the ferry routes before he really relaxes. Most of the time, unless we're going west to Superior, or to the eastern islands, we don't even come into this channel."

From Bayfield, Anderson headed southeast to pass close by the south end of Madeline Island, largest of the Apostle Islands. As they rounded the end of Madeline, the party in the cabin heard the engines throttle back. Kay Anderson snagged another beer which she opened and the three climbed the ladder to the flying bridge where Anderson accepted the can his wife offered and shook Tanner's hand.

"Welcome aboard, welcome." He spread his arms. "Isn't this grand? Who would ever have thought, hey sweetheart, that we'd be runnin' a real company in such a great part of the world?" His enthusiasm and honest welcome set the tone for the rest of the afternoon.

"This lake and the beauty of the region are some of the reasons George got interested in this project and partly why he and the others started CRR," said Kay.

Responding to a questioning look from Tanner, Kay

Anderson went on. "George's family has always lived in southern Wisconsin, down near Lake Geneva, but he was in school at Madison when one of his uncles died. In the man's effects somebody found a pile of papers on his genealogical research. I forget just how they came to George, but he read them and got interested. Several members of George's family had lived near Ashland. Some of them worked in the forests or the mills."

"I did a paper for some class, using the research as the basis," said George. "But I want to point out the Michigan light. It's the first lighthouse built in the islands."

"When was that?" asked Mary.

"1857," responded George, guiding the big cruiser in a wide circle that brought them close off the dock jutting out from the small island. They could all see the steep set of stairs leading up the cliff toward the tower. Mary made marks on a small map of the islands she had brought with her.

With a glance at the sky and then at his radar screen, George Anderson headed west toward one of the biggest of the Apostles, Stockton Island. He handed Tanner a pair of bright yellow binoculars. "Take a look. Dead ahead you'll see the high cliffs of Quarry Bay. It's a popular spot for campers, and it's a good anchorage against any rough weather except something out of the southeast. Something we almost never get."

Mary made another note.

"We'll—"

Whatever George was about to say was interrupted by a loud chiming sound from a pouch on a shelf beside George where he stood at the wheel.

"George, I asked you not to bring the phone!" Kay snapped.

"Sorry," Anderson said. The chime sounded again, loud, insistent.

"Here, Kay. Take the wheel. I'll handle this quickly. I promise."

Kay Anderson sent a sharp look at her husband, then slipped around him and took control of the boat. As the northeast end of Madeline Island fell away on the port side, she curved left toward the middle of the three islands that lay across their path.

"This is Hermit directly ahead. You can't see it from here, but there was a big quarry on this side of the island where they got the sandstone for building."

Mary rose to stand beside the other woman. Her gaze turned from Hermit toward the north and the watery space between the islands that led to the widening vista of vast heaving blue expanse that was the inland sea called Lake Superior. Then she said, "That was in the 1880s, wasn't it?"

"That's right, Mary. The stone is called brownstone. There are other old quarries on the islands. The federal Lake Shore headquarters building in Bayfield is built from brownstone quarried in the islands. The mining companies also shipped it south for buildings in Chicago, Milwaukee, the Twin Cities, and of course, Ashland."

A few minutes later, as the launch ran down the channel between Madeline and Basswood islands, George Anderson reappeared from below. The sun was fading in the west and the temperature was dropping almost as fast. The two couples moved to the lower steering station, a roomy enclosed cabin where the noise of the well-insulated engine was only a pleasant background hum.

Between them, the Andersons were a bounty of knowledge about the history and current times of the Apostle Islands and the surrounding area.

"Did you know Captain Hickock came to Ashland?" queried George at one point. "Yessir, old Wild Bill came to Ashland several times and in the twenties he tried to broker a deal between the logging interests and the Indians. There were sawmills on the Bad River reservation then, and they and the Indians at Red Rock still held some of the best timber remaining in these parts. By then, of course, the mills at Ashland were looking every which way for more raw product. The tugs were even draggin' log booms across from the Canadian side. A couple of times the Schroeder mill was shut down and everybody was laid off when deliveries didn't arrive on time."

"That was something I wondered about," said Mary, smoothly returning the conversation to present-day specifics. "Your brochures suggest that there's a huge supply of timber still on the bottom of the lake, just waiting to be harvested. If so, why hasn't someone been there already?"

Tanner saw a glance pass between the Andersons and wondered if there was a slippery scam in the offing, but Anderson repeated what Mary and Tanner already knew from their research back in Seattle.

"There are several answers to your question. Early on, lost timber was just ignored by the companies working around the area. The forests must have seemed inexhaustible. The islands could be logged all year long. When the ice broke in the spring, steam tugs came and hauled the timber to the mills. Today of course we know there aren't endless quantities of anything, well, except possibly our desire for more wood.

"In the early twenties, one of the Ashland mills, looking for more product, sent loggers out on barges in Chequamegon Bay with special long pikes to probe the bottom near Ashland. They snagged some of the sunken timber, but the depression stopped all that. And of course they couldn't get to anything much below twenty feet of water unless they brought in expensive diving apparatus. Today, scuba gear makes a huge difference. It's down in the deeper, colder water where the least deterioration takes place. Those logs are surprisingly well-preserved. The divers set flotation bags to raise the stuff from deep water. We hire local divers to locate the timber but we've brought in other divers during the season."

Tanner looked down at the blue and white water rushing by. He couldn't see the bottom, and he wondered what they might be passing over at that very minute. "That's right, I don't imagine you can do much in the way of recovery when the lake is frozen."

Anderson nodded. "The cold water makes it difficult for divers to work long periods below the surface even in the summer."

"A short season, plus having to use divers to locate the logs, must add substantially to your operating costs, doesn't it?" said Mary.

George nodded. "True, and you'll see that reflected in the figures when you meet with Arne, but our projections show pretty conclusively that even with higher costs of doing business, the demand for the wood will continue to more than offset the expenses.

"There's a lot of first-quality wood down there. In the late nineteenth century," Anderson went on, "steam-powered tug boats dragged log booms of timber from the gathering places on the islands and from some of the mainland bays to the mills, principally in Ashland. Hardwoods don't float well, so those logs had to be supported by the pine and other softwoods. If there wasn't a storm, and things went okay, the tug would arrive with nearly all the timber it started out with. But sometimes..." Anderson's voice trailed off and he busied himself for a moment with the business of piloting his launch, making minute adjustments to course and speed.

"Sometimes storms came up," said Kay Anderson, continuing the narrative. She interrupted herself to point over the right side. "Over there is Bayfield." They all gazed through the gathering darkness at the cluster of lights sprinkled up the slope that marked the town. Lower, just above the water, they could see the red and green lights signaling the harbor entrance.

"Then those more distant lights off to the left must be the marina at Pike's Bay," said Tanner.

"That's right. We're running down the bay toward Ashland in a trough that's over fifty feet deep. Tugs carried supplies and pulled the log booms down this same route. Sometimes there were storms. This lake can be very dangerous, you know, especially because of the cold water. One of George's relatives was lost in these waters. A great-great-uncle was a logger who lived in Bayfield for a while."

"Really," said Mary.

"Yes, he disappeared in 1896. Nobody knows what happened. George's family has a few letters from when he first came up from Chicago to be a logger. But the next year the letters stopped and nobody ever heard from him again."

"How tragic," Mary murmured. "To have a relative just drop off the earth like that."

"Well," George said, "it's not like I ever knew the man, or knew anybody who did. He wasn't married, s' far as we know, so it's just one of those family mysteries."

He switched back to CRR. "At times the loss of timber from the booms could be pretty high. I've read about tugs arriving in Ashland missing almost forty percent of what they started out with. A lot of that timber went to the bottom of the lake and just stayed there. That's the timber we're harvesting."

"The difficulty, of course, is money," said Kay. "Always money. Now that CRR has made advances in the harvesting of that sunken wood, others are trying to get in on the act. Some of them are better financed."

"Just how do you go about locating the wood?" asked Mary.

"It's a little like a treasure hunt for lost ships, or any kind of underwater archeology," said George. "We define a search area, based on calculations and research among logging company records. On such and such a date, the tug Mable left Red Rock with a tow of ten thousand logs of mixed type. Passing Pike's Bay, the captain notes heavy seas and a sudden squall that pushes the boom up beside the tug. He's forced to cut the boom loose or risk being holed and sunk. The boom disintegrates and the whole kaboodle is lost." He smiled. "That's an extreme example, of course."

"Was the Whitney Corporation cooperative?" asked Mary.

"Yep," said George. "Sent us copies of everything they could find, apparently."

"Didn't a lot of the timber wash ashore?" asked Tanner.

"Sure, but it was scattered from hell to breakfast and once the butt-end markings that identified who owned the logs was sheared—or sawed—off, proving ownership was impossible. I bet a lot of the buildings up and down these shores were built from salvaged timber. And of course, a good deal of the prime wood just sank. It's still down there."

"And that's what CRR is after."

"Exactly. Of course, it's a finite resource, just like the timber here was to Whitney and Weyerhaeuser and the rest of the logging companies. When the useable stuff on the bottom is gone, we'll shut down or move on."

"How long do you figure it will take to raise what you can use?"

"Our underwater surveys tell us there's enough

timber in the lake to keep the company in business for ten or fifteen years. Longer, if we have to keep fighting the environmental lobby and other bureaucracies in court," said Anderson with a disgusted tone.

Chapter 7

"How'd you sleep?" Tanner went into the steamy bathroom. Mary, clad only in her rosy-toned skin dotted with sparkling water droplets, stepped from the shower and held up her luminous face for a kiss.

"Like the proverbial log. All that fresh air last night really put me out. Besides, maybe you haven't noticed, but this is a very quiet town at night."

"I noticed a couple of things during that boat trip. I think Anderson would like to attract you as an investor, but something else is going on. I intercepted too many meaningful glances between Anderson and his wife during the evening."

"Let's go get some breakfast. I think you're right, but now I need to feed my inner child. There'll be time for assessment a little later," Mary said.

They breakfasted at the Pier Plaza along the main street just up the shore from the city dock. A cheerful college-aged waitress served them coffee, toast, and cereal. While they ate, sitting at the big window that faced northeast toward the busy harbor and the lake, Mary read the paper and Tanner watched the people coming and going.

"Busy little town today," he commented. "I'll bet we could charter a sailboat here. There's a Sails, Inc. sign on the building across the street from the restaurant. I'm pretty sure they're a sailboat charter company."

"There's a yacht club on Madeline Island," Mary said, lowering the paper and nodding toward the window. "They rent out some of the yachts docked there. Plus, I read about a company called Superior Charters. I think they're located at that marina in Pike's Bay, the one we passed on the way in."

Tanner's cell phone rang.

"You and George," Mary grinned. "Did you catch the look Kay flashed at George when his cell phone rang on the boat?" She returned to her newspaper.

To Tanner's ear the voice on the other end of the line sounded intense and a little nervous. "Tanner... Is this Michael Tanner?"

Tanner admitted that it was.

"You the Tanner thinking about going to work for that new lumber mill over to Ashland?"

"Who'm I speaking to?"

"My name is McGregor, Ted McGregor. I need to meet with you, sir. At...at the earliest opportunity."

"In regard to what, if I may ask?"

"In regard...in regard to that company, Chequamegon Resource?" The voice sounded young, but he pronounced through the "a" in Chequamegon with a 'shw' sound, something Tanner had already learned was the way local people said it. "Believe me, what I have to say is very important. There are some very important factors you need to consider before you go ahead...sir."

Tanner was about to brush the man off, but the thought occurred that he might learn some useful information so he said, "Well, Mr. McGregor. I don't make a habit of meeting strangers to talk about my business, but this morning I'll make an exception. Can you meet me in half an hour? There's a restaurant on the main street of Bayfield. I think it's called Rittenhouse Avenue. The place is just up the street from the harbor. It's called The

Pier. Or Pier Plaza. Do you know it?"

"Yes, sir, I do. I'd much prefer to meet you somewhere more private, say your rooms at Bayfield by the Lake? Or in the lounge at the Bayfield Inn?"

"No, I don't think so. I'll be in the restaurant, at a table farthest from the door. I'll be there, whether you choose to meet me or not. I assume, since you've tracked me down that you know what I look like. Fair enough?"

He waited, listening to the electronic silence on the line, but there was no response, so he ended the call and replaced the phone in the pocket of his jacket. Tanner looked at Mary.

"Man named McGregor. Has something extremely important to say to me about CRR, apparently. I'll see him here at the restaurant in half an hour."

"Or not, sounded like."

"He wanted more privacy." Tanner smiled. "I figure if he wants to shoot me, he'll have to risk a public forum."

"Michael!" Mary looked at her husband with mild shock in her face. "Don't even joke about such things."

"It's likely this'll turn out to be nothing. But you never know. Maybe I'll learn something useful. If not, well, I have nothing important on my schedule at the moment."

"This is one meeting where I suspect my presence will be unwelcome."

"Not by me, my love. What will you do instead?"

"I'm off to see if I can find out some more local history. I want to get a sense of what went on here during the logging days. Maybe I can get a better idea of how much timber there is on the bottom of this lake. I'm not inclined to just take George's word on it. I seem to recall a museum in that town we came through—Washburn? What say we meet back at the condo around noon?"

Mary took the car, heading south along the bay, and

Tanner ordered another cup of coffee and a dessert roll. While he ate he kept a sharp eye out to see if anyone was giving more than casual attention to his presence. He changed his position at the table to put his back to the street so he could see the entrance without twisting around.

* * *

In Washburn, fifteen miles down the road from Bayfield, while Mary stopped to gas up the Lexus and inquire about a bookstore, in the back of her mind she worried about Michael, waiting alone in the Bayfield restaurant.

Karlyn's Gallery along the main street was open and she found several locally written books, and a lot of gorgeous watercolors and pottery in addition to the shelves of written materials. For even more historical information, she was directed to the Washburn museum, housed in a handsome brownstone, a former bank building. There she found pamphlets, books and other ephemera. She bought several, including a heftier work called *Tales of Lake Superior: The Early Days.*

* * *

At five minutes after ten, while Mary was in Washburn, Tanner watched a slender young man with short curly blond hair and a sparse blond beard enter the restaurant. The man was wearing a dark blue *Save the Whales* sweatshirt over faded and well-worn blue jeans. His feet were encased in heavy-soled dark brown hiking boots that looked new. The only thing in his hands was a sweat-stained billed cap.

The man stopped and surveyed the half-empty room. Tanner lowered his eyes to his coffee cup and watched through his lashes. After a moment of hesitation the man made a beeline directly for Tanner's table.

"Excuse me, are you Michael Tanner?"

Tanner nodded. This was not the voice of the man who had called and made this appointment. "Yes, I'm Michael Tanner. What can I do for you?"

"My name is Ted McGregor, and I appreciate you seeing me on such short notice like this."

The waitress appeared at the table with a coffee pot. She gestured at Tanner's cup and he nodded. "I guess you'd better sit down and tell me what this is all about."

McGregor sat, and said to the waitress, "A pot of tea would be nice." He placed his cap on the corner of the table.

"Frankly, Mr. McGregor, I only agreed to see you because I'm curious. Now I'm starting to wonder if it was a bad idea. You don't sound like the man who made the appointment this morning on the telephone. Unless there are two Ted McGregors here in Bayfield, which seems unlikely."

"Yes. I'm sorry about that. Using my name that way was a mistake. The man, boy, really, who called you was afraid you wouldn't listen at all unless he used my name. He hasn't much experience. But let me explain what this is all about.

"I am part of an international environmental organization called People For the Earth. Here." McGregor made sudden move to his hip pocket and produced a bent white business card with raised green lettering. He thrust it at Tanner who looked at it but didn't offer to take it. It confirmed what McGregor had just said. Tanner, active in support of various environmental groups in Washington State and elsewhere in the Northwest, had never heard of the PFE, so he remained silent and waited for McGregor to continue.

McGregor put the card in his shirt pocket with a jerky move. Then he said, "You've probably never heard of us. We are mainly interested in the deforestation problem and cleaning up the water of the planet—cleaning up pollution everywhere."

"Well, I admire your goals, but I don't see what that has to do with me, or with my firm. I'm just traveling up here with my wife. Seeing the country. You know how it is." Tanner smiled and spread his hands disingenuously.

"That won't wash, Mr. Tanner," McGregor said forcefully. He was seated on the front edge of his chair, back straight and now he leaned forward a little. "We know you are the CEO of Tanner and Associates, a big important Seattle PR firm. We also know your wife is an heir to the Whitney family lumber and shipping operation that pillaged all the northern forests in the last century. And we know you're here to set up a campaign to help Chequamegon Resource Recovery really get off the ground and try to take all that sunken timber off the bottom of the lake."

Tanner bristled at the mention of his wife's family, but said nothing. He wondered how McGregor had gotten his information so fast.

McGregor flashed a quick smile at the waitress who set down a small pot of tea.

Tanner had heard McGregor pronounce Chequamegon with a hard 'c' and 'q' which marked him as an outsider. The man splashed some tea into his cup and went on. "I wanted to talk to you now because things are moving faster than we thought they would. Apparently CRR has made a pitch to a new investor and my information says they're interested. New money will give them the ability to crank up their operation. We've been able to keep 'em pretty well bottled up for almost three years now. You must help us stop them. They're gonna ruin the natural habitat. Don't you see? At the very least, if you agree with our concerns, we hope you'll withdraw from this job."

McGregor was staring at him with an intense gaze. Tanner recognized that McGregor was zealous in pursuit of his goals and there was little or nothing to be gained by arguing with the man. "I don't know where you get your information, but I'm surprised. I would have expected you to support CRR, since the logs they want to harvest are already cut. Where's the harm? It will mean reduced cutting of old growth forests, won't it? If they expand it'll bring new jobs to the area. Looks to me like a winning idea."

"Where's the harm? I guess you don't get it, Mr. Tanner. That timber has been on the bottom of Lake Superior for a hundred years, in most cases. Now it supports an ecosystem that's grown up depending on those logs. A fragile ecosystem. If it's disturbed by removing the timber, the balance of nature will be ruptured, quite possibly ruin the lake. We can't allow that to happen. Superior is the largest freshwater lake on the continent, did you know that? You have to help us. If you refuse, I warn you, there will be a disaster." McGregor's voice had risen and people at nearby tables were looking at them.

Tanner was growing uncomfortable under the man's harangue. "All right, McGregor. Just calm down. Do you have any literature? Any studies to back up your claims? I'll be interested in any information you can provide. I—"

"Ahh, you're just like the others," McGregor interrupted angrily. "We thought you were better than the bureaucrats! That you'd understand how important this is. Why can't you accept the facts in front of you and go with it?" He lunged up out of his chair and turned away. Abruptly he swung back and leaned over Tanner who had remained seated. Tanner saw McGregor wipe the frustration and anger off his face with a conscious effort. Back in control of himself, for a silent moment he stared into Tanner's face. "Listen, Tanner, and remember this." His voice had dropped to a low, almost menacing tone. "Mark my words. If you and Anderson persist, something terrible will happen!"

The man spun on his heel and stalked away. Tanner watched McGregor go. Flamboyant as he sounded, Tanner felt in his bones that McGregor hadn't made an idle threat. He picked up his coffee and took a sip. It was cold and bitter.

* * *

Mary Whitney unlocked the door to their condo. She'd glanced up the street toward The Pier when she'd returned to Bayfield, hoping to glimpse Tanner through the window, but she didn't see him. She unloaded her recent purchases and stacked them on a table. Then she sat down and opened *Tales of Lake Superior.*

* * *

Merlin Ames squinted over the frayed wool scarf that covered his face just below his eyes. He rubbed a mittened hand over his ice-speckled eyebrows. There was supposed to be a logging road through the forest right ahead. A road that meandered mostly northwest toward the big lake, but by the dear Lord, he was blessed if he could see it. Merlin Ames blew out his breath in mild exasperation, waving away the cloud of steam the cold temperature created. If the horse remains upright, he thought, somehow the Lord will provide.

Intinerant preacher, Merlin Ames, jiggled the stiff

reins and his horse stepped ahead once more, breasting through deep drifts of the white powder. The snow that had begun sometime during the previous night was still falling. Thankfully, there was little wind in this deep forest of pine and hemlock. To Ames' practiced eye, this part of the forest still held a large number of tall, straight trees and little evidence of the loggers' axes. Experience told him the land wouldn't be left alone for so long. There must be a logging camp within riding distance. He hoped he was right. Neither he nor his faithful horse could last much longer without warm shelter. Gathering his determination and ignoring the growing numbness in his booted feet, Ames pressed on through the gray light.

* * *

Mary Whitney smiled and closed the book. The stories were more fun to read than the drab statistical abstract she'd also picked up at the museum. She felt the need for some tea so she went to the small kitchen in the condo and brewed up a pot. Through the big picture window, she watched a Coast Guard patrol craft heading down the bay in the general direction of Washburn, its warning light flashing. When the tea was ready, she took pot and cup back to the big sofa and reclaimed her book.

* * *

When Reverend Ames finally rode out of the forest and into camp almost half-frozen that Saturday afternoon, he immediately encountered a crisis. He hardly had time to dismount and stagger into the empty bunkhouse. The bunkhouse, sheltering nearly fifty members of the Whitney logging crew, was quiet. Most of the men were out in the woods at their various jobs and the few in camp, mostly cooks and helpers, dragged Ames off his horse and into the warmth of the cookshack. A swamper saw to his weary mount. But for that, most seemed surly and uncommunicative. While he thawed, Reverend Ames explained that he had been urged by the county sheriff to visit this particular camp as soon as possible. The sheriff had heard unsettling rumors about serious trouble at this camp and he wanted an outsider's report. When Reverend Ames pressed his enquiry, he learned that one of the loggers, a man named Tompkins, a man who farmed in the short summer somewhere near Iron Lake, had accused a teamster of trifling with Tompkins' teenage daughter.

Although the teamster, Jarl Rylstone by name, had vigorously denied the accusation, he wouldn't account for his whereabouts during one crucial afternoon. He should have been skidding cut timber to the nearby riverbank, but his team had been idle for several hours, according to other men in camp. The accusation was splitting the camp into factions, some siding with logger Tompkins and others with Rylstone. Several fights had broken out in recent days and, although the itinerant preacher had never dealt with something this serious, he was not inexperienced in dealing with high-tension disagreements among loggers forced to live in close quarters for long stretches at a time. The surprising thing was that there weren't more fights and even murders. In the deep forest, with bitter cold weather often in the mix, with dozens if not hundreds of sharpened axes, knives, and saws readily to hand, it was easy to manufacture an accident, if one wanted to rid one's presence of a rival, or one who had transgressed. The big woods of northern Wisconsin was, after all, a frontier settlement where the rule of law was distant and tenuous.

* * *

Mary read on, a tiny smile playing at the corners of her mouth. Lunchtime came and went. Being close to the locations mentioned in the chronicle, recognizing some of the place names, she was transported back to an earlier century. Present time fled by unnoticed, and it was only the darkening of the day outside the window when a small cloud passed that brought her back to reality. It was already afternoon. Where, she wondered, had Michael got to? Hungry, she decided not to wait for Tanner, but left to find a restaurant.

* * *

The eighteen-foot aluminum runabout with the legend SUPERIOR DIVE neatly lettered on each side bobbed gently in the protected waters of the bay. John Wharton, a Rice, Wisconsin, diving champion of a decade ago, hummed a soft tune as he went about the routine business of keeping track of his partner deep in the water below. This was their second dive of the day, surveying the bottom for CRR, locating the best timber to raise. It was almost time for lunch. He knew the barge would appear in an hour or so from Ashland with the flotation bags and the latest clutch of photographers and reporters. By diving to locate good timber to raise before the press arrived, as George instructed, they were assured of the best photo opportunities and the most effective results for the press. Wharton grinned, thinking that Anderson was a master of milking the press for maximum exposure. He glanced over the side again to find the trail of bubbles that marked the location of the diver below.

The black shape trailing a noisy garland of bubbles cast an uncertain shadow over the lake bottom. The shadow twisted and turned, sometimes gracefully, sometimes awkwardly, peering at the forest giants lying akimbo like an abandoned game of giant pickup sticks on the lake bottom. Even with the sun high in the summer sky, little light reached the littered bottom of the lake. Huge boulders anchored the nearly mud-free floor of the bay. Between and upon the boulders and the lake bottom, long massive fingers of wood lay askew, one or two swaying gently in passing currents. The dense cold waters of the lake pressed down on the tree trunks, holding them to the bottom, loath to let go after so long.

The diver swam on through the clear water, gloved fingers brushing gently over the hundred-year-old timber. Lake Superior, cold, unforgiving, dangerous. Lake Superior, where the dead remained, never rejected by the pure icy waters. The diver glanced at his watch. Only a few minutes longer. The cold was creeping in through his suit, starting to numb his fingers and toes. Insidious, silent, a subtle warning. The earth continued its patient rotation, shifting the shadows from the sun in almost unnoticeable increments. The shadow of a huge tree-trunk, more than twenty feet across, shifted slightly to the east, revealing the bottom of the bay and a clump of rubble partially covered by another massive trunk. Light filtering through the water seemed to give life to the rubble. The diver swam closer and found himself staring into the vacant gaze of empty eye sockets.

Recoiling, he blew out a tremendous bubble of air and shot toward the surface. Long minutes later, when he surfaced near the aluminum boat that was his tender, Raul Mendez ripped off his mask.

"Holy mother!" he called. "There's a body."

"Raul, my man, calm down. Breathe or you'll hyperventilate. What are you shouting about?" Wharton leaned over the gunwale of the boat and frowned down at the agonized face of his partner. He reached to help Raul up the ladder hanging over the side.

Mendez clambered awkwardly out of the water, hampered by the big swim fins attached to his feet. He grabbed two big gasps of air and said in a strangled voice, "A body! I swam right into a skeleton." He blew out another great breath. "I came straight up, this must be almost exactly the spot. Put a float over to mark it."

Wharton picked up a small anchor secured to an orange detergent bottle by a long thin line and dropped it over the side. While Mendez slumped, still slightly stunned in the bottom of the boat, he picked up a portable GPS unit. With a few practiced taps, he brought up their latitude and longitude from the satellites and secured it in the unit's memory. "I'll get on the horn to the Coast Guard. Any idea who it is?

"It ain't exactly a body, you know?" Mendez took a couple of big, calming breaths and said. "I mean, actually, what I saw was a skull. Just a skull, man. It looked like it was coming for me. Freaked me out, man."

"Just a trick of the light." Wharton reached the Coast Guard station at Bayfield and relayed the news. Then he cradled the radio mike and reached out to gently punch his friend and partner on the shoulder. "Just relax an' take it easy. They'll be here in a minute. Man, this'll freak Anderson. After everything else, findin' a body isn't gonna help speed up timber recovery at all. Not at all."

In the distance, the rising wail of a boat siren disturbed the tranquility of the day.

Chapter 8

Tanner watched Ted McGregor leave the restaurant and disappear up the street. Then he rose from the table. While fishing in the pocket of his jeans for some cash to leave as a tip, an old man sitting nearby who had observed the confrontation put out a hand and tugged gently at Tanner's sleeve. "That McGregor. Too much passion, not enough sense," he said quietly.

"You know McGregor? Was that man, in fact, Ted McGregor?"

The old man nodded solemnly displaying just the barest smile on his creased face. "And you are the famous Michael Tanner, a public relations medicine man. From Seattle."

Tanner stared at the old man and nodded back. A feeling came to him then that he was being laughed at in a gentle fashion. "You have me at a disadvantage, sir. It seems as though just about everybody here in Bayfield knows me and, perhaps, my business?"

The old man smiled again and shrugged. "Small towns, you know. But of course, the drums have been active for days now."

"The drums," repeated Tanner.

"Yes. We Indians have always had a very good system of communication, you know." He dipped a hand into the pocket of his jean jacket and pulled out a small cell phone which he showed to Tanner.

Tanner blinked and chuckled. "Drums. I see. I wonder, would you spare me a few moments?"

"That's why I came down this morning from Red Cliff. From the Rez. We knew that McGregor was meeting you."

"You knew I was meeting Ted McGregor here in this restaurant? Now I'm very curious. How did you find out?"

"We knew for sure that he'd called you. We're still pretty good at following a trail, even in the twenty-first century."

Tanner nodded. "I'll just bet you are. I'm pleased to meet you. I have several questions you might be able to help me answer." He stuck out his hand and the older man took it gently, saying, "You can call me Joe, Mr. Tanner. Injun Joe. Sit down, won't you?" Tanner couldn't help smiling again. An Indian who'd read Mark Twain and one with a ready sense of humor.

"With all due respect, I think I'll decline that offer," Tanner responded with a smile. "But I'll call you Joe if you'll call me Michael."

"I think it would be a good idea, Michael, for you to meet other members of my band," said Joe, after they'd been served more coffee. "That's the true reason I came looking for you. We knew you and Mary Whitney are staying across the street and just as I drove up I observed the two of you going to this restaurant. I decided to skulk about for a while to see what I might observe. It's an old Indian trait, you know."

Tanner nodded and smiled some more. Over still more coffee and then some toast, the two men quietly discussed the expansion of the Red Cliff marina, and the coming season of the Green Bay Packers and the Seattle Mariners. They talked too of old logging treaties and the changes brought on by the passage of time.

"It's hard to believe, in a way," said Joe. "Not too many years ago, in the last century, the shores of Chequamegon Bay looked a lot different. In Bayfield there were sawmills and lake freighters docked here frequently. Down in Washburn, the lake shore had a box factory and more'n a dozen saw mills. There were several railroad spurs running alongside the buildings and back into the forest."

"That's sort of amazing, when you look at the place now," said Tanner. "I'm more used to seeing the rotting remains of that kind of industrial activity after companies pull out."

Joe said, "At one time there was a big crib where the freighters unloaded coal for the logging engines and for the factories. About where the marina is in Washburn. Michael, I can contact the council office to call a meeting if you could come with me now. And, if you don't mind riding in an old Indian's old pickup truck, I'll take you up to Red Cliff and bring you back after our meeting." He took out his cell phone and pressed a button. His eyes watched Tanner while he briefly conferred in Ojibwa with whomever was at the other end.

On the short ride to the Red Cliff tribal center, Joe and Tanner made little conversation. The truck's muffler was almost completely rusted out and a lot of engine noise came up through the cracked floorboards. As they rounded a curve on the forested highway, Joe suddenly slowed as a graceful doe leaped out of the woods and crossed to the other side. Instead of starting right up, he waited. "There is almost always more than one," he said, "and in this case––ah." He pointed to the left and Tanner saw two small fawns picking their way nervously to the brushy edge of the road.

After a moment eyeing the truck, they scampered across to safety at their mother's side. Joe and Tanner glanced at each other with satisfaction and the truck engine roared as Joe shifted into gear.

Fifteen minutes later, when they arrived at the reservation, there was no one there to meet them. Still later, as the participants began to straggle in, Tanner realized the meeting could be a lengthy one. He stepped outside and used his own cell phone to call Mary. She didn't answer so he assumed she'd turned her phone off. He left a message that he wouldn't be back in time for lunch.

* * *

Tanner walked out of the big building with the smoothly rounded red roof into the late afternoon sun in company with Joe and several other members of the Indian Band. Although the formal meeting had ended, Tanner was intent on ensuring there was no misunderstanding between him and the others.

"Just to be sure I'm clear on your position; you aren't happy with the harvesting of those logs from the bottom of the lake, but you recognize the realities. And, I take it, you're reasonably satisfied with the deals you've struck."

"We believe that the spirits of our ancestors live in the trees of the forest. Whether the tree is growing on the land or has rested beneath the waters of the lake for many years doesn't alter that," said a tall wiry man who had been mostly silent during the meeting.

Tanner had found the Indian leaders to be thoughtful and well-informed about the company and the environmental concerns, and now Tanner had a better sense of the Red Cliff band's position.

"What about the Bad River Indians? Do you know how they feel?"

"The treaties that affect us are similar and we have had many pow-wows of course," said a dark-skinned member of the council.

"Yes," said Joe, patting his jacket pocket where he carried his cell phone.

When the meeting concluded, he and Tanner clambered into the man's old GMC pickup and Joe drove him back down Highway 13 to town. As they crested a hill on the highway just outside town, Tanner looked southeast toward the lake and Long Island. In the near distance he saw a cluster of boats that seemed to be resting on the water, surrounding a Coast Guard ship and a dive boat.

Inside their apartment he found Mary standing in their rented living room, arms crossed over her chest, watching him come through the door. As he went toward her, she said, "I got your message. I think this is the first time you've ever stood me up for a lunch date."

"At least I called. What did you do for lunch?"

"I went over to the lounge at Bayfield Inn. Had a sandwich. Thought I'd see if there were any good-looking men around I could pick up."

"And?" Tanner leaned forward and kissed Mary's cheek.

"Slim pickings. Oh, there was a cute young cop there, but he was on duty. Where have you been, sailor?"

Tanner shrugged out of his light jacket and hung it on a nearby chair. "After meeting with that McGregor fellow, I was abducted by an old Indian."

"Excuse me?"

Tanner explained. "A man I know only as Injun Joe invited me—"

"Injun Joe? As in Mark Twain?"

Tanner nodded. "That's what he said to call him. I opted for just Joe. Anyway, he invited me up to Red Cliff for a meeting with some representatives of the tribe after

McGregor stormed out. That's where I've been. Meeting at the reservation." Tanner went into the kitchen. "Can I fix you a scotch and water?'

"Yes, thank you. How did the meeting with McGregor go?"

"He's young, quite possibly dedicated to environmental causes, and says he represents something called PFE, People for the Earth. Ever hear of it?"

Mary thought for a moment. "No, but if they're legitimate I bet I can find them on the Internet. I'll just have to hook up the laptop and do a search."

"Anyway, he wanted me to back off from helping CRR at the least. I got the impression he would be happy to recruit Tanner and Associates to aid their anti-pollution causes. We never got that far because I asked him for some evidence that the harvest of these logs would disturb the lake's ecosystem. 'Destroy' was the word he used. He got huffy and stormed out of the restaurant when I asked for some documentation."

"But there was no gunplay, I take it."

"No, but he did pause long enough to offer me a dire warning. Might even have been a threat." Tanner returned from the kitchen with their drinks and shrugged to show he wasn't taking McGregor's words seriously. "This McGregor I met in the restaurant wasn't the man who called me. He seemed to know a good deal about us, about both of us. He also seems to have information that an important new investor is being courted by CRR, although he didn't mention your name in connection with that."

"A source inside the company?"

"That's my guess. We'll have to see how it plays out. Incidentally, Joe confirmed for me that the man I met at the restaurant really was who he said he was. I can't decide whether this McGregor is dangerous or not but this business is getting more complicated by the hour. So, tell me about your day."

Mary took her drink from Tanner and they settled on the davenport before the big picture window.

"I found this lovely gallery in Washburn where the woman was very helpful. She sent me to the town's museum. When logging was big in this part of the country, there were mills all up and down this coast. Ashland had the biggest, but this whole bay was a pretty busy place in those days."

"So my friend Joe informed me. I'm still amazed there's so little evidence of that left along the lake shore."

"Something else I learned, there's a place called Barkdale, or something like that," Mary said. "It was a munitions factory."

"No kidding? Where?"

"The plant was located south of Washburn. Over a thousand acres, apparently. It was in operation until the seventies. You can't see it from the highway, but there it was. Dupont started it as a source of reliable gunpowder back in the 'teens. There's a nicely rendered display of the place in the museum in Washburn. They have a diorama of the waterfront too at about the time milling was most active."

The telephone on a side table rang.

Tanner rolled over on the couch and reached a long arm for the phone. Charles Eddington's voice sounded urgently in Tanner's ear.

"There's been a discovery. In the bay. They've found a body among the logs!"

"Whoa, Mr. Eddington. Slow down."

"Mr. Tanner, this is just terrible. This kind of publicity could seriously damage the company's image. We—I really need your help on this."

"Start at the beginning, Charles," Tanner said evenly. "If I'm to help you I need the whole story."

"Today we had a local contract diver cruising some of our lease-holds in Chequamegon Bay. We need to get some more red oak into the kilns and George wants to kind of stir up the media again."

"I see."

Eddington paused. Then he went on in a lower voice. "I hope you're keeping all this in confidence."

"That goes without saying."

"Even though we don't have a contract yet?"

"Even though."

Eddington blew out his breath in a gusty sigh and seemed to relax some. "Okay. There's another element here. Most people don't know that George had family links to this area a long time ago. It seems a distant relative was working up here and then disappeared."

"I know. George told us that story while we were cruising on his boat the other evening."

"Oh, well, good." Eddington sounded even more relaxed. "Lately, George seems more and more interested in finding out about his missing relative. Sometimes he even goes off when he should be attending to company business. He'll deny it, of course. Now, finding this body will really throw things into a cocked hat.

"I assume the authorities will seal off the area, won't let anyone near the site. That'll curtail recovery operations. Still, if we're careful to set the right tone, CRR could get some good public relations out of this. I'm going out to the site in the bay. Can you join me there? I'll send a launch."

"Sure, I'll come. I can meet the boat at the gas dock here in Bayfield."

"Excellent. I can't thank you enough. I'll send one of our boats when I get on the water. It shouldn't take more than a half hour to get there."

Tanner put down the receiver and turned to Mary.

"Interesting. A diver turned up a body among the logs in the bay. Do you want to come along? Out to the barge?"

"I don't think so. Now that I'm a potential investor, you and I had better be a little more separate in our dealings with the company. I want to get in touch with my people in Seattle and I can do that by phone. It's only three on the coast. Besides, I have no desire to gaze upon dead bodies. You go and report back."

Tanner changed to jeans and rubber-soled slip-ons, clothing more appropriate for climbing about boats, and walked to the nearby marina. Even though shadows were rapidly lengthening, there were several hours of daylight left in this eventful day and the heat had moderated very little. As he went down the small hill past the brick marina office and shower room, Ted McGregor stepped up beside him.

"Mr. McGregor."

"I told you something might happen. Maybe this body will convince you those people need to be stopped."

Tanner turned to face McGregor. "Let's not make any irrational statements. There's probably no connection at all between CRR and this alleged body. I'd advise you to be very careful and not make irresponsible accusations. Now excuse me, I've a boat to catch." Tanner stepped around the other man and went down the ramp to the gas dock. Over McGregor's shoulder, he'd seen a launch rapidly approaching the dock from the direction of the harbor entrance.

Tanner grabbed a short line tossed to him by one of the two men in the boat. "Mr. Tanner," the other called.

"Yes."

"Charlie Eddington. We met the other day at CRR, but I wasn't sure you'd recognize me. Climb aboard and we'll get going. I decided it would be quicker to just come here and pick you up myself."

The boat driver expertly backed away from the dock, turned about and headed to the marina entrance. Once through the breakwater and into the lake, he throttled up to full, teeth-jarring speed, and they skipped across the low waves to the southeast, pointing directly at the cluster of boats anchored north and west of the Long Island light.

As they approached, Tanner identified boats from the Apostle Island Lake Shore Park Service, the Coast Guard, and the Bayfield County Sheriff's Department. A sheriff's deputy confronted them as they nosed in between two boats tied to the rusty barge that was the center of the activity.

"Officer," called Eddington. "We're here for the company. This is our barge and it's our diver who found the body."

The young deputy nodded. It wasn't necessary to identify the company. Everybody who lived along the bay had heard about CRR. "Sure," he said. "Come aboard, but stay out of the way, okay?"

Eddington, followed by Tanner, clambered aboard. Tanner carried a painter and passed it around a handy cleat and handed it back to the boat driver. Then the two men walked forward to the open part of the barge where a small group was clustered.

"Who has top authority?" asked Tanner in a low voice.

"I checked," Eddington said. "The bottom of the lake is Wisconsin territory, so the county sheriff gets it. I think this is Ashland County. I don't know the sheriff personally, but his name is Ferguson, Sheriff Patrick Ferguson. If it's Bayfield County, the sheriff is Tom Morton."

"Okay," Tanner nodded. "Let's see what we can find out."

At the center of attention was a man identified as

Raul Mendez, a local diver who first sighted the body. His partner, John Wharton, had gone down to retrieve the body after the Coast Guard boat arrived. There'd been a small problem since the object hadn't stayed in exactly the same place after being disturbed by Mendez. Wharton had eventually found the skull and was now back on the bottom looking for more bones.

An older man wearing the star of the Bayfield County Sheriff was huddled with a Coast Guard officer and other uniformed people. He raised one hand to get some attention and quell the murmuring. "Okay. Here's the story. There's no body yet. Just a skull, which we now have." He pointed to an object on the deck at his feet covered with a piece of wet canvas. "We're gonna put a whole chunk of this bay off-limits to boaters and certainly to divers and to fishing. We'll map out a search area and with the help of the Park service and the Coast Guard, we'll try to keep everybody away until we've had divers down again to survey the scene."

"Are you pulling in divers from downstate?" asked an unidentified reporter.

"Not at this time," responded the Sheriff. "Mendez and Wharton have agreed to go down again as often as possible, depending on what's necessary. They'll put their contract with CRR on hold for a day or so. It's not that deep here, so it shouldn't take long, if the weather holds. We'll pull in more local divers who are used to the lake if we need 'em."

"How long do you want the area patrolled?" asked the Coast Guard officer.

"Can't say, Henry. After some dives tomorrow we'll have a better idea."

Eddington stepped between two men and said, "I'm Charles Eddington, representing CRR. If you want to use this barge as a platform and any of our underwater video gear or anything else, just ask."

"Thanks, Mr. Eddington, I appreciate that," said the Sheriff. His gaze shifted to Tanner.

Eddington saw the look and went on, "This is Michael Tanner. He's working with CRR in a public relations and marketing capacity. I hope it'll be all right if he observes your investigation here."

The Sheriff nodded. "We don't want a lot of people out here, but I have no objections at the moment. Meanwhile, we'll leave everything as it is right now and start again at first light."

"Excuse me, Sheriff Ferguson?" asked Tanner from his new-found stature. "I assume you've considered the fact that this location isn't out of reach of a diver from the shore, so you'll post a guard tonight to discourage any tampering."

It was apparent that if the Sheriff had considered leaving a guard, he was the only one aboard the barge who had. "Thank you, Mr. Tanner. We're doing just that."

As the small group began to disperse, Tanner walked to where the Sheriff was detailing a deputy to stay on the barge. "I'll send Josh about midnight to relieve you. But you and him are the only available deputies right now and besides, you two have more water patrol experience. We'll find some heavier clothes for you and I'll send a boat back before dark with a portable spotlight and some food and water. Mr. Tanner?"

"I wonder if you can tell me anything else about the body Mendez found."

"Mr. Tanner, in the strictest confidence you understand, here's what I know for sure. It's not a body, it's a head. A skull. It appears to be undamaged except for a hole in the back. My experience tells me the hole was probably caused by a bullet. I think it's been in the water a long time. I'm betting we don't find anything else down there. But we'll make a search. The skull will be sent to the state's forensic lab tonight."

"Thank you, Sheriff. I appreciate the confidence."

"Well, don't disappoint me." He turned away.

Tanner went to Eddington and said, "If you want my advice, I'd say nothing to anyone, including people in the company. We don't know who the skull belongs to, whether it has a connection to CRR. Later, we may be able to capitalize on the finding of the skull, but that's pretty chancy until we know a lot more."

Eddington and Tanner stepped aboard the boat that had brought them to the scene and cast off. Then Tanner said, "One more thing. I suggest no one at CRR volunteer anything to the media. Speculation and rumor can be damaging. What you hope is that any connection of this discovery to CRR is kept tenuous at the moment. Sure, publicity is publicity, but this is the kind of publicity that can come back to bite you."

Eddington nodded that he understood perfectly.

Chapter 9

The smooth black asphalt twisted and turned, winding through the tall hemlock and pine trees. Sun spattered down through the trees onto the road. Mary looked with pleasure at the patterns. The morning after the discovery of the skull in the bay, Tanner had gone back to the anchored barge to talk with the diver who had discovered it. Mary was on her own, exploring more of Bayfield County.

Since she and Tanner had come to northern Wisconsin, she'd been focusing on the business aspects of CRR and whether the company was worthy of her recommendation to the Whitney venture capital office. There was more to come, she knew. It reminded her of why she had listened closely to her granduncle and grandfather as a young girl growing up in a wealthy Seattle family. The two crusty adventurers were second generation Whitneys who'd been prominently involved in the day-to-day activities of an expanding enterprise. Both had been of similar mind regarding the lovely young woman who had shown an independent attitude and more than idle interest in the affairs of the company. In spite of parental concerns, both old men had taken Mary Whitney to sea, into the warehouses and onto the lands held by the Whitney Corporation. They'd spent long hours talking with her about their history and their legacy.

Out of those conversations and experiences, Mary

had come to understand both the rapacious nature of the robber baron era in America and an attending obligation, whether born of guilt or a fundamental goodness.

Mary Whitney had come to believe that her nature was not to spend her life either as a Wall Street wife or in the business world of Seattle, inhabited by the corporate leaders of Whitney and other large entities. Today, she was, in one sense, again fleeing that world by taking a solitary exploratory trip into part of the northern Wisconsin wilderness.

She drove the Lexus off the highway and onto a gravel side road and stopped. Shading her eyes, she looked up at the leafy canopy overhead. For a moment she conjured up what the forest must have looked like a hundred and fifty years before her logging ancestors and other lumbermen had swarmed into these woods with their shining axes and sharp saws. It had been a tall forest with a thick cover of needles and leaves, so that the sun had difficulty penetrating to the ground and there was little underbrush. Even now there was evidence that the forest was steadily reclaiming untouched lands. Mary drove slowly into the grove.

Here the tree trunks were closer together and low branches brushed the top of the car. A few hundred yards down the narrowing gravel road, she stopped and consulted the map in her lap. Apparently the cartographers at Rand McNally hadn't seen fit to include this particular wandering gravel lane. Well, no matter, it obviously went somewhere. And if it didn't, she'd just turn around and go back to the highway.

Half an hour later she wasn't so sure of her decision to follow this path less traveled. The gravel had become more and more sparse and finally petered out into a track, mostly of muddy ruts. She looked through the bug-spattered windshield at a fork just ahead of her front bumper. The road descended into a wide pool of murky water. Out of it two muddy paths went in different directions. Either one could lead to somewhere useful. Or not. The large brown puddle faded away into the underbrush growing right up to the edges of the track. She couldn't see the limits of the little pond and there was no indication of how deep the water might be. Great, she thought, at least I don't have to worry about traffic piling up behind me. I'll just turn around and go back the way I came.

She backed up several feet and then stopped to think about where she might get off the track to reverse her direction. She didn't recall passing any clearings and she hadn't been paying attention to the mileage she'd gone. How far from the paved road was she? Mary switched off the motor and opened the driver's side door. She was reminded again of the stillness of the big woods. Nearby insects and other small critters, disturbed by the passing car, were silent for the moment. Even the air was still.

The first to resume were the insects, then small birds began to twitter in the nearby brush. For a few minutes, Mary and the trees communed. She felt a connection to this place. People who worked for her family had worked here, felling trees, skidding logs to the shore. There was resonance, just as when she had first dipped her toes in Lake Superior on the beach at Washburn.

Mary stepped out of the driver's seat and stood listening. If there was a road nearby, there was no traffic on it. As far as she could tell, no other human was within a hundred miles. She smiled faintly and went to investigate the roadside. Immediately off the muddy track the ground was spongy and grew progressively softer as Mary pushed her way through the undergrowth. Recent rains had loosened the earth so it looked as though driving off the track to turn around was not a good idea. The car would likely sink to its axles and she'd be stuck.

Mary walked down the slight incline ahead of the Lexus to the edge of the large puddle of water where the track forked. Along the way she found a dead branch by the side of the road. Sacrificing her clean white tennis shoes, she stepped into the mud and probed the bottom of the pond, finding it to be not more than a couple of inches deep and apparently solid under a thin layer of silt. She figured she could drive through that.

Back in the Lexus, gunning the engine, she slammed and slithered through the pond, sending a great wave of muddy water up onto the windshield. Dripping and growling, the Lexus made it through the water and she skidded into the left hand fork. Twenty minutes later Mary knew she'd chosen the wrong path.

The track had degenerated into a deeply rutted, meandering trace that ended in a wall of brush in front of her bumper. There was no gap in the bushes and small saplings barred her way. It was obviously the end of this road. The ground was drier here and Mary got the Lexus turned around, but only a few yards back along the ruts she felt the rear end of the vehicle suddenly slide toward the edge of the cleared track. When she gunned the engine, the Lexus bounced on the greasy mud, scraped over a patch of bare earth and grounded on the high center of the track. The body was just high enough to take away traction to the wheels. Damn it, she thought. It was getting late in the afternoon and she was stuck somewhere in a northern Wisconsin wilderness. What's more, no one, including herself, knew where she was. Now here's a situation in which I definitely could use my cell phone, Mary mused. So much for leaving it behind.

With the engine off, the only sound was the ticking of the cooling metal and the hum of insects. Mosquitoes descended on her where she stood peering into the trunk, looking for any kind of tool to help her extricate the Lexus. The jack appeared to be the only useful item. She went to the front of the car and decided that if she jacked up each wheel, there'd be enough space to shove branches and even some dirt into the ruts and so raise the car off the mound of earth that prevented the wheels from gaining traction.

She went to work and, after many minutes, had filled in the rut under the left front wheel. When she let the jack down, the trash and branches she'd shoved under the tire compressed several inches but held the car up enough. Progress! Her hands were filthy, she had smudges on her face and on her slacks, and sweat was running down her cheeks.

"You took the wrong fork," said a quiet voice from the other side of the Lexus.

Mary jumped what felt like several feet and felt her heart hammer in her chest. Whirling, she saw a lean, jeans-clad figure standing there, his white t-shirt tight across his chest. Mary's eyes seemed to sear the appearance of this suddenly materialized stranger into her brain. He was wearing muddy cowboy boots and a western-style hat with a broad brim that shadowed his face. He carried a rifle or a shotgun over one shoulder.

"Oh! My God! You startled me! I almost had a heart attack." She stood there with the jack handle in one hand, feet apart, ready to jump for the bushes.

"Minnesota plate," the man said, shifting his stance. "You're a stranger 'round here." He wasn't asking questions. "It's pretty easy to get lost in these woods if you don't know your way." The man swayed forward and came a few steps down the side of the car toward Mary. She took a step away. Her grip tightened on the jack handle.

The stranger took his hat off and wiped his brow with the other hand. She could see his straight black hair caught in a short braid by a colorful beaded circlet. His dark eyes, strong chin, and seamed, leathery face bespoke a man who spent a good deal of time in the out of doors. He squinted at her. "This here's Indian land. Red Rock." He waved one arm around him, never loosening his grip on the weapon.

"My name is Mary Whitney. I'm visiting here with my husband, Michael Tanner."

"Looking for more timber to take?"

"Excuse me, I don't—"

"Whitney people came here many years ago. Your people took much of the forest in these parts. Now you want to recover the timber that sank in the lake, am I right?"

"You know about that?"

"Of course. Come on, you jack up the other side while I get more brush and sticks to hold up the wheel." The man carefully leaned his rifle against a nearby sapling and walked into the brush. When he returned with a huge bundle of downed branches, Mary had the wheel jacked up out of the hole. In short order the Lexus was standing free on all four tires.

The stranger retrieved his rifle and came around to the driver's side of the car where Mary sat. He stood a few feet away and pointed. "Go back down this track a little way until you come to a faint trail leading only to the left. It's more grass than dirt, but it's higher ground so it's dry and safe. It will take you to the gravel. Go right on the gravel and you will get to the highway in about a mile."

"Thank you so much for your help." Although she was still cautious about the man, Mary said, "Can I offer you a ride?"

"No, that wouldn't be a good idea. But please remember where all that timber at the bottom of the big lake came from, and what it now hides." The man raised one hand, settled his hat more firmly on his head and then walked without a backward glance into the brush and disappeared.

Mary Whitney sat staring after him for a long thoughtful moment. Then she started the car and drove cautiously back down the muddy track the way she had come. Soon she had gained the highway and was heading back to Bayfield.

* * *

Night came early and still the snow fell. The teams of loggers straggled in from the surrounding forest and went immediately to their places in the mess hall. The evening meal of roast beef with potatoes and gravy came hot to the tables, and there was almost no conversation beyond a grunt or two. A few men sent curious glances in Ames' direction and he knew his presence and his purpose would be known throughout the camp before many more hours had passed.

After supper, the camp foreman took Ames out back. He lit a lantern and they broke a trail through the thickly falling snow to a small shed. It was very cold. Ames wondered if the temperature was still falling.

The two men had to struggle together to get the shed door opened against the new snow. Once inside the foreman explained that there had been a fight of some kind and a man had been killed. The body was stored in the shed until the County Sheriff arrived to take charge.

Ames had sensed the uneasy atmosphere of the camp. Some of the men obviously felt hostility and suspicion toward others in camp. The poisonous situation was gradually infecting the entire camp. Could Ames not somehow bring a little peace? If the men made more trouble, if there were more accusations or fights, this crew would fail to get the timber out and the company owners would be upset. Ames thought he could try. He'd change his planned sermon for tomorrow, Sunday morning.

The foreman looked hard at Ames through his raveled graying beard and hung the lantern on a nearby peg. Then he turned and with difficulty lifted a stiff and frozen piece of canvas off a mound at one side of the shed. Ames had seen his share of death and injury after ten years of traveling to the farms and camps of northern Wisconsin, but this was bad.

The body lay face up, hands loosely placed at his belt. His trousers were dark heavy wool, stiff with frozen sweat and grime. His torso was clothed in a checkered shirt, with a heavy mackinaw over that. There were dark splotches all over the man's clothes, splotches Ames took to be frozen blood. In the center of his chest was a small hatchet.

* * *

Mary shivered and slipped a scrap of paper between the pages and closed the book. She glanced out the window and then at her watch. Suddenly she was ravenous, and there was no way to know when Tanner would reappear. She went downstairs and out into the heat of the late afternoon. Ten minutes later she was seated at a table in one corner of Grunke's. A tall pilsner glass, one-third empty, was at her right hand, and the remains of a crisp green salad of tomatoes, lettuce, chopped green onions, and bell peppers was on the plate before her.

She wiped her mouth on the napkin and considered that, with her inner being temporarily satisfied, she would return to the Reverend Ames narrative. When she looked up, Ted McGregor was standing nearby, frowning down at her.

"Excuse me?" Mary said pleasantly. "Was there something you wanted?"

"My name is McGregor, Ted McGregor. I met your husband a few days ago. May I join you?"

Mary looked up at the young man. "I don't think so. You may have business with my—Mr. Tanner, but not with me. I'd like to enjoy my meal alone, if you don't mind."

McGregor leaned forward, resting his hands on the table. "But I do mind. You are supposed to be concerned about the environment, isn't that right? That's what I hear, anyway. So why are you avoiding me? Why aren't you out there trying to stop that company and Tanner from messing up the lake?" His voice was rising.

"Look, Mr. McGregor, I'm here on a vacation. That's all. Now, you'd better leave."

"Yeah? So you've been seduced by the money, just like everybody else. I—"

"Excuse me," said a voice from behind Mary. She twisted around to see one of the restaurant managers coming toward them. "You're disturbing the other people. If you want to yell at each other, take it outside."

Mary shook her head and said, "No, I think Mr. McGregor was just on his way out."

McGregor started to go on and then, faced with the larger, older manager of Grunke's, flapped his arms in disgust and turned to stomp out. As he left he flung a parting shot over his shoulder. "This isn't over. You'll see."

Chapter 10

"This is really an amazing process," Tanner remarked, watching the crew of the big barge going efficiently about their tasks. A second barge leased to CRR had been moved into position outside the restricted area where divers were searching for more human remains.

He stood on the prow of the commercial power boat *Island Hunter*. Earlier that morning, the *Island Hunter* had maneuvered a fifty-foot floating crane into its designated position. Thick, dirty anchor cables splayed out into the water from each corner of the barge, a barge that had seen better days. From the crane's deck mount to the formerly white and now heavily dented sides of the barge itself, dirt and rust dripped everywhere.

"She ain't pretty, but she works good," said a hard-hatted man noticing Tanner's gaze. He spat tobacco juice over the side and swung awkwardly up into the operator's seat eight feet above the deck of the barge. Except for the crane mounted at one end, the barge was just a large open well with steel walls about five feet high. All the members of the crew wore hard hats and lifejackets.

"We're about to get a look at timber that was cut over a hundred years ago," George Anderson, standing a few feet away, said. He continued, "It's also amazing to realize that the timber we're bringing up started growing when Columbus was alive. You know, our operation is going to help save the few remaining old growth forests.

I always get a little bump right here," he touched his breastbone, "when they bring up another log. We'll see the butt markings and learn who cut it where and when, and who owned it."

"You said you feel as though you're completing what the loggers started a hundred years ago," said Tanner.

"Well, sure." Anderson gave a slight shrug. "A little hyperbole never hurts, you know, but it is true. And we aren't disturbing the balance of the environment or any spotted owls, either."

"I have to tell you, George, I got a little bump right here," mimicking Anderson's gesture, "when I watched the news on TV this morning," said Tanner.

Anderson glanced at Tanner as if he didn't know what he was referring to until he registered the look on Tanner's face. "Oh, you mean the piece about finding that skull?"

"Exactly. As I recall my conversation with Mr. Eddington, my advice was to avoid the press until we know a lot more."

"Well, you're right, I guess. I shoulda resisted getting historical with that reporter."

"Not to say hysterical. You don't want CRR to be seen as exploiting the discovery of that skull. You could have all kinds of reactions. Suppose it turns out to be a member of one of the Indian bands in the area? Suppose the state decides they don't want this kind of notoriety and it would be easier if you just went away? You should be very cautious from here on. How'd the reporter get to you? And so fast?"

"She said she got a tip. Said the caller told her one of our divers had made an ugly discovery. That it was probably a murder."

"Did she say who called in the tip?"

Anderson shook his head. Tanner glanced across

the water toward the other barge and said, "How's your search for additional investors doing these days?" When he looked back at Anderson, he thought Anderson's face had blanched a bit.

He waved a hand in a casual manner. "Well, the stock market's been depressed for a while, you know. Means possible investors don't have as much free cash as they might. We've been hampered by all the bureaucracy that got in our way. We're almost three years behind my projections. But last week things started to turn around. The market's uptick has helped. I'm starting to get calls again." He stopped and looked at Tanner silently for a moment. "I get it. You think I talked to that reporter to get publicity and hype the investment?"

Tanner shrugged. "The thought occurred. Mainly, though, I want you to understand that if my company signs on to this project, we expect all company officers to run media contacts through us. At least until we get the campaign up and running."

The diver aboard SUPERIOR DIVES, from the charter company contracted for this recovery operation, finished his preparations. Raul Mendez flashed a big smile and a thumbs up at the people aboard the other craft and slipped over the side. He'd been relieved of his assignment when the Wisconsin authorities decided to bring in a police underwater team to search for additional evidence where the skull had been retrieved.

Mendez sank from sight in the water carrying a hammer, ring bolt, and a big yellow and blue plastic flotation bag. He would select a log, hammer the ring bolt into the log at one end, and attach the flotation bag. Then he'd connect a hose from a compressor on the barge to the flotation bag and the bag would be pumped full of air. When there was enough air in the bag, it would drag the log to the surface. There the claw on the barge's crane would grab the log and hoist it into the belly of the barge. The sequence would be repeated several times over the next few hours until a full load could be transported to the harbor at Ashland.

"This isn't what you'd class as easy work, is it, George?" said Tanner.

"No, and there's some element of risk, particularly if we get too eager and don't follow the procedure. But we haven't had any serious accidents. These guys are all experienced professionals. They'd better be. I'm paying them plenty."

"That's one of the things we're wondering about. I heard from my people in Seattle, you know, and one of the questions is about the cost of recovery."

"Teddy mentioned that. It costs more to harvest these sunken treasures than it does to cut timber in the forests."

"But you can charge more," said Tanner.

"Right. Once it's dried out, the wood is more valuable. The hardwoods. Not every log attracts the big bucks you read about in some of those articles. We have to be careful about our costs but the economics are okay so far. And you'll see when you tour the plant that we use every bit of the wood we recover, down to the sawdust generated by the cutting and planing operations."

There was a whoop and a huge splashing sound. Like a small whale, the yellow flotation bag and its attached log exploded to the surface. George Anderson peered at it through a small pair of powerful binoculars. "That's seriously old," he said. "No saw marks, which means it's one of the real early ones. Red oak from the look of it. Just what we need right now."

Anderson's cell phone trilled and he flipped it open, turning away for a little privacy as he did so. Tanner continued to watch the operation, admiring the care of the crane operator when he maneuvered the huge gaping jaws of the clam bucket over the bobbing end of the log and clamped on. When it was stabilized, Raul Mendez swam to the log and unhooked the flotation bag and deflated it. Then he flipped over and sank out of sight, returning to the bottom of the lake to snare another piece of history.

Anderson pointed toward Ashland, and Tanner saw coming toward them a launch with a big red bubble on the top of a metal bracket over its bridge. The police cruiser swung parallel to the barge and the driver expertly dropped his speed and slid to a stop.

The Ashland County sheriff put up a hand and then grabbed the gunwale of the *Island Hunter* beside Tanner's feet. "Well there's not-so-good news and some bad news," he said, "depending on your position, I guess. The bad news is this. We've got a preliminary report on the examination of that skull Mendez brought up yesterday. It appears to have a bullet hole in the back of the head. The other news is that it is pretty old. Maybe a hundred years. There's still no sign of any more of the skeleton but we're going to keep the off-limits signs until the state guys are convinced they aren't going to find any more bones."

"Thanks, Sheriff. I appreciate the update," said Anderson. He was smiling widely. Tanner knew George was thinking that finding that old skull would make little or no difference to CRR's fortunes. For a moment Tanner wondered if there was a sensitive way, in good taste, to take advantage of the find.

The sheriff let go of the gunwale and the boat turned to head toward the other barge.

"Looks like you dodged a bullet," Tanner said.

"Yep, I'm relieved, I don't mind telling you. We're expanding our operations, you know. The company is perched on the edge of global expansion. Did you know they're finding sunken timber in lots of places all over the country? Hell, if I can find enough new investment capital, we'll even start signing some overseas contracts." He shot Tanner a meaningful look. "This is going to be big, Tanner, really big. Investors who get in now are going to make a lot of money."

Midafternoon, after several hours watching the harvest of big logs from the lake, Tanner had himself ferried back to Bayfield. About to depart the still-working barge, Tanner said, "Look, George, I seem to have slid into working for you in an unconventional manner. I still want to think over a few things and talk to Mary about it, but I think you'll be able to count on my help. We've the weekend just ahead, so let's meet Monday morning and go over contract details."

Anderson's face lit up in a wide grin and he reached out and grabbed Tanner's hand. "Great!" he said. "That's just great. We'll make a terrific team."

When Tanner walked up from the marina dock to their condo apartment, he found Mary sitting wrapped in a robe, tending to her toenails. He stopped for a moment to admire her long legs that emerged from the skirt of the pale yellow robe. "I had a small adventure, and I met your Mr. McGregor," she said smiling up at him as Tanner crossed the carpet and bent down for a kiss.

* * *

Over a drink at a loud boisterous Maggie's, crowded with sailors and vacationers, Mary said, "I still don't know about the investment part of this, but I've talked to a friend of mine at the foundation. She's a lawyer, heads up the research team for the investment office of the foundation. Very sharp. Anyway, what do you think?"

"I can understand George's and the other's

enthusiasm for this project. They're dabbling in history, it's environmentally clean, and it's a new idea."

"Attractive on most counts."

Tanner nodded. "I could almost feel the excitement on that barge this morning, even from the hired workers who have really nothing invested."

"But what do you think about George and the rest?"

Tanner smiled at Mary. "What I think is that George is a bit of a hustler. Some of the others are as well. CRR is still a relatively new enterprise and it could go belly up in a trice. George isn't about to let that happen if he can avoid it."

"What about the original investors? How many are still in there, waiting for a payoff?"

"That I expect your financial wizards to tell us. Right now I don't think we'll be taking an equity position and George hasn't proposed that we do."

Mary nodded and drained her glass. "Maybe he doesn't have to since I expressed interest on behalf of Whitney."

"There is that. Well now, we have the weekend ahead of us. What would you like to do?" Tanner traced an aimless pattern on the back of her hand where it lay on the table between them.

"I'd like to see more of these islands. Let's try to get out on the water during the weekend. We did say this was going to be a vacation as well as a working trip, right?"

"My very thought. Let's go back to the condo and see what we can come up with."

"I've been collecting some flyers," said Mary, "and there are several possibilities. We can book on the boat tour that goes around all the islands, get a full historical picture. The tour boat leaves from right down there at the end of the commercial dock. There's also a schooner that makes short excursions into the islands.

"But what I'd really like to do is charter a sailboat. If we hurry, maybe we can even get a boat tonight," Mary said. "There's lots of daylight left."

Back at their apartment, Tanner took up the telephone and called the local marina office. The boy who answered gave them the number for Superior Charters, just down the road a couple of miles. Superior Charters, it turned out, had a cancellation. The woman on the telephone told Tanner there was a nice twenty-six-foot Paceship available for the weekend. It was an older boat, she said, but well-maintained and quite comfortable. She agreed to wait for them past closing if necessary while they scrambled for provisions for a two-day sail among the Apostle Islands.

Chapter 11

Two hours later, Tanner and Mary were being checked out on *Spindrift*, a red-hulled sloop with a tiller and an outboard engine.

"Oh, this'll be interesting," Mary said to Fred Craft, a small active man with innumerable laugh lines around his eyes who stood on the finger dock beside *Spindrift's* bow. Craft, a Superior Charters employee, was helping them explore the boat. "It's been a long time since we've sailed on anything this small."

Kraft nodded enthusiastically. "You'll find her a lot more nimble than your bigger boats. Of course, she's not as fast as what you're used to, but you'll have a good time."

"Draft?" asked Tanner.

"Four feet. We monitor channel 16 from seven in the morning to ten at night, and of course the Coast Guard is awake twenty-four-seven." The marina man nodded and smiled.

"What's the weather going to be like?" Mary swung a hamper aboard from the two-wheeled cart they were using to transport rain gear and their small duffels to the open cockpit. Tanner was standing in the galley, stowing their meal makings in the small icebox and in cavities under the cabin cushions.

"Ten to fifteen knots of southerly winds day and night. This time of the year they'll probably shift back and forth from southwest to south and you're likely to have some calms along about sundown." He cocked an experienced eye at the sky. "Looks like the wind might hold today, though. Fairly calm water. Nothing uncommon. Sunny and more of the same for the next couple of days. You should have a great weekend on the water."

"Anything else?"

"Well, since you're unfamiliar with the area, be cautious about sailing after dark. There are pond nets and other uncharted obstacles that can be a problem if you hit one. These nav charts are accurate about everything else. There's a hump in the bottom right here in the approach to the marina." His callused finger stabbed the chart he was holding for Mary to examine. "Since the lake is lower than usual this spring, you better not try to go over it. In normal times, your four-foot draft would clear it easily. Have a good sail. Oh, and don't forget to watch for the ferries when you pass between Bayfield and Madeline. One other thing we always remind people. The lake is icy cold just about everywhere except in shallow bays where it's just ordinary cold. Even the bays don't warm up until late summer." Craft grinned at them again, loosed the bow lines and pushed *Spindrift* back out of her slip. Mary already had the outboard idling and she slowly backed the little boat out and then turned toward the gap in the marina breakwater.

"This boat must be over twenty years old," said Tanner from his squatting position on the foredeck where he was stowing mooring lines and examining the anchor tackle.

"Even so, she looks well-maintained," Mary said. "Hand me those fenders. I'll stow them in the lazarette."

Under Mary's guiding hand, *Spindrift* zipped out through the gap in the concrete breakwater and they headed northwest. Tanner sorted out the lines and had a big jib up and filled with the breeze as they approached Bayfield a short while later. He paused in his preparations for raising the main and put the bright yellow binoculars to his eyes. He located the superstructure of one ferry at the Bayfield dock, and swept the shore beside the Bayfield marina. Then he looked east to see a second ferry just leaving the shelter of Madeline Island. For the permanent residents of the island, the ferries that ran between La Pointe on the southern end of Madeline and Bayfield were the only way to get from their homes to the mainland and back. Satisfied they could pass over the ferry route with time to spare, Tanner turned his attention to the main halyard and smartly hauled the mainsail up the mast. Looking up from cleating off the main, he looked toward Bayfield again and saw a man standing on the edge of the breakwater with binoculars pressed to his face. He seemed to be staring right at *Spindrift.*

Two hours later, with a brisk breeze from their starboard quarter, *Spindrift* was gliding contentedly up the west channel between the mainland and Basswood Island. With a small bottle of water in one hand, Tanner sprawled in the stern of the boat, taking his turn at the tiller. Late in the day as it was, the sun still shone bright and hot from a clear sky, and both Tanner and Mary slathered on sunscreen. The green hills that cascaded down to the water's edge of the island were bathed in a golden glow.

They'd quickly discovered the idiosyncrasies of the Paceship. They had a big genoa bellied out forward of the main and were getting a teriffic ride along the island. There were no sailboats on this side of Basswood and only an occasional powerboat went by, turning the deep blue of Lake Superior's water momentarily white.

"This is neat," said Mary. She was crouched on the cabin roof by the mast. "We get a much more immediate sense of the water and our speed in a smaller boat like this. Ow!" A small wave sent icy spray over the side, giving Mary a good sprinkling of Lake Superior's enduringly cold water. "That was a little too immediate."

"We're heading toward Oak Island," Tanner said, adjusting their course. "We might make it to the north end of Oak, or we could turn east and go to the deep bay on Stockton. You have any preferences?"

Mary leaned over and took the chart. "Actually, I don't, so long as we can anchor somewhere for supper. I don't much like the idea of trying to make a hot meal in an unfamiliar galley while we're under way. Besides, we have to anchor for the night so let's pick a good spot."

Tanner glanced at the sails and then at the chart Mary held out after sliding down from the cabin roof to the seat beside him. She snaked one arm around his waist and hugged him. "If this wind holds, Stockton looks like the better choice for tonight. I'll whip up a few snacks and we'll plan a late dinner after we anchor. That suit ya, sailor?"

"Suits me just fine, matey, especially if you can fish me out a can of beer from the reefer." Tanner admired the curves of Mary's backside in her tight shorts as she leaned through the hatch and snagged him a beer.

* * *

Racing the coming night, Mary adjusted their course. The wind freshened and the little sloop chuckled as she raced on, bow cleaving the water and splitting the small waves. White water occasionally slopped up over the bow and wetted the genoa.

Below in the main cabin which served as galley, salon, and sleeping quarters, Tanner grinned and braced himself against one of the bunks. He flipped up the cover of the ice box, pulled out the bottle of pinot grigio and filled two plastic glasses from the rack over the tiny stove.

When he regained the cockpit and glanced around, he saw they had made excellent progress toward their anchorage. The blue water sparkled in the low slanting sunlight and their shadow raced ahead of them, dappled by the restless water. Watching Mary handle the boat, Tanner saw the concentration and pleasure in her face. Her smile widened when she brought her eyes down to his.

"Fun," she said. "I like the quick way this boat handles. It's so different from the *Sea Queen*."

The radio crackled to life. "*Spindrift, Spindrift, Spindrift*. Paceship *Spindrift*, come in, please." The call was repeated again before Tanner remembered that their boat was named *Spindrift*. He dropped back to the cabin floor and thumbed the mike.

"This is *Spindrift*, over."

"*Spindrift*, this is Superior Charters. Switch to Channel 62 please.

Tanner did as requested and reestablished the link.

"*Spindrift*, we have a caller requesting that you contact him as soon as possible. I have a phone number for you."

"Ah, roger, Superior Charters. Give me the name and number. You'll have to tell the caller I have no phone out here. I can't call until we get back to the marina." Standing in the hatch, Tanner glanced up at Mary who gave him a big thumbs up when he mentioned not having a cell phone aboard.

"What's your location, *Spindrift*?"

"We're southwest of Stockton, heading generally in that direction. I expect that's where we'll anchor for the night. Over."

"Stand by," crackled the radio.

After a moment, the marina radio operator came

back on. "*Spindrift*, I wasn't able to relay the message. Your caller has hung up."

"Roger that. If it's important they'll call again. Out."

Tanner replaced the mike on its hook. They passed between Hermit Island and Stockton, and Mary tacked. They carried on across the wide expanse of the channel, heading northeast toward the deeply indented harbor called Quarry Bay on Stockton's eastern shore. On all sides they saw other sailboats, some motoring, others content to drift along with the light breeze as they made their way to various destinations. A large cabin cruiser, multiple fishing rods festooning the rear rail, lumbered by, rocking *Spindrift* gently in its wake.

"I have a new thought," said Mary. "How about organizing the makings for some super sandwiches while I get us to Quarry Bay? We'll do a cold supper our first night out and just forget dinner."

"Consider it done."

"How's about a little more wine for the helm before you start rooting around in that ice box?" Mary held out her glass. Tanner reached the bottle of wine up through the hatch. Mary took it and wedged it in a corner of the cockpit with an extra cushion and a bungee. Tanner paused to listen to the gurgle of the water along the hull of the sailboat. For a moment he allowed his memory to drift back to another time on another body of water, with a different woman he'd called wife. Still remembering, he turned to his task of creating fat sandwiches of sliced turkey, cheese, lettuce, and tomato.

On deck, he arranged the big cutting board he'd discovered under the stove to hold paper plates and food. Mary held the tiller between her knees while she took big bites from her sandwich. "Good sandwich. I'll ship out with you any time."

Tanner nodded enthusiastically. "It's not just all this fresh air, either. I think you have to have first-class provisions to keep the crew happy." He glanced around. "Anything especially interesting happen while I was below?"

"A few boats went by. Lots of nice views. Great trees on that island. A picture-postcard evening. I hope we can get out to Devil's Island. I understand the caves are interesting."

Tanner had brought up the boat's bright yellow binoculars and was now methodically sweeping the horizon. Occasionally he paused to study a boat traveling in the channel.

"What?" said Mary, aware as usual of Tanner's moods. "You looking for a different ride?"

Taking the glasses away from his face, Tanner said, "Nope. I was just thinking about that radio message. Do you remember what I said?"

"Not exactly. Something about heading toward Stockton for the night. Why?"

"I can't put my finger on it. Who did we tell we were coming out here this weekend?"

Mary frowned in thought. "No one. It was all sort of last minute."

"So how did whoever called Superior Charters know we were out here on a boat named *Spindrift*?"

"I see what you're getting at. The people at the charter company know, of course. I just told the caretaker at the condo we'd be gone for the weekend. Even I didn't know the name of the boat." She was silent for a moment. "I suppose somebody in the office might have overheard. But if you were watching us sail out you could call and ask for us. They'd relay a message and tell you what boat we're on, wouldn't they?"

"That's just what I was thinking. I don't recall

anyone else in the marina office, but there might have been. If that's how they found out, it means someone must have followed us, to the grocery store and then to the boat. Odd, don't you think?"

"Very." said Mary. "Why would anybody follow us? Who? McGregor or his friends? Are we involved in something we don't know about?" Her lips quirked momentarily at the absurdity of her statement. "Unless you have our exact location, course, and speed, finding us out here isn't going to be easy, even with this red hull. We know how hard it is to find another boat on a big piece of water."

Tanner nodded. "Right. Unfortunately, I told the radio operator where we were going to anchor for the night. At least I mentioned Stockton Island."

"How concerned are you? Do you think somebody is trying to keep track of us?"

Tanner shrugged and exchanged binoculars for his own sandwich. "I don't know, hon, it's just one more thing and an odd feeling I get every once in a while."

"You mean like someone is watching you?"

"Yeah, I guess. You feel it?"

"No, I can't say I have." Mary made a quick visual sweep of the surrounding area. "Stand by to tack."

Tanner set his sandwich down and turned to the winches that controlled the jib sheets. "Ready."

A moment later Mary said, "Tacking." She swung the tiller over and *Spindrift* obediently shifted from an easterly course to almost due north to bring them directly into the mouth of Quarry Bay. The jib rattled across the boat and Mary slacked the boom while Tanner adjusted the sheets.

"Looks like a few boats ahead of us." Tanner consulted the chart the marina owner had provided. "There's a park service dock right in the throat of the bay

with a campground behind it. On your right is the mouth
of a small creek. Probably going to be marshy there and a
mushy bottom. The rest of the bay is sand bottom. Unless
the wind shifts to the southeast tonight, I think you can
park us just about anywhere."

"Do you want to go ashore?"

"Not tonight. I'm tired. How about you?"

"Fresh air and all this work sailing will do that to
you."

"Maybe tomorrow on one of the other islands."

"Agreed. If you'll bring the dinghy up, we'll get
this motor going and drop sails."

Moving with quiet efficiency and few words, even
on the unfamiliar boat, Tanner and Mary dropped their sails
and motored deeper into Quarry Bay. The sun had
disappeared and darkness was almost upon them.
Masthead anchor and cabin lights sparkled across the
water. The smell of charcoal and the sound of laughing
voices drifted across the water. After a slow tour of the
bay, while they collected friendly waves from sailors
relaxing on their anchored boats, Mary chose a spot. In ten
feet of water, she brought *Spindrift* to a stop. Tanner eased
the anchor over the bow and watched it sink to the bottom
in the clear water. Then Mary backed *Spindrift* until they
felt the anchor take firm hold. She killed the motor and
began to tidy up the cockpit, lashing the tiller down to keep
it quiet. On the foredeck, Tanner tied off the jib in a neat
bundle. While they secured things on deck, night fell
around them.

In the darkness, sitting companionably side by side
in the cockpit, Mary murmured. "How do you feel about
more food? Those sandwiches were so filling, I'm not in
the least hungry."

"The same, but I think a good brandy would be in
order and then I'm ready to turn in."

"I think I'll forego the brandy this time," Mary said. She rose and stretched.

When Tanner returned to the cockpit with his own small glass of liqueur, he saw Mary sitting on the cabin roof gazing at the water. Communing with Lake Superior again, he thought with a smile.

* * *

Around three o'clock in the morning, the moon departed and the night became as black and quiet as the inside of a closet. Tanner awoke with a start, unable to say what had disturbed him. From the bunk across the narrow space, he heard Mary's regular sleep rhythm. He swung his bare feet to the crowded floor of the cabin, hissing softly at the cold fiberglass underfoot.

When he poked his head out of the hatch, disturbing the netting they'd hung over the opening to discourage mosquitoes, Tanner saw that several other boats had arrived after they had put down their hook and were arrayed under twinkling masthead anchor lights across the bay behind *Spindrift.* Somewhere in the quiet night, Tanner heard the mutter of a small motor. The sound was moving back and forth and once circled *Spindrift's* location. It never came closer and eventually drifted out of earshot. Tanner decided it must have been boaters lately arrived from shore trying to locate their ship. He shivered and went back to his warm bunk.

Chapter 12

The wind had freshened overnight and now whistled brightly up the slot between Stockton and Michigan Island from the southwest. Most of the boats turned southeast, back toward the mainland. Tanner and Mary Whitney chose a different route, sailing almost due east until they could make a northerly tack and clear the bulbous peninsula off Stockton named Presque Isle. The sun rose, heating the air and the water and lending its color to the lake.

Tanner stood at the tiller. He glanced up into the sky over Stockton. "Mary, look," he called, bringing her to the hatch. He pointed skyward.

There, high overhead, with wings wide spread, two bald eagles rode the thermals, circling again and again over the island and the lake.

"Beautiful," said Mary. "Looking for breakfast, don't you think?"

"Yep." Tanner rubbed his stomach in a suggestive manner. "Me too."

Mary laughed. "Patience, my love. Delectable multi-fruit compote with hot coffee on the side is on the way."

Minutes later, with the boom let out over the starboard rail and her sails filled, *Spindrift* sailed out from behind Stockton and headed north toward Outer Island, hurried on by the wind at her back.

Mary took the tiller and turned her face to the wind and the sun while Tanner cleared away breakfast. When he'd made himself comfortable on cushions in the cockpit, Mary said, "I meant to tell you. I had a call yesterday from the coast. Edmund is coming."

"Edmund?"

"Yes, Edmund Hochstein. From Seattle." Mary made a sour face.

"Edmund Hockstein. This is a person to whom I have been introduced?"

"Once at least. At our wedding."

"An old family retainer, is he?"

Mary laughed. "No, you dolt. He's president of the foundation. An attorney. Tall, sort of stork-like? Remember?"

"Ah, my famous recollective powers are kicking in. Sure. He seemed, I don't know, uncertain of me and my motives."

"Like he thought maybe you were a fortune hunter?"

"Possibly. I also gathered he didn't much care for my profession. He never really said so, I just detected a faint aura of distaste when we were introduced. He's coming here? What for, if I may ask."

"He's going to check out my latest investment idea."

Tanner grimaced. "Of course! You said you were going to call in somebody. But does he usually fly around the country at your bidding?"

"No, it's unusual. He doesn't usually go on-site."

"Why now? Any clue?"

"Nope. Maybe he just wants a break from the comforts of Seattle."

Tanner smiled. "Is there anything we should do in this connection?"

"No, his travel people have taken care of housing and so on. I think he'll be staying in Ashland. In a way, it's good because it relieves me of having to spend much more time going over the company financials. We'll probably have dinner with him one night early next week. It's curious, though, Edmund coming here. It's usually someone like Lloyd. Lloyd Casjens."

"Ah. That's right, you did say he was the one you talked to. Him I like."

* * *

"Take the tiller, my man, and I'll read to you a little of the history I have uncovered."

They changed places and Mary took a notebook from the pocket of her shorts. "You see that long spit of sand?"

"Sure."

"In 1950, a steamer named *Faithful* was scuttled right at the end of the sand spit."

"No kidding."

"The hull is now a barrier, so I guess the sand is slowly growing over it. *Faithful* was a ferry, a tug and an all-around working steamer. Not very big."

"I suppose these islands were all logged off at one time?"

"Some of the islands, like this one, were large enough that they even built a short railroad on it to transport logs from the inland cutting camps to the shore."

"And then logs were towed in booms to Ashland. Hence, CRR." Tanner adjusted their course so they crossed the sandbar into the shallow bay on its east side.

"There's a funny story," said Mary. "There's quite a grade coming down here from the middle. The train was made up with the engine inland so they backed down after the logs were loaded. The story goes that the engineer didn't like the brakeman so he'd get the line of cars up to speed and come flying down the tracks toward the water. The brakeman had to really climb on the hand brakes to keep his car from going in the lake. Sometimes I guess it was a near thing."

Tanner grinned, tacked and steered *Spindrift* back to an upwind course along the western side of the island. They became aware of the thrumming of a large marine engine. Looking back over his shoulder, Tanner saw a fast speedboat tearing across the water toward them, throwing out a wide wake. As the boat passed without slackening speed, the two men and two women aboard waved vigorously. Mary and Tanner returned the greeting while *Spindrift* bounced briefly in the wash from the other boat and the sails cracked.

"Let's sail over to Devil's Island," Mary said.

"Okay. Course?"

She looked west through the binoculars and then consulted the chart. "I make it a little above due west, say about 290 degrees. We'll go south of North Twin and north of Rocky. With this wind, we should make it around noon."

"Aye aye, Cap'n, 290 it is," growled Tanner and swung the tiller. *Spindrift's* vanishing wake carved an arc in the water while Mary adjusted the sails. Big rollers swept out of the northeast, rocking the boat as the winds hurried them on their way.

By eleven, it was clear they'd never make Devil's Island by noon. With the blue sky holding a bright sun, almost unshaded by any but an occasional small cotton-ball white cloud, their cruise across the northern edge of the Apostle Islands was idyllic. After a time, over the rustle of the wind around their ears, they could hear the odd moans and random booms that helped give the island its name and its reputation.

All along its shores the underlying rock, laid down originally as sediment, had eroded over thousands of years. Variations in the hardness led to the formation of odd rock shapes and caves, caves that were open to the weather and especially to the almost ceaseless wave action of Lake Superior. When the water levels were right, and the wind blew a certain way, the whole island resonated with the booms and moans from the caves. It sometimes sounded like a gathering of spirits. For the superstitious and those inclined to believe in the unknown and the unexplainable, Devil's Island is aptly named.

"The addition of the fog signal with this lighthouse adds to the mystique," Tanner said.

"There's no keeper at this lighthouse. They activate the horn from somewhere else. By radio, I guess."

"Look," he pointed. "I can see big rusty ringbolts in the rock."

Mary trained binoculars on the shore line. "Look at those long ledges of rock. They're like steps leading up to the vegetation level. Those ringbolts must have been used by boats that brought the keeper and his supplies. Wait a minute." She sat up straight and refocused the binoculars. "There's somebody there. On the island."

Tanner smiled. "Wave hello."

"It's a man and he's already waving in a sort of intense way."

"I see him. Here, let me come about and we'll sail right up to the landing."

Mary waved at the man who was now scrambling down to the water's edge, jumping over the low growth and skidding to a stop. He continued to wave.

Tanner released the sheet and spilled wind from the bellying main to slow *Spindrift*. "The wind's up and we're on a lee shore here. See if you can make out what the guy wants."

Mary went forward to stand before the mast and yelled across the frothy water. "Hello. Is everything all right? Do you need something?"

The island caves boomed then and the man's response went unheard. Mary waved and cupped one hand over her ear. Tanner eased the tiller to point *Spindrift* higher into the wind. He wondered if he ought to start the engine, but then they wouldn't be able to hear the man. Waves slapped at the hull, sending cold spray onto the deck.

"He said something about a radio. Now he's disappeared," called Mary and then she returned to the cockpit to stand beside Tanner. He pulled in the main sheet and fell off the wind to give *Spindrift* more speed and maneuverability. They sailed up to the end where the beacon stood and turned back, as close as they dared get to the rocky shore.

The man reappeared with what looked like a pillowcase. On it he'd printed

RADIO DED NEED PICKUP

"I better go ashore and find out what's going on," said Mary. "Can we anchor here?"

Tanner shook his head. "The wind's wrong. Are you sure you want to try this?"

Her response was to reach into the lazarette and pull out the collapsible oars for the dinghy.

Tanner again tacked to beat upwind toward the end of the little island. The sound of the waves booming against the nearby caves was now more frequent as the wind and the waves rose.

Mary tightened the straps on her life jacket and stepped over the lifeline onto the boarding ladder at the stern. When she reached the last step and got into the little rubber dinghy they'd been towing, Tanner grabbed a quart bottle of fresh water and handed it down. "Here. I know they can drink lake water, but this will be better. You hang on here until I get us a little farther upwind." When she released the tether a few minutes later, Tanner had swung the sailboat so Mary had a small piece of calm water, protected from the wind by *Spindrift's* hull.

"Mary?"

She looked up at Tanner and grinned.

"Don't go out of sight. Okay?"

She nodded and dug the oars into the water. As soon as she was out of the shelter of *Spindrift*, the wind began to push the little dinghy quickly along the shore. Strongly rowing upwind, Mary was no match for the rising wind but finally beached the dinghy several yards down the island from the landing.

The stranger had been keeping pace with Mary but it took a minute for him to get through the closely growing barrier of bushes. Tanner watched as Mary handed over the water jug and talked with him. He didn't see anything out of the ordinary, except that the man seemed a little less agitated now. Tanner lost sight of them for a few minutes as he again tacked around and bore down on them, now at even higher speed, as the wind continued to strengthen. He glanced at the overhead sky and the thickening clouds. His sailing senses warned that he'd need to reef the main before too long.

Yet again Tanner tacked back upwind to keep station near where Mary and the man were talking. Then without looking back Mary pushed the dinghy off the shore and began to row out onto the lake. Tanner was upwind at the farthest point from the dinghy at that moment. Mary apparently hadn't realized how much higher the wind had risen while she was ashore. The wind caught the dinghy and Tanner saw immediately that she had no hope of rowing out to *Spindrift*. The waves began to toss the dinghy about and though Mary struggled valiantly, there was no way she'd row upwind to *Spindrift*. Even a course across the wind was impossible.

Tanner yanked the tiller over and let the main run out so the big sail took as much wind as possible. He considered starting the outboard and then decided the running motor posed more of a complication than he wanted to deal with.

Tanner looked ahead where Mary in the bobbing dinghy was at least 100 yards away. She waved and bent to her rowing. Tanner realized she was trying to get as far from the island as possible to give Tanner more maneuvering room. He calculated his course to intersect that of the now wildly bobbing dinghy. But he miscalculated Mary's progress and *Spindrift* slid by out of reach. Tanner watched as Mary glanced over her shoulder, shook her head and began to row even harder.

Tanner circled back upwind. Unable to see the dinghy over the bow and afraid he'd run her down, he closed to within twenty yards and simply dropped the mainsail. *Spindrift* slowed and stopped. The sloop began to wallow heavily and the jib banged loudly back and forth. Tanner leaned over the port side in the lee of the wind where he hoped she'd be. Nothing but roiled water.

"Ahoy, there, sailor. Permission to come aboard?" came the welcome shout.

Tanner jumped to the other side of the sailboat to find Mary clinging to the coaming just forward of the cockpit.

"I dunno, lady. Any reason why you should?"

Mary grinned and handed up the dinghy painter so Tanner could ease the little rubber boat back to the ladder. He tied it off and took the oars from Mary. Then he grabbed her shoulder and helped her scramble up the ladder and into the cockpit.

"Hey, babe. You're shivering."

"That lake is cold!"

Both turned their eyes to the surrounding lake and the island. *Spindrift* was rapidly drifting downwind, all the while wallowing and heaving. Her bare masthead made wide eccentric circles against the graying sky.

Mary grabbed the tiller and Tanner the main halyard. Minutes later, trim and beating upwind, *Spindrift* returned to her position just off the landing rocks. The stranger was standing there with the water jug, watching and waving.

"What's his story?"

"He and his wife are camping on their honeymoon. They were going to call the water taxi by radio when they wanted to return to the mainland. But yesterday, they discovered their radio is on the blink. I said we'd radio in for them, but with the lake like this, the water taxi might not get here until tomorrow."

"I take it they're low on water?"

"Yep. I'm going to change into something dry," said Mary. "Then I'll radio Bayfield. Then let's find an anchorage for the night."

Rescue mission accomplished and relayed to the honeymooners, *Spindrift* fell off the wind and hightailed it into the middle of the Apostles.

Tanner had been studying the chart between swigs of hot soup. "The wind is shifting toward the east and will stay there, or go a little north, according to weather radio. Let's beat east over to Cat for the night. Looks like there's a nice anchorage right along the tail."

"Sounds fine."

While they were crossing west of South Twin, another powerboat with two men buzzed across their stern. Tanner watched them for several minutes as they went by. There were no friendly waves of shared camaraderie between the occupants of the two boats. "I don't see any fishing poles on that one," said Tanner.

"You're still bothered by that radio call, aren't you?"

"Along with some other things," Tanner admitted. "There are a bunch of unconnected incidents. First, George had all that detail about us. On a couple of occasions I thought I sensed somebody paying more than passing interest to us. The radio call. I still think George is holding something back. Maybe I'm paranoid."

"And those feelings are the reason you wanted me to stay in sight on Devil's Island," Mary said.

"Right. My gut feelings. It's probably just motion sickness."

* * *

Late in the afternoon, the sun having reemerged, Tanner steered *Spindrift* toward the tail of the cat, a long sandbar that was home to hundreds of gulls. Mary, in her bikini, lay somnolent on the foredeck, protected from the wind by the jib. Tanner had brought *Spindrift* close to the western shore, so that only small breezes filled the sail and sent them drifting along toward their intended anchorage.

"I suppose I'll have to do the anchor bit," came Mary's sleepy voice.

"Tanner smiled. "That would be appreciated, although I can handle it alone."

"Nah. I got it."

Tanner steered directly toward the island shore and Mary slipped the anchor over the bow. "Bottom," she sang out, peering over the lifeline at the water.

Tanner put the tiller hard over and reversed his direction, dragging the anchor around until it buried itself in the sand. At the same time, he secured the boom and dropped the main. *Spindrift* came up tight against the anchor line and stopped in the calm water.

Mary came back to the cockpit. "A favor, milord."

"Sure," said Tanner. He turned back from lashing the tiller to the back stay to see Mary diving neatly over the lifelines into the lake.

"Yoww! This is really cold!" Her shout of pain when she surfaced bounced off the nearby land. "I should have a wet suit. Or a dry suit. Or a hot shower." She rolled slackly over on her stomach and began to swim vigorously along the length of the boat, turning at the bow to swim back along the other side. When she reached the swim ladder at *Spindrift's* stern, she grabbed on and looked up at Tanner's laughing face.

"You're nuts, lady. What's the favor?"

"Would you rig the sun shower? That water is nice and hot now."

"Consider it done."

The black plastic bag with attached nozzle was designed to be set in the sun for several hours to heat the water inside, so sailors or campers could have a warm shower on sunny days. Tanner rigged it to the main sheet and hoisted it up the mast, a few feet above the deck.

Meanwhile, Mary swarmed, shivering, up the ladder and crouched out of the breeze in the cockpit. "How far away are those boats?" she asked, taking her bathroom kit and clambering to the deck beside the mast.

"Far enough they'll need binoculars," Tanner said, knowing what she was about to do.

Mary stripped off her bikini and, lithe, naked, and silvery in the reflected light from the sky, lathered herself with liquid soap. She rinsed with hot water from the sun shower bag and soaped her hair again. When she was through, Tanner handed up a big fluffy bath towel, hearing faint whistles and a cheer from the nearest sailboat headed their way.

Wrapped from neck to knee in the towel, Mary stepped down from the deck and smirked, "There's plenty of water left."

Tanner took her place, but because the oncoming boats were now in easy hailing distance, he elected to retain his swimming trunks during his brief shower. When he returned to the cockpit, Mary had two big glasses of gin and tonic waiting, along with crackers, cheese, and smoked whitefish.

The first boat in sailed a loop around *Spindrift*. It was a forty-foot Beneteau with several couples aboard. They nodded and waved, and Tanner could see appreciative smiles on the faces of some of those aboard.

"I've been thinking about your vague feelings," said Mary. "Let's assume it isn't *mal de mer*. If there are dark forces at work here, who's doing the work of the devil?"

"I'd expect it to be a board member," said Tanner. "Somebody with an ax to grind and maybe a way to profit if the company collapses."

"Something for me to be watching out for when I examine CRR financials. Personally, I think there are just three candidates."

"You want another drink before you expound?" asked Tanner.

"Why yes, thank you. Yup. I think it's Stan Krizyinsky, that eastern European smoothy with the heavy, penetrating gaze."

"The one who licked your hand."

Mary giggled. "Or it's long lanky boyish-looking Eddington—Charles. Or it could be that really dark, almost saturnine, guy. Richard Kemperer."

"Kemperer? The cabinetmaker?" Tanner rubbed his nose. "Huh. Interesting choices. I'm not sure I agree with you. What about Anderson?"

"George? Nope. He's hiding something all right, but his heart and soul are in CRR and whatever he's not telling us, it's because he thinks it's for the good of the company."

Boats continued to arrive off Cat Island until there were nearly a dozen at anchor. Late in the afternoon, a pair of power boats roared in, slowing to idle as they wove their way among the anchored sloops to ground on the beach. Small tents soon appeared on the sand along with camp stoves, a scattering of children and a dog. In the space of a couple of hours, the population of the long narrow sandspit had evolved from gulls and other birds to a small group of human beings.

After nightfall, the temperature dropped. Dinghies from some of the anchored sailboats ferried people ashore, and soon a bonfire was glowing on the spit. Laughter and camaraderie came off the landed group, along with the faint sound of a practiced guitar.

Tanner and Mary chose to stay aboard *Spindrift* side by side in the cockpit, each with an after-dinner brandy.

"We've watched the creation of an instant community," murmured Mary tickling Tanner's ear with her tongue.

"And it's still growing," said Tanner, nodding in the direction of two more sets of running lights out on the lake.

"Tomorrow everyone here will scatter and tomorrow night, a new group of boaters and campers will appear."

"It's sort of magical, isn't it?"

"I remember something you said once when we were in Toba Sound. I think that's when I first knew for sure that our lives were going to be inseparable." Mary blew in Tanner's ear.

Tanner smiled in the dark, then turned his head and laid his lips softly on Mary's cheek. "Have I ever told you how glad I am?"

Mary stood and together, arms about each other, they watched two late arriving boats set their anchors. The lake was glassy smooth, resting, cradling the anchored boats in serene contemplation of whatever the new day would bring.

Chapter 13

The pastoral scene of the night before had undergone a radical change, Mary discovered when she poked her head out of the hatch the next morning and looked around. There was no sun, no blue sky overhead. Instead there was a seamless gray cloud in every direction. Cat Island had disappeared. Boats still at anchor nearby were invisible. It was as if they'd been transported to a completely isolated anchorage out of sight of the rest of the world.

The air temperature was in the brisk range and the billowing gray fog that enveloped *Spindrift* seemed limitless and moist. Everything they touched was damp. Condensation glistened on the cabin roof and on the wooden arm of the tiller.

"Time to break out Mr. Magellan," said Mary, stepping back down the ladder. She was referring to a battery powered GPS receiver they had brought along.

She took the small black case from her duffel and returned to the cockpit. Another quick glance around brought the ghostly outlines of two nearby boats, but their outlines faded in and out of view as clouds of denser fog drifted by. Now she heard sounds from other boats farther out on the lake. Tanner joined her in the cockpit and wiped ineffectually at the damp cushions. From even greater distance they both heard the sounds of fast-moving powerboats.

"Either this fog bank is limited, or people up here are just charging blindly about."

"Maybe they have good radar they know how to use," said Tanner, handing her a partially peeled banana.

"Is this boat equipped with a fog horn?" she asked.

Tanner went back below and pawed through a couple of drawers and a storage space near the radio. "I don't see anything. Is there any wind at all?"

"Just a bit. I'm going to raise the main and sail over the anchor." A moment later, she exclaimed, "Oh, look!"

Tanner glanced through the hatch and saw, high overhead, a small patch of brilliant blue sky that seemed centered over *Spindrift's* mast. He went up to the cockpit, glanced forward where Mary was hauling the dripping anchor back aboard. He pushed the tiller to one side. *Spindrift*, her main sail filling and sagging listlessly in the almost still air, made a slow turn and pointed her bow toward the open lake.

They listened intently as they ghosted over the still water, gathering a small bit of way, but except for the distant hum of power boats, the world was eerily silent. Mary and Tanner were reluctant to disturb the quietude, and they murmured to each other almost in whispers.

"What's my course?"

Mary glanced at the compass and replied, "About 240. I bet we won't get any significant wind until we pass Stockton." She peered at the GPS screen and made a pencil mark on the chart to indicate their position.

It took two hours in the almost windless conditions for *Spindrift* to finally reach the southern end of Stockton Island. It was an ethereal journey through the fog, with blue sky overhead on a lake that was calm and peaceful and covered with fog. As they neared the end of the island, a freshening breeze fanned their faces. *Spindrift* was moving faster. They raised the jib and, smiling at one another, trimmed the sails to beat upwind against the southwesterly.

The fog thinned and tiny wavelets, sometimes capped by white froth, appeared. A chuckling sound arose from the bow as *Spindrift* heeled slightly and picked up speed.

"There's land close by," Mary said suddenly. "I can smell heat and the dust."

Tanner checked the chart. "It must be Hermit Island." He leaned over the side and peered ahead.

"Worried?" Mary asked.

"I wouldn't want to hit a hermit."

"Look there," said Mary pointing over the starboard side. Indistinct trees and, lower down, a rocky shore became visible. "Still plenty of water under us, almost a hundred feet. Whoa!"

"A new nautical term?"

Mary smiled. "No, but the bottom is rapidly shoaling."

"Chart says we can stay on this course and sail right by. The GPS agrees."

The shoreline receded as *Spindrift* sailed into the North Channel and began to beat her way south in the bright sun, leaving behind the gray fog bank. The day passed quickly while they explored the shores of nearby islands, marked interesting-looking anchorages on their chart, and discussed future possible voyages in the islands.

"I think we have to start for home," said Mary, glancing at her watch.

"Tanner swallowed the last of his sandwich and nodded. "It's been a great weekend. We'll have to come back here again for a longer stay." He put the tiller over and *Spindrift* responded, turning eastward toward Bayfield and Chequamegon Bay.

Lower down, traffic picked up considerably as

boaters and fisherfolk came down both channels, heading for home. They watched for several minutes to fix the approximate crossing times of the ferries that traveled back and forth from Bayfield to Madeline island.

"Let's cross to the end of Madeline here and then cut across east of Bayfield. It'll only take a little longer."

"Longer is okay," Mary responded. She adjusted their course and they headed across the prevailing breeze.

"Is this breeze going to hold, you think?"

"I'll crank up the motor, just in case," said Tanner. He leaned over the transom and pressed the starter on the outboard. It obediently snarled into action. By eight, the wind had shifted again to the south and they crossed the water between Madeline and the mainland on a comfortable beam reach. Now in the shadow of the Wisconsin hills, Mary switched on the running lights. Overhead a plane droned east, heading toward the small private airstrip on the island.

It was full dark by the time they arrived off Pike's Bay and the entrance to the Superior Charters Marina. Tanner luffed into the wind and Mary dropped the sails. The sound of the outboard made talking difficult so they relied, as was their custom, on hand signals although it was almost too dark to see them.

Moving at dead slow pace, the couple motored *Spindrift* into the marina and then into its assigned slip. Mary secured the bow line and stepped back aboard. She put her face up next to Tanner's and bussed his nose.

"Thanks, sailor. Lovely weekend."

"Likewise to you, ma'am," he responded.

Efficiently they smoothly packed up their belongings and secured *Spindrift*. There was still plenty of movement in and out of the marina, so neither paid any attention to the rusting pickup that followed them back to Bayfield.

Chapter 14

The following morning, Tanner and Mary drove to the CRR building, a former Louisiana Pacific wood manufacturing plant on the eastern outskirts of Ashland. There they found Richard Kemperer waiting. A small, nervous man was with him.

"This is Antonio Prada. Our shop manager. He's in charge of the crew here."

"I'm very pleased to make your acquaintance," said Prada, enthusiastically shaking hands and bouncing up and down on the balls of his feet. "We'll give you a complete tour, but first perhaps you'd like to see the videos of our harvesting operations?"

"Since we've already been to the barge working in Chequamegon Bay, I think we can skip that step for now. Perhaps later, just to see how the divers work underwater," smiled Mary.

"I'm going to excuse myself for a few minutes," said Kemperer. "Something has just come up that needs my attention. I'll catch up with you." He walked back toward the front door.

Antonio Prada led Tanner and Mary up a flight of stairs and down a narrow hallway. There seemed to be a barely suppressed air of excitement in the offices. People strode quickly back and forth. A man in a long shiny ponytail skipped around them and slapped a tiny yellow Post-It on the window of an office door without a pause. Voices rose and fell with evident good humor. Copy machines chattered and a couple of telephones rang in an empty office. Prada gestured to two men in another room who were hunched over drawing boards.

"Designers," he said. "We're starting to get orders for new products. Some of them have to have drawings before we can manufacture anything."

"So CRR isn't just harvesting timber," said Mary.

"Oh, no. Besides recovering and reclaiming lost timber we're also manufacturing all kinds of things from that timber. You'll see later on. And, of course, we supply manufacturers and building contractors with paneling and flooring."

A young man stuck his head around the corner of the corridor and shouted, "Hey! The stock is moving up! We're gettin' rich!"

Prada smiled. "Employees can elect to be paid partially in stock, you know, so we all have great interest in what's happening with the market. Technically there's no public market in CRR stock, but under certain conditions some current investors might be looking to buy or sell."

They went through a heavy steel door into a huge cavern of a room. The contrast with the close, active office structure they had just left was considerable. The dark gray concrete floor was largely empty. Against a far wall, huge mounds of logs of different size and dimension rested, indifferent to their surroundings. Here and there, isolated in islands of light, large, brooding, complicated-appearing machines stood silent. High above them, sunlight strained to filter down from the grimy skylights. From where they stood on the balcony fifteen feet above it, the floor seemed to stretch out for hundreds of feet in either direction, fading away into the dimness.

Antonio Prada led the way down the steep stairway to the factory floor. Their steps rang on the steel treads and echoed across the space. "This was a plywood and chipboard manufacturing plant for Louisiana Pacific. They left town years ago and the place had been vacant since. George got the city to sell him the whole plant for about five hundred bucks. Now he says they overcharged him." Prada grinned. "You can't imagine what a mess this place was when we first moved in."

Glancing around, Tanner noticed long strips of insulation hanging off the walls. In other places, pieces of shiny gray duct tape had been used to patch holes in old drywall. They walked around a huge water stain that was still damp.

"Leaky roof?" Mary asked.

"Yep." Prada nodded vigorously and smiled. "This place was empty for a lot of years. We're patching the place up bit by bit, but it's a slow process. I don't mind telling you, it's been a rough three years. Money's been tight, but now that the bureaucrats have figured out that we know what we're doing and issued the permits, things will get much better." He slammed his considerable weight against a big metal door in the wall and they went out into a vast asphalt-covered yard surrounded by a high shiny wire fence. Strands of sagging barbed wire topped the fence.

Along one side of the space, well removed from the building they'd just exited, was a long, shiny, steel, box-like building. "That's the drying kiln," Prada said, pointing. "It holds several thousand board feet of wood. We'll have more of those once things really get cranking. The wood's been in water and mud for hundreds of years, you know, and it has to be dried carefully to preserve it in the best possible condition."

Railroad tracks alongside the kiln led through the fence at the back of the yard and disappeared in a long curve to the east. Soiled wood pallets were stacked elsewhere in the lot in several untidy piles. Tanner saw two trucks and various other vehicles scattered about. Some of the vehicles appeared to be permanently attached to the cracked asphalt. A small sailboat, its mast in a cradle alongside, stood forlornly in one corner.

"I guess George told you that we're starting to handle wood from all over the country, right?"

Mary nodded.

"Most of it comes by rail. Some we're storing inside until we can get it ready to dry, but a lot of it just goes right into the kiln. That's why the tracks run right over there." He pointed at the track end barrier, which was only a few feet from the end wall of the building. Prada turned and said. "Okay, let's go back inside and I'll show you some interesting pieces we've recovered."

In the cavernous building, they skirted several small piles of what appeared to be trash and some large, dangerous-looking machines. They walked toward the east wall, where huge stacks of gray logs rested inside heavy welded steel cribs. Most of the logs had their ends squared off and were piled in sixteen to twenty-foot lengths. They rested on platforms of steel I-beams. Several were twice the height of a man and reached up into the gloom above the hanging lights.

"These piles remind me of the skids I've seen loggers make up in the woods," Mary said. "I've seen pictures of similar piles from the logging days up behind Washburn."

"That's right," Prada responded. He laid a hand reverently on the stack before them. "Think of it. This stack was cut near here in the late 1880s. It's old growth.

That means it was growing when Columbus crossed the
Atlantic. Think of that. One of the things you've noticed
is how these stacks look. If you compare pictures of
modern logging, you'll still see piles of logs, but the logs
aren't this big."

"George said something about old cypress from
Georgia or Florida?" asked Tanner.

Prada nodded vigorously. "Come over here." He
slid between two stacks of logs.

"I don't know," Mary said doubtfully. "Is this safe?
It looks like the only thing holding up the ends are these
steel beams."

"You're right, Ms. Whitney, but those I-beams are
welded together and carefully braced. I assure you these
cribs are safe. George insisted that we overbuild. He's
very safety-conscious." He smiled and pushed his weight
against the logs. There was a faint creaking sound from
inside the stack but the logs didn't move at all.

"Now I want to show you this recent acquisition.
George is determined to be as efficient as possible with all
the wood we acquire. Even the sawdust from the mill is
going to be used." Prada stopped beside a machine. "This
is our computer controlled band mill. It cuts boards to very
tight tolerances. Our milling operation is very flexible and
complete. We can supply several grades of flooring and
paneling, depending on the needs of the contractors."

"I understand you're getting inquiries from all over
the country now," probed Mary. "Is that right?"

"From all over the world," corrected Prada. "A few
months ago a representative of several French violin
manufacturers was here. He wanted to know if we could
supply the kind of wood his companies require to make the
finest violins."

"Why the special interest?" asked Mary.

"Some researchers believe that old-time violin

makers like Stradivari buried their materials in water for as long as a year, in order to change the acoustic characteristics of the wood. We have wood that's been underwater for a hundred years."

Tanner got the impression that Prada was standing taller and had puffed out his chest a little. "I get it. The water eventually replaces some of the softer cellulose or something, in the wood, so when the wood dries out you end up with lots of little echo chambers."

Prada nodded and Mary raised an interrogatory eyebrow.

Tanner shrugged. "In the PR business, you pick up all sorts of odd bits of information."

The trio moved on.

"That's pretty much it for this part of the operation. Now, I'll take you to what George calls the artifact room and the gift shop so you can see some of the specialty products we're making."

They passed through two heavy steel counter-weighted doors into the front offices. In a crowded room, a VCR and a television sat in one corner, and shelves and cabinets lined the paneled walls.

"All the wood you see in here, the shelves, cabinets and wall paneling, were made by our company from timbers we recovered. Did you notice the wood paneling on the outside when you drove up? That's all knotty birch out of Lake Superior," said Prada waving one hand around him.

"Expensive," murmured Mary, stepping into the room and looking at a wood-framed picture on the wall.

"Yeah, but George insisted that we use our own lumber. It causes lots of comment."

Mary was looking at a picture of a younger George clad in a scuba dry suit with tank goggles and fins, sitting on a huge, shiny, wet log. Behind him was a vast expanse of blue water.

"I take it George does a lot of the recovery himself," she said.

"Sure. Not so much now, but he still dives now and then, just to keep his skills sharp. He's always been a diver, you know, since he was a kid. In fact, he was part of the group that found that big old Spanish treasure ship. Maybe you read about it? The one they found in the Caribbean?"

Prada looked toward the door. "I don't know what's happened to Dick—Mr. Kemperer. Why don't you sit down and watch this video of one of George's dives? It's pretty interesting. And I'll see if I can find him."

Prada grabbed a video cassette off a shelf over the TV and slammed it into the VCR. Before Tanner and Mary could find chairs, Prada had skipped to the door and disappeared around the jamb, flipping off the overhead lights as he left.

Tanner sank onto a folding chair and said, "Sort of acting nervous, wasn't he?"

"Yes, I think he wanted Kemperer to be doing the duty."

A shadow filled the open doorway and Richard Kemperer walked in. "Sorry to have abandoned you like that. We seem to have suffered another bout of vandalism and I had to speak with the police."

"Vandalism?" queried Mary, turning her attention away from the TV and the languid scenes of Anderson in scuba gear floating among scattered mounds of logs somewhere under the lake.

"Yes, it happens periodically. So far there's been nothing really serious. A fence cut, a few pieces of timber stolen, eggs thrown at the front of the building. Juvenile stuff, mostly."

"Do you have any idea who's doing it?"

Kemperer nodded. "Some, but nothing concrete. We think local Indians and maybe the environmentalists who have opposed us from the beginning are harassing us. I wanted to hire a security firm to stake out the place and catch whoever's doing this, but George is more relaxed about the whole thing. And, I suspect he doesn't want to escalate things by getting some of these people arrested."

"What about disgruntled investors?"

Kemperer shot a spiky glance at Mary and then smiled when he saw she wasn't entirely serious. "Of course, we do have a few of those. George can get pretty enthusiastic, as you already know, and occasionally he promises too much. How'd the tour go?"

"Your Mr. Prada is a good guide," said Tanner. "He gave us a complete look at your operations here. What happened in this latest vandalism?"

Kemperer shrugged and eased his pant legs over his knees. "You're very direct, aren't you? Somebody scaled the fence and tried to smash the doors on the big drying kiln. We can't decide whether they were trying to jam the doors closed or get inside to disrupt the drying process. In any event, they didn't succeed."

The video came to an end and Mary stood up. "Thank you, Mr. Kemperer, for your hospitality." She extended her arm and Kemperer clasped her hand in both of his. He ushered them to the door, still holding Mary's hand.

In the car, Mary fastened her seat belt and said, "I don't like that man."

"Really? Why is that?"

"Oh, a lot of small things. He held my hand too long. Used both of his. There was something in his eyes. I got the impression he wanted to touch me. I also think he lied when he left us to Mr. Prada's care."

"We probably got a better tour because of it."

Tanner glanced at Mary and guided the car down Lake Shore drive. "I've heard of a really good small restaurant along here somewhere. Let's put our notes together about these people over a good lunch."

Chapter 15

At ten after four Tuesday morning, when the sun had just begun its serene travel through the northern Wisconsin sky, several propane tanks inside the CRR factory blew up.

One tank tore through the north wall of the old warehouse that housed Chequamegon Resource Recovery. Another went up like a rocket through the sheet metal roof. It soared over the buildings across Lakeshore Drive and landed in the mud at the edge of the lake. No one was about at that hour, so there were no injuries, but trash and wood chips on the floor beside the storage cage were ignited and fed by the escaping propane. Vented by the new holes in the wall and roof, the trash sent up a thick column of smelly smoke.

Other tanks overheated and blew off their valves. Some of them impersonated small lethal rockets. Those skittered across the floor and caromed off partitions and machine bases, sending lumber and small tools flying. One of the tanks hit the small kiln door a glancing blow and knocked it off its hinges, but the wood inside was still so wet, it resisted the nearby flames and only emitted a thick cloud of smoke and steam. CRR was fortunate that the rocketing propane tanks had not set afire the huge piles of dried wood stored elsewhere in the cavernous warehouse.

Why none of the smoke and heat sensors installed throughout the building had triggered alarms was a still unanswered question. Because the tanks were small, the damage was minimal.

The explosions and rocketing tanks woke sleeping dogs in Ashland for a quarter mile around and disrupted the hunting paths of three feral cats that had taken up residence in the vacant lot behind the big kiln. The erupting tanks blew debris over a wide area, but most of it landed in the nearly empty lot behind the warehouse.

When Ashland fire crews arrived there was little for them to do. The propane in the tanks, still bleeding out inside the storage cage was dissipating into the outside air, and the trash had not become fully involved so the fires were still small.

In Bayfield, unaware of fire or explosion, Tanner and Mary Whitney went about their routines, deciding that morning to patch together breakfast from the stores they'd picked up the evening before and leftovers from their weekend aboard *Spindrift*.

Tanner brought bowls of cereal and fruit to the tiny table in the bay window of the room.

Mary looked up over the top of yesterday's *New York Times* and said, "I see Bill Gates and Microsoft are starting a new round of jousting with the Justice Department over the monopoly ruling. I've meant to ask, why aren't Tanner and Associates the PR firm for Microsoft?"

Tanner smiled and shrugged. "We've never pitched a proposal."

"Why is that? I'd have thought King County's most successful PR firm and Redmond's biggest and most successful corporation would be an ideal marriage."

Tanner sat down and poured milk in his cereal bowl. "We did a small project for them a few years back, but they got so big, they're like Lake Superior. They create their own weather. We just decided not to compete in that arena, and we didn't want to be tied to a single large client. Now they have their own internal operation."

The telephone rang. When Tanner picked up, he heard George Anderson's voice.

"There's been an incident," he said.

"Another one?"

"This wasn't just vandalism. I think this was an attempt to seriously hurt us. Several propane tanks at the factory blew up early this morning. There's other damage, but I don't know how much yet. We aren't running a night shift right now, so there wasn't anybody at the plant. No injuries, thank God. I'm on my way out there." He sighed in Tanner's ear. "More bad PR. I'd appreciate it if you'd come on out."

"I'll meet you at the warehouse." Tanner hung up the telephone and related the news to Mary.

"That's terrible! Was anybody hurt?"

"No. It happened during the night or early morning. Apparently the place was empty."

"Thank goodness for that. Do you get the impression this company is being besieged?"

"I think I'll reserve judgment for the moment." Tanner was throwing his clothes on. "Do you want to come along?"

Mary shook her head. "No thanks. I wonder about the timing. You might keep that in the back of your mind while you poke around out there. Call me later."

Tanner slurped up the remains of his coffee and went to the door.

"And don't take any risks, you hear?" Mary called after him as the door slammed shut.

At the factory on Lakeshore Drive, Tanner met George Anderson in the parking lot. The fire trucks were still there although the fires appeared to be out. The whole neighborhood smelled of smoke and wet wood.

Anderson had his head together with two men. Tanner recognized George's brother Arne, and the plant manager, Antonio Prada. They broke off their conversation as Tanner approached and turned toward him. From their body language they appeared to be having some sort of disagreement.

"I got here as soon as I could. What happened?"

Anderson placed his soot-blackened hands on his hips, smudging his blue jeans. He had a long dark smear on one cheek. "I wish to hell I knew. I've had propane tanks here on the property for years and we've never had a problem. Come back here, I want you to look at this." Arne Anderson acknowledged Tanner and turned away toward the front of the building where the offices and show rooms were located.

Prada, Tanner, and George Anderson walked around the building to the back yard and the shed where the propane tanks were stored. A fire truck stood beside the damaged shed attached to the back of the warehouse. Black scorch marks covered most of the aluminum siding of the shed. A few marks extended all the way up the sides of the warehouse to the roof.

A fireman with a white CHIEF shield on his fire hat turned toward the men as they approached. "It's a lucky thing, George. If this had happened while there were a lot of people around, it could have been a disaster. By the way, it looks like your housekeeping has broken down."

Anderson frowned at the chief. "What's that supposed to mean?"

"It means sawdust and scrap wood and some untidy piles of lumber."

"Wait a minute. Ever since your initial inspection we've been following your suggestions carefully. No scraps, no greasy rags, we sweep up every day. Besides, you know I'm going to use all that scrap for some high-end products."

The fire chief took off his helmet and smoothed back his graying wisps of hair. "Yeah, and our recent inspections have found the place to be nice and clean. But this morning...are you building an office or a room of some kind under the stairs on the south wall?"

"Yeah," said George, "it's going to be an office for the shop foreman and a small tool storage area. Why?"

"It's a mess, that's why. Sawdust, framing lumber, and but-ends of logs. Piles of stuff."

Anderson shook his head. "It sure wasn't like that yesterday morning when I was here with a potential investor. I want to take a look at it."

Anderson, Tanner and the chief turned toward the small door nearby and Anderson took a couple of rapid strides into the warehouse. Tanner and the chief followed closely. Just inside they were met by a fireman coming across the puddled floor. He stopped when he saw the men and waited until they reached him.

Then he leaned forward and said in a low voice, "You'd better take a look at this, Chief. We've found a body under the rubble."

The small crowd of firemen and CRR workers stood aside. Tanner stopped beside the framed-in wall of the office. No drywall or paneling had been installed, so it was easy to see into the entire room which was cluttered with scrap wood, old timbers, and loose electrical cabling. In the corner, directly beneath the upstairs landing against the back wall, it appeared that some broken sheets of paneling had been thrown over some framing lumber and even scraps from the factory floor. The untidy heap was leaning against the block wall that formed one side of the small office. When the fireman shined his big lantern at the pile, everyone there could see part of an old wooden office chair under the pile. A hand rested on the arm of the chair, and on the floor they could see part of one leg and a booted foot.

"Oh, shit," sighed Anderson.

"Everybody get back," ordered the chief. Gingerly he stepped over the clutter on the floor and reached to touch the hand. "He's cold, all right. Nothing we can do now, so somebody call the station and get the police over here. The rest of you men go back to whatever you were doing."

He came carefully back out of the space and looked at Anderson. "George? Look familiar? Anybody missing you know of?"

"I'll have to check upstairs again, but that's the first thing I thought of when I got the call. Somebody would have told me by now if anyone's missing. We're like a family, you know? It must be someone who broke in, or a visitor who got left here when we locked up last night."

"Is that likely?" asked Tanner.

"No," George admitted, "but if you wanted to stay, it wouldn't be all that hard to hide until everybody had left."

"But why do that? Unless you were looking to steal a computer or rifle through the offices," said Tanner. He took the lantern from a fireman and turned it on what he could see of the body. He aimed the lantern at the jeans-clad leg and the new-looking brown hiking boot. His stomach tightened.

"We do lock up some stuff, most of the time. But the goods in the gift shop wouldn't be worth stealing. Hard to sell." Anderson rubbed his head, frowning deeply. "I just don't know. It must be a vagrant." He let out a huge sighing breath.

A fireman approached the chief and drew him aside,

talking in a low voice. Tanner couldn't hear what the man said. The chief nodded and looked at George. "More bad news," he said quietly. "We found traces of an accelerant around the storage shed. No question now, this fire was deliberately set."

Tanner was watching Anderson when the fire chief delivered his news. As far as he could tell, it looked like George was still focused on the body in the office space. Anderson rubbed his forehead.

"If the whole place had gone up, that body wouldn't have been located so soon," Tanner said.

"We're gonna suspend everything, now the fire's out, George," said the chief, "until the proper authorities get here. But I'll keep one engine company here for a while, just in case. We may have to call in an arson expert from Milwaukee, but that remains to be seen." He waved to some of his men who were still crowded around and they cleared out.

Tanner and Anderson went up the steel staircase and into the main offices which were uncharacteristically silent while staff waited for more news. Anderson's secretary put down the telephone and said, "George, I just reconfirmed. Nobody's missing, so whoever they found in the warehouse wasn't an employee."

"Well, that's some comfort," Anderson said. He led the way into his small cramped office.

"George, I'm getting some very strange feelings about this whole business. It's time you and I had a talk," Tanner said.

Anderson squinted and rubbed his forehead again. The smell of smoke was evident throughout the offices. "Okay, I guess now is as good a time as any while we wait for the police."

"This whole project started off with your call to me in Seattle. At that time I thought it a little peculiar that you had such a depth of information about me and about Mary. In fact, the only reason Mary and I are here is because you piqued our curiosity. I've never had a potential client start out by giving me such a run-down on my interests and on my wife's. It made us wonder. What gives?"

Anderson looked at Tanner for a silent moment. "Well... I'm just not sure what to say. I have to respect certain confidences, you know? It was part of a deal I made a while ago." He paused, obviously stalling, and Tanner leaned forward to prod him.

"Look, George, I know about—"

"Excuse me, George," called his secretary from the corridor, "the police are here, about the dead man?"

With relief plainly etched across his face, Anderson seized on the interruption and almost ran from the office, saying, "C'mon, Tanner."

On the factory floor, they stood to one side while the police and firemen removed the lumber and other materials from the body. A deputy sheriff and the man from the medical examiner were also present, watching closely. A big uniformed officer with the Ashland patch on the shoulder of his shirt beckoned Anderson and Tanner closer.

"Either of you two know this man?"

Tanner glanced down and even through the dried blood smeared on his face, he recognized Ted McGregor. He looked at George, who let out a huge sigh and said in a firm voice, "Yes. I know him. That's McGregor. Ted McGregor."

Tanner nodded. "I met him once—in Bayfield. He introduced himself as Ted McGregor. He said he represented an organization called People for the Earth."

The Ashland policeman said, "George, we better go upstairs and I'll take your statement."

Anderson nodded after a silent moment. Then he

said, "I want you in on this, Tanner."

"He seems to want me in on everything but what I'm supposed to be doing," muttered Tanner as he followed George back to his factory office.

Chapter 16

Baraks was not on the National Register of Historic Buildings. Nor had it ever made the Michelin Guide to fine restaurants. When Tanner and Mary drove out of the woods and into the graveled parking lot, their rented Lexus jounced through another pothole, splashing water from the previous night's rain up onto the windshield. Muddy water ran down the window on Mary's side.

"Whoops," laughed Mary, grabbing the overhead handhold.

Tanner switched off the engine and they looked through the dirty windshield at their destination. A tired neon sign flickered out BARAK. The sign was mounted over a single door in the long log wall that faced the parking area. There were no windows across the front.

"Not exactly the most welcoming picture," Tanner muttered. "I wonder why Kay wanted to meet us way out here?" They were somewhere near Moqua, of that he was pretty sure. Mrs. Anderson's directions had been precise and clear so they'd had no trouble finding the place, but it didn't seem to be on their map of Wisconsin. There had been the suggestion of an element of adventure when she'd called, especially after a day of dealing with Ashland authorities in the wake of the death and fire at Chequamegon Resource Recovery.

But now, with the big woods blocking out most of

the rapidly diminishing sunlight, the atmosphere had turned decidedly gloomy. They were far enough from the big lake that the humidity and the heat of the day added to their growing feeling of unease.

"Well," said Mary in a resolute tone, "we'll never learn anything sitting out here. Let's go, sailor." She gracefully exited the car, swirling her full skirt around her hips as she did so.

There were a few pickup trucks and SUVs parked closer to the building. They were of various ages and looked as if they'd always been strangers to a hose or carwash. A couple of the vehicles looked as if the only thing holding them together was the mud caked on the fenders and the rust around the door hinges. A single light fixture that gave off little light hung askew over the entrance. The only other light radiated from the letters of the sign on the roof, which barely beat back the coming night and cast an unhealthy pallor over the rutted lot.

Tanner yanked open the heavy door—it didn't give way with ease—then he stepped back for Mary to precede him. Inside were a couple dozen people, all men, most seated on stools at the bar. A few interrupted their conversations or their drinking to look around at the newcomers. Tanner could feel the waves of appraisal wash over him.

Directly ahead, under three long-bladed ceiling fans that struggled to move the thick air, a wooden bar fronted a gaudy neon-and-mirror-festooned wall of shelves. The shelves were crowded with an assortment of bottles. Some of the neon flickered and buzzed companionably with the outside sign. Tanner momentarily flashed back to his days of heavy drinking when he'd nearly lost everything after the murder of Beth, his first wife. His step faltered for just a moment. This roadhouse had the same kind of stultifying atmosphere he'd encountered on more than one occasion in waterfront places around Puget Sound. His nose was assailed by the mingled odors of stale beer and old grime.

Mary straightened a little more erect under the appraising looks and strode confidently across the uneven plank floor toward the bar. Tanner followed and swept the room with a quick glance. There was a wide entrance to what appeared to be another room off to their right, but there were no lights beyond the entrance and it was just a wide black hole. An old-fashioned Wurlitzer jukebox, loaded with 45s, sat to one side flashing its multi-colored lights at the dark empty room. Wall sconces, some with burned-out bulbs, marched at head height around the perimeter of the place. Over the square arch between the barroom and the dark room, a banner proclaimed LADIES NIGHT-EVERY WEDNESDAY. It sagged against the wall. In smaller caps underneath, Tanner read DRINK'S HALF PRICE.

The main barroom floor space in front of the bar itself was taken up by a collection of tables and chairs which might once have been a matching set, but had long since succumbed to years of wear. Replacements suggested periodic searching through thrift shops and garage sales. The interior walls of the building were peeled logs, grown dark with smoke and grime. All together, neither the room nor its occupants offered a friendly welcoming scene.

Mary stopped and looked around questioningly at Tanner. The woman they were to meet was not in sight, so Tanner made a little hand motion to indicate they could sit anywhere Mary was comfortable. She went to one side to choose a table that appeared to be clean, halfway between the bar and the door. She sat and looked up at Tanner. "I'd like a beer, I think. In a bottle. You needn't bother with a glass." A thin smile came and went.

Tanner grinned. "No glass? My, my." He went to

the bar and looked at the bartender.

The man wiped his big hands on a towel and strolled over to say, "Yeah?"

"Heinekens, if you've got it. Otherwise, two Buds will be fine."

"Bud," said the man. "We don't hold with that foreign stuff." His tone was mildly reproving. He reached into a big cooler behind him and pulled out two long-necked brown bottles and thumped them on the bar. "Four bucks," he said.

Tanner gave him a five and waved off the four quarters the bartender returned. The bartender turned belatedly to offer a glass, but Tanner had already started back to the table.

The door opened and banged closed behind three men who glanced curiously at Tanner and Mary. A moment later, the door opened again and Kay Anderson stepped inside. Tanner stood up to get her attention. Her gaze traveled around the room as if she was checking the rest of the occupants. Then she turned and walked toward them.

Mary nodded and Kay sank into a chair, ignoring Tanner's proffered hand. "Thank you for coming. I know this is an imposition, but I think I am about to burst unless I talk to someone, and I can't go to our lawyer. He's handling CRR and if I went to another attorney in town, the news would be all over within twenty-four hours."

She took a deep breath and went on, "It's a little ridiculous, skulking around out here to this road house, but people do talk and I don't want George or anybody on the board hearing about our meeting until you are ready to tell them. I'm very sure no one in the company comes out here."

Mary said, "Is there any news about the fire or Ted McGregor?"

Kay Anderson shook her head slowly. "No. The police will be around as soon as the medical examiner finishes. You know, a lot of people are jealous of George. Some of them think he's just a con artist. I suppose it was all that treasure hunting in the Caribbean."

"He certainly is enthusiastic about this project," said Tanner. "Can I get you a drink?"

"Thanks. A beer would be fine right now."

When Tanner returned with a third bottle of Budweiser, Mrs. Anderson resumed talking in a low voice, leaning across the table. Her fingers were entwined on the table and Tanner noted her knuckles went from red to white to red over and over. Kay Anderson seemed drawn taut as a bowstring.

"When George told me that the body they found this morning was that Ted McGregor, I felt I had to talk about some of this. The trouble is, I don't know how much I don't know. You see what I'm saying?" She took a healthy swig from her bottle. "The fire chief told George they're certain the fire this morning was set. What they don't know yet is whether it was set by Ted McGregor or somebody else. In a way, it doesn't matter, because a lot of people know McGregor was trying to stop the company from bringing up those logs. And since everybody knows McGregor and George have been fighting—"

"I didn't know that," interrupted Tanner. "I met once with McGregor, just a couple of days ago. He seemed pretty prickly, but he never mentioned knowing George."

"They have had some real confrontations," said Kay, "not fist fights, but they ran into each other at the hotel in Ashland one day and the argument got loud. I wasn't there, but according to George and some others who were, McGregor started shouting in George's face so George shoved the man out of the way. Then I guess McGregor shoved back."

Kay Anderson sighed and shook her head. "George can be hotheaded at times and he's a little frustrated by all the delays. But he's not a murderer!" She downed more beer. Tanner noted that her bottle was more than half empty.

Kay's voice had gotten louder and Tanner saw a couple men at the bar raise their heads. "Were the police called? When McGregor and George got into it?"

Kay shook her head. "No. The men with George separated them."

"Did McGregor have anybody with him?"

Kay Anderson thought a moment. "I don't know. Nobody mentioned that. Of course, George wasn't the one who told me about the incident. I heard something at the office and asked Stan. He was present and he told me what had happened."

"Is that Stanley Krizyinsky?" said Mary.

"Yes."

"Were there other confrontations?" asked Tanner.

"Some," Kay nodded. "I heard them, or at least I heard George, shouting over the telephone one time, and he's mentioned a couple of others."

"Does the company get hate mail?"

Kay looked at Tanner and frowned. "I don't know, but I don't think so."

Mary laid a gentle hand on top of Kay's clasped fingers. "We mustn't jump to conclusions. It's understandable that George is worried that the fire and the skull they found in the bay and now McGregor's death will scare investors away."

Kay nodded, looking still more miserable as Mary went on, "I've told George that the Whitney Foundation is sending someone in to examine the company. Our representative should be here tomorrow or the next day. He's not going to be swayed very much by anything other than what he sees in the financial records and his own investigation."

Her words didn't seem to help. Kay still looked miserable. She took a sip of beer and said, "I'm prepared for it if Ted McGregor was murdered."

"Wait a minute," said Tanner. "I haven't heard even a suggestion that McGregor was murdered."

"I know," said Kay, "but if that is what happened, George will be a suspect. A lot of people don't like George. Even people who are making money from the company. I know he's brash, and his humor is off kilter sometimes. And sometimes he uses that ridiculous down-home sort of country-boy style. I've tried to get him to stop it."

"Try not to worry about McGregor until we know more," Tanner went on. "Have a lot of local people invested in CRR?" asked Tanner.

Kay nodded. "Quite a few. But only people who could afford to lose their investments put up significant amounts. Most local people invested less than a thousand dollars each. There are all kinds of rules, you know."

"Has George recently sold any significant amount of his stock?" asked Mary.

Kay shook her head again and finished her beer. "Can I have another, please?" Tanner looked at her and she smiled. "I'm not a lush, Mr. Tanner. I didn't drink at dinner and I think I can handle two beers. But to answer your question, no, he hasn't. I know that's a rumor going around that after the company went public, George and some of the others dumped their stock at a huge profit. I don't believe any of that happened. I'm sure I would know if George did that. Most of the stock is in my name."

"You aren't joint owners?"

Kay shook her head. "Not now. Something about taxes and risk and insurance. I keep our personal books and do the banking, but I don't fully understand these stock things. We have a financial planner and a good CPA who takes care of all that. But George and I have other legal arrangements between us. He doesn't like to give up control of any of his projects, you know."

"What about the people who work there? They're partially paid in stock. They must be worried about the financial health of CRR. Some of them might resent the time it's taking to take the company public and make a market in the stock," said Tanner.

Kay nodded again. "That's true. I think most of the carping comes from a few people around the bay who are suspicious of everything new, whether they invested or not. It doesn't make any sense for people with money in the company to wreck it. They'd lose everything just like we would." She sighed and took a sip from her bottle of beer.

"But all this financial business isn't why I wanted to talk to you privately. I'm afraid George hasn't been completely forthcoming with you and I want to clear the air."

While Tanner and Mary glanced at each other with mild alarm, Kay Anderson took a long slug of beer and then sighed.

"I know, I'm stalling. But here's the story. When the company started, George talked to a lot of potential investors. Some invested and some didn't. The usual. We didn't know for a while if we'd raise enough to make it."

Tanner nodded. "That's pretty much how it goes with new ventures."

"Exactly. I don't remember the exact figure but something like three-quarters of all new companies fail in the first couple of years. At one point it looked as if George would have to sell the whole thing, lose control. That bothered him a lot."

"Was that while you were riding out all the

regulatory business with the state and negotiating with the local Indians?" asked Tanner.

"That's right. George never anticipated it would take so long. One day he came home from a trip to New York and his mood was completely changed. You'd have thought he found a gold mine. In a way, I guess he had. I met him at the airport in Duluth. I could tell he was excited, but the whole way home he wouldn't tell me much except to say our troubles were over and he'd explain at the office to everybody at once."

"It sounds like he'd corralled a big investor," said Mary.

"That's right, he had. It was a big one with huge resources. We still owned a bare majority position, but there were some options he'd agreed to which worried me. But George was convinced by this investor that if things went well with the company, we'd never have to worry about the options."

"But this investor wanted some things in return, right?" said Mary.

"Sure. He wanted a seat on the board and he insisted that he be kept anonymous. None of that is particularly unusual, but George had to agree to an odd condition."

Tanner had a sudden premonition. "One of the conditions was that George had to persuade Tanner and Associates to get on board as CRR's PR firm."

Kay opened her mouth and looked at him in astonishment.

Mary's face was grim and her eyes flashed. "Kay, what's the name of this investor?"

Kay Anderson shook her head. "George didn't tell me, but after I saw the company name on some papers on his desk, I asked. It's called The Phoenix Fund, or something like that. Why? Is it important?"

With a quick glance at Tanner, Mary leaned forward a little and said, "I want to be sure of this. The Phoenix Fund is where my ex-husband works. In fact, he is the Phoenix, if it's the same venture firm."

Kay looked back with bewilderment. "The name George told me was Tobias. I'm afraid I don't remember his first name."

Mary sat back and said sourly. "That's him all right. Edwin Tobias. Our divorce was, shall I say, not amicable."

"I'll bet George was instructed to keep that information from us as long as possible," said Tanner.

"Would you have refused the job if you'd known about Phoenix?"

Tanner shrugged. "Probably. The reason we came out here was because George had so much personal information when he called me. We wanted to find out why that was. Well, now we know the source. My company doesn't take on jobs all over the country. We have plenty of work at home in King County. I don't get this. What possible reason could ET have for wanting us involved?"

"I can think of a couple of reasons." Mary paused and took a drink of beer while she organized her thoughts. "He already knew a lot about how I think and he must have remembered that the Whitneys cleared some of this land. He could easily find out about you," her hand reached out and tapped Tanner's, "and the firm. Could he have concocted a scheme to take some kind of revenge on me? Or on both of us?" She looked at Tanner and he saw the concern in her eyes.

"That seems pretty far-fetched to me," Tanner said.

"You don't know my ex."

"Tanner and Associates has been successful," Tanner said, noting Kay Anderson's quizzical expression, "so we have a fairly high profile in Seattle. Besides, I was involved in an investigation on the Inside Passage last year, so anyone wanting detailed information about me wouldn't have to work very hard to get it. But the whole idea of Phoenix wanting Tanner and Associates as a condition of investment is bizarre." Tanner frowned. "How would ET know you'd become interested enough to consider investing? He couldn't even guarantee I'd take on the public relations contract."

Kay had been silent for several minutes. Now she said, "Do you mean the Phoenix Investment isn't real? We're counting on that money. In fact we're borrowing against the letter of intent Phoenix gave us."

"I assume your firm's lawyer looked at the documents, Kay," said Mary. "But I think you'd better tell George what we've talked about. When Mr. Hochstein gets here, I'll fill him in. He has ways to find out more about this, and maybe some ways to get Mr. Tobias out of your hair at the right time."

The three of them rose and went toward the door. Tanner's gaze drifted over the men in the barroom, including a scruffy-looking man who'd followed Kay Anderson into Barak's by a few minutes.

"I've seen that fellow before," Tanner mused. "I wonder where it was."

Chapter 17

Kay Anderson glanced at the man Tanner was talking about and said, "Oh, that's Wally Zane. He's a local handyman. Sort of a drifter. He turns up here and there around the area and does odd jobs when he feels like it. As far as I know, he doesn't seem to hold a regular job. He drives a pickup truck that's so old and beat up, nobody knows how it runs at all."

"What's his story?"

Kay frowned as Tanner pulled open the big door and they exited into the thick night. "Nothing serious that I know of. He worked at CRR for a few months last year. But George had to let him go. He only showed up when he felt like it. Extreme unreliability, George said." She pointed across the gravel lot. "There, that's his truck."

The vehicle in question was an older Chevy pickup of uncertain color. Between the rust, the grime and the sun-faded surface, the truck appeared to be grayish pink. The outside mirror on the driver's side had been broken and only an empty chrome shell remained.

Tanner stood back when Kay Anderson unlocked her Cadillac and slid into the driver's seat. When she lowered the window and looked up at them, a small, wistful smile drifted across her face.

"Thanks for listening. I feel a lot better, knowing you have the picture now." She twisted the key and drove out of the lot.

Mary looked after her and said, "Is she okay to drive, do you think?"

Tanner gazed at the disappearing Cadillac. "I guess so. She's a pretty together woman, even with two beers. It must have cost her a good deal to tell us about Phoenix. I wonder if we do have the whole picture. For example, she said Phoenix required a seat on the board of CRR. Who would that be?"

Mary was silent for several minutes while Tanner piloted the Lexus through the trees to the highway. "I guess now we know why she and George were acting a little odd on our boat ride right after we got here. Have you signed a contract?"

Tanner glanced at her. "No, we're going to do that tomorrow at their office. Assuming there aren't any last-minute disagreements over the terms. Are you having some reservations?"

"I guess I am. Now that we know Edwin has his fat fingers in the pie, I'm more than a little uneasy. And remember, that's partly why we came out here. To learn more about why Anderson had so much personal detail about us." She sighed.

"Fat fingers? Is he really?"

Mary shook her head. "Fat? No, that's just my expression. I've never described him to you, have I?"

"No. But I've never asked, either."

"He's about your height, slim, prematurely gray. Wears his hair fashionably short. Wire-framed glasses. Regular features, and always dressed to the exact nines. If you see him, you'll register his expensive duds. An expensive weasel."

Bright lights from a vehicle behind them flashed in Tanner's eyes and he adjusted the rear-view mirror.

"Since it's come up, I'll tell you a little about my New York life with corporate raider ET."

Unseen in the dim light from the Lexus dashboard, Tanner's eyebrows went up. There was a bitter undertone to Mary's voice and she'd never used such language before in reference to her former husband. They rode in silence for a time.

"About all I know is that you were married to Tobias for a year."

A sigh. "A little over a year. Just long enough for me to discover he was—is—a highly focused and driven man. Obsessive wouldn't be out of place here." Mary turned in and leaned against the door, drawing her leg up on the padded edge of the seat. She had to unbuckle the seatbelt.

"Edwin Tobias is descended from a long line of obsessives. You know the type. They're men who made it their business to get an education at top schools and then to succeed in business. Most went to Harvard or Yale or Columbia and then to law school or they got a graduate business degree by way of Wharton or one of the other top graduate business programs. In the process they learned to speak well, use charming manners, and then to have mostly successful careers."

Tanner grinned. "You aren't condemning everyone who followed that path, are you?"

"Of course not. But there seems to be a certain kind of individual who follows the pattern. Most started with wealth and got more. Nothing wrong with that either, you know. I don't subscribe to the notion that wealth necessarily corrupts. But underneath the veneer, I think most of the Tobias men, at least those I encountered, are little better than cavemen. Brutes."

"I'm surprised to hear you say that. Now that I know you, I'm surprised you fell for such a character."

Mary chuckled ruefully. "I was younger then and I suppose I was dazzled by the East Coast glitter. I'd only been out of college a couple of years and remember, in spite of my rough and tumble relatives at home, I'd led a fairly sheltered life. Plus, those people are very smooth. They have good manners, as I said, and they can sweep a girl off her feet, if she isn't paying close attention. I saw it happen with girls being dated by Edwin's younger brothers. I was wined and dined and rushed unmercifully, once Edwin decided I would make a suitable bride." She paused then, remembering her former life.

"Parties, gifts, that sort of thing?"

"Oh yes, and some of the gifts were outrageously expensive, even to a Whitney. My engagement ring was really ostentatious. But it was the rest of it. Mention casually you're interested in a sold-out Broadway show? A pair of aisle seats, center section, show up hidden in a great bouquet of flowers two days later. We attended just about every major show or gallery opening while he was courting me. And if he seemed just a little bored, or more interested in who was there to see or be seen with, so what? Did I need to do some casual shopping? Hey, ET arranged for a driver to whisk me around. I got endless, flattering attention. I loved it. I admit it. Who wouldn't?"

"Anyway, after our wedding, which was not in Seattle, I take pains to mention. It was on Catalina. Phoenix, which was fairly new then, had just invested in some big deal on the island, so we combined the wedding with a little business trip." Mary fell silent.

Tanner noted the following vehicle was creeping closer on the dark winding road. He snugged up his seat belt.

"It's funny," she said. "You know I've avoided talking about that part of my life except occasional little bits here and there."

"I have noticed. I am interested, but I've always had the feeling you weren't quite ready. I figured that one day when you wanted to tell me, you would. Or not. It was your life and I don't have any particular right to know."

Mary leaned over and patted Tanner's thigh. "That's one of the things I've always liked about you. Interested but never nosy."

"That's me, Mr. Perfect."

"Oh, now I never said that. Wait'll we get home. I have a list." Mary stopped, organizing her thoughts. "There's no big scandal, you understand. I would have told you about that right away if there were. Anyway, after the wedding, Edwin's attitude toward me began to change. And I began to see similarities to the way his father treated his mother. He gradually grew distant. Most of the other women in the family got the same treatment.

"I don't mean we were abused. We were just dismissed. Edwin and the other men were almost always charming and generous. But what we Tobias women thought was of no consequence. I grew up in an family of participation. We talked about everything, just like you and I do. Not the Tobiases. No way. And sailing. Hah. Why are you slowing down?"

"The guy behind me is hanging on my bumper, so I'm going to let him pass." But Tanner felt his pulse increase.

The vehicle behind them didn't pass immediately. After hanging inches off their back bumper, drifting back as much as a quarter mile, then moving up and tailgating again, the driver flicked on his high beams and roared around the Lexus in a near miss. Leaving a trail of scorched oil in the air, the truck disappeared down a hill and around a steep curve at the bottom. Mary and Tanner watched the truck whiz by. Mary straightened in her seat and hooked up the seat belt, tugging it tighter over her lap.

"Some old duffer in a pickup," said Mary. Tanner

heard the false lightness in her tone. "Hard to be sure in the headlights, but that looked a lot like the truck Kay Anderson pointed out back at Barak's."

A mile further on, Tanner saw his headlights reflect off a vehicle parked in a tiny clearing just off the edge of the pavement. Mary looked at it as they passed.

"Old truck. Pickup, I think," she said. "Could have been the one that was tailgating. Anyway, I told you that I hassled Edwin about a sailboat until he agreed to let me buy the *Sea Queen*. I used my own money for it." She stopped then for a minute, then said quietly. "I'm glad I'm telling you all this. It feels good to talk about it. Oh, by the way. You don't have to worry about buying me expensive gifts. I don't seem to hang on to them anyway."

Tanner smiled in the dark at the mixture of seriousness and amusement in her voice.

"I gave 'em all back. Including the ring. When I started the divorce."

"Everything?"

"Everything. I think that's what made Edwin the maddest. I'd moved out of our Fifth Avenue place to an apartment and the papers had been filed. We met at his attorney's office. My lawyer didn't think that was such a hot idea but I insisted."

"On their territory."

"We walked in and before anyone could say anything, I placed a typed list and a box on the table. Every piece of jewelry, and affidavits for the car and a few family heirlooms I'd been given. Every stinkin' piece. He looked at the list, looked at me and he turned a lovely purple shade. His lawyer took the list and compared it to one Edwin must have prepared. Turned out there wasn't anything to negotiate. I wasn't asking for alimony and I didn't even ask for the things my family had given him." Mary laughed a short, hard sound. "He and his lawyer just sort of sat there with their mouths open with nothing to say.

"Then my lawyer told Edwin to sign the agreement right now or we'd go to the SEC."

"The Securities and Exchange Commission?"

"Edwin and Phoenix were always fudging the rules and he had no way of knowing for sure how much I knew, how much I might have overheard at the dinner table, or one of the family gatherings where we all sat around like decorations. He couldn't afford to bet against me. Edwin Tobias is not a gambler, unless he has a sure thing. Anyway, they signed and I signed a paper agreeing to be silent about anything to do with Phoenix. Then I closed the apartment and flew back to Seattle. After that, the lawyers scrapped over stuff Edwin said was missing. He wanted to attach the boat, and so on. In the end, we had to threaten to sue over other stuff besides Phoenix. Phooo! Later I heard he ranted about me and the Whitneys for weeks after the split. In fact, now that I remember, I had an email from a girlfriend in New York just before we flew out here. She mentioned that Edwin was still bitter about the divorce." She blew out her breath as headlights bloomed in the back window of the Lexus.

Mary twisted around in her seat and looked out the back window. Her voice rose slightly. "There's another one with a funny headlight, or it's the same truck that passed us earlier."

This time the following vehicle neither slowed nor pulled out to pass. It sped up. It slammed into the rear of the Lexus, throwing it forward and to the right.

"My God, Michael!"

Tanner cursed, stomped on the gas and wrenched the car back to the center of the pavement. "Hang on!" he yelled.

Twice more the driver of the other vehicle slammed into the back of the Lexus, apparently attempting to force it off the road into the trees.

The other driver suddenly cut to the left. The headlights rocked as he tried to pull alongside. Tanner, driving a more powerful sedan, managed to stay ahead of him.

"I don't think I want to let him pass again."

There was a sharp crack, heard faintly under the sound of their engine.

"That was a shot, Michael! He's shooting at us!"

"Mary, get down as low as you can."

She slammed one hand against the dashboard and bent over. Her other hand clutched the handhold on the passenger door. Tanner floored the accelerator and the Lexus leaped ahead. Tanner screamed around a curve, right-side tires chattering in loose gravel and the truck behind them again slammed into the Lexus' rear end. Twice more on winding sections of the highway, Tanner was forced to slow down and twice more the game of deadly tag allowed the other driver to pull alongside the Lexus. Tanner had to manhandle the car down the highway, wishing he was driving his more responsive Porsche.

Around one more dark curve, the lights of Bayfield bloomed over the forest in the night sky. The driver of the pickup suddenly aborted his attacks and screeched off on a side road. Tanner took his foot off the gas and glanced at Mary who was still crouching low in her seat. "He seems to have disappeared. Are you okay?"

"Whoo," Mary breathed. "I don't like these wild rides any more. What's going on here? Homicidal Wisconsin truckers?" She laughed shakily.

"Damn it," Tanner muttered. "I'd like to chase that bastard down, but he's obviously armed." He flexed his fingers and looked at Mary in the corner of the car, breathing deeply to calm herself. Tanner felt the adrenaline bleeding away.

"Michael, who was that?" Mary said, voice shrill in the darkness. "All this talk about road rage aside, no local drunk would act like that. I think we've become targets."

"Yeah, I'm sure you're right. That truck looked a lot like the one Kay pointed out back at Baraks."

Chapter 18

"Michael! What in the world are you doing?" Mary goggled up at her husband. From his standing perch on the end of the bed in their rented condo, he grinned down at her. Tanner was naked, stretching his arms overhead. His long fingertips just reached the ceiling when he bounced lightly on the mattress.

He sketched an even wider grin. "I feel really good this morning," bouncing more vigorously, "and a few stretches just add to my sense of well-being. We've learned some important stuff, cleared a little fog, and escaped a mad Wisconsin driver."

"Uh huh. I'll remember this. If I feel a need to liven you up, I'll just get some yokel to try to run us off a dark road. Gets you going, does it? I poured you some coffee and there's a slice of bread in the toaster. All you have to do is press down on the lever at the end."

"Of the toaster."

"Exactly. I'm for the shower. If Mr. Hochstein calls, find out when and where he wants to meet today."

"Your wish is my whatever," Tanner responded, still bouncing on the bed, arms outstretched for balance.

Mary surveyed his body up and down again and giggled. Then she padded into the bathroom. Tanner grinned after her, hopped down from the bed, threw on his light robe and strolled into the kitchen. As he reached to depress the toaster lever, the telephone rang.

"Tanner."

"Michael? Edmund Hochstein here. I've just now landed at the Duluth airport. I've reserved a car so I'll be in Ashland a little later. I hope we can meet immediately."

"Of course, Mr. Hochstein. We were told to expect Lloyd Casjens. Is there any reason you decided to come yourself?"

"Yes, I am aware of the original plan. I decided, after some preliminary examination, it would be preferable if I came out. Mr. Casjens will be busy elsewhere."

The Whitney Foundation was sending in the first team. Interesting, thought Tanner. His thoughts turned to Edmund Hochstein. Edmund Hochstein was the only person Tanner always addressed as mister. Mary usually called him Mister Hochstein as well. Certainly, Hochstein, who towered over just about everyone at six and a half feet tall, cast an intimidating presence wherever he went. He seemed to have a similar effect to when a well-dressed, striking woman entered a room. Conversations would die down, and people would turn to look at the new arrival.

Hochstein was very thin, approaching emaciation, with a head topped by a mane of thick, silver hair that he wore swept back above a protruding and nearly unlined forehead. His large head was filled by a capacious brain, a superior intellect, and his dark, slightly ophthalmic eyes were large and piercing. Tanner had wondered if the tinted, heavy-framed glasses he wore were more of a prop than a necessity. His richly tonal baritone voice could be piercing as well. In Tanner's experience, Edmund Hochstein, attorney at law and president of the Whitney Foundation, had no sense of humor whatever.

"I assume you are carrying a cell phone?" Tanner asked.

"Naturally."

"When you get to the junction of Highway 2 and 63

to Hayward, give us a call. We'll drive over to Ashland and meet you at your hotel. I assume you are at the Chequamegon?"

"Yes, quite. The Chequamegon."

Tanner didn't bother to correct Hochstein's pronunciation.

"I have reserved a small suite. It is a waterfront hotel, is it not? The Chequamegon?"

"Yes. The current hotel is a reconstruction, owing to a fire many years ago that destroyed the original."

"Michael, I judge from the communications I have had with Mrs. Tanner that the two of you are not staying in Ashland, but rather in Bayfield across the bay?"

"Right."

"Isn't that a trifle inconvenient?"

"It hasn't been, so far. But we can discuss it if necessary. Mary and I will see you later today at your hotel."

"Thank you. I see my transportation is ready. Goodbye."

* * *

Tanner and Mary waited in the lobby of the Chequamegon Hotel. Unlike grander or more modern establishments, this hotel lobby was small, with pillars, nooks and crannies, lots of dark paneling, and plenty of overstuffed chairs and intimate sofas. The reception desk was ornate and almost hidden from the entrance behind a partial wall and a pillar. Tanner was sitting, knees crossed, in a chair that was so soft he'd sunk onto the end of his spine. Mary was pacing back and forth.

"Mary, are you really so nervous at the prospect of seeing Ed Hochstein?"

"I guess I am. What I can't figure out is why he

came instead of Lloyd. It's bad enough to learn my ex-husband is involved, but now Hochstein as well." She waved a hand. "He's in his seventies, you know." She spun on her heels to pace a few steps toward the glassed in verandah that looked out on the bay. Her long skirt swirled around her. "He never approved of Tobias. He told me the man was a fortune hunter."

"Is that really true?" Tanner wondered for a moment how much sway this old man really had over Mary. Hochstein and the Whitney Foundation had never been the subject of an in-depth discussion between them. But it had always been his impression that Mary Whitney was one very independent woman. "So, what did he have to say about me, I wonder?"

Mary stopped pacing for a moment to smile at Tanner. "Oh, he adores you. Told me at our wedding this was a match made in heaven."

"He has a nice turn of a phrase. Funny, I never quite got that positive an impression."

There came the sound of the penetrating, well-recognized voice from the direction of the small elevator in one corner of the lobby and Tanner struggled up from the sofa. Around the pillar stalked Edmund Hochstein.

He raised both hands, smiled, and clasped Mary's hand, saying, "Ah my dear, my dear. It has been far too long. You are looking well. Very well." He leaned down and kissed her cheek. Hochstein's eyes flicked over Mary's shoulder and landed on Tanner. "Michael. Good to see you, my boy. You too appear to be in splendid health."

Tanner nodded and the two men shook hands. Hochstein was impeccably attired as always in a dark gray suit, sparkling white shirt, and suitably conservative tie. He carried a knobby black cane adorned with the head of a beaked bird, perhaps a hawk or a falcon. The carved head, covered with dull gold gilt, was curved just enough so Hochstein could hook it over one wrist when he took hold of Mary's hands. Tanner noticed a small group of locals entering the lobby and heading for the downstairs club. Their glances stumbled over the cadaverous Hochstein, so obviously a wealthy outsider. When he looked back, Hockstein had raised Mary's hand to his lips in a lingering kiss.

"I understand there is a bar of some considerable local repute in the basement of this hotel, where we can talk and have a small libation. Am I correct?"

"That's true," said Tanner. "It's called Molly Cooper's."

The trio went downstairs to a pleasant room with large windows that looked out on Chequamegon Bay and found a table well away from the others.

After they ordered, Mary said, "Is your room satisfactory?"

Hochstein nodded. "Quite, my dear. I would have preferred a suite, but there were none available." He surveyed the barroom, a watering hole with a faint roaring twenties decor. "Do either of you know who Molly Cooper was?"

"I haven't run across her in the historical stuff I'm reading," said Mary, shaking her head.

Hochstein's lips curved up and then down. "During the heyday of the lumbering years, Whitney and the other companies that cleared the forests of the region weren't particular about the people they hired. They just wanted reliable workers. Many of the men were single and some appear to have had a sizable roistering quotient. Ashland, as well as other communities around the bay, catered to most of their needs, and some of the townspeople weren't above cashing in on the pay of the loggers when they came out of the forests.

"One of the most enterprising appears to have been a woman named Molly Cooper. There were a great many liquor establishments and more than a few bawdy houses in town. Apparently this Cooper woman gradually acquired several boarding houses for women who worked in the community and she became something of a local celebrity. It seems some boarding houses served other, umm, less polite functions. I suppose naming this place after her is one way the local populace has of getting in touch with their less straightlaced roots."

Tanner was a little surprised at Hochstein's knowledge. He, or somebody at Whitney, had been doing some in-depth research.

Delicately, Hochstein tasted his drink and nodded approval. "Now to current business. The principal investor in Chequamegon Resource Recovery, apart from those actively running the enterprise, whom I understand you have already met, is an East Coast venture capital firm called Phoenix."

Mary nodded and Hochstein returned the nod saying, "I gather this is not news, nor is the fact that the principal stockholder of Phoenix is your former husband, Edwin Tobias III." His thin lips turned down. "I should add that we have been following Mr. Tobias off and on for some time, owing to your, um, shall we say, unfortunate previous association."

"You don't have to dance around the subject. It was several years ago and I'm quite over him." Mary glanced at Tanner who smiled, signaling his understanding and level of comfort with the topic.

Hochstein's eyes flitted like a hummingbird between Mary and Tanner. "Yes. It is inevitable, in the world of finance, that we are all at least aware of each other. Whitney has never done business with Phoenix, nor with any other Tobias enterprise. They have a certain predatory attitude, I'm afraid, which I find rather distasteful. Nevertheless, we are, as I say, aware of Phoenix, and in the same manner, they are aware of Whitney Enterprises. It is common practice for investment funds to stay apprized of the competition. In this regard, I should say we are somewhat perplexed."

"Oh?" said Mary. "About what?"

Hochstein sipped his drink and peered over the rim of the glass. For a moment Tanner thought he saw a twinkle in the other man's eyes. He blinked and it was gone, a passing illusion.

"It is my impression that this sunken timber recovery proposition has high front-end costs and is somewhat risky. There have been continuing questions raised by Native Americans and environmental protection groups. There have been delays. It does not seem to be the sort of investment Phoenix would be interested in supporting.

"Whitney's investment in this present enterprise, should it come about, will be the first time our two entities have joined forces. I have to say, right at the beginning, that we have some other concerns about the Tobiases. Phoenix itself has never run afoul of the myriad regulations we all must be cognizant of, but I must be frank. The Tobias reputation leans somewhere toward the freebooter and swashbuckling style. The family has run afoul of SEC and other regulatory agency rules from time to time. Given all the circumstances we shall proceed with great caution in this enterprise."

"I read that Edwin himself was being looked at by the SEC."

Hochstein nodded again. "Yes, that is true."

"Is Phoenix involved?"

"We do not know. The SEC is extremely reticent about revealing anything regarding its ongoing investigations. Even the published fact that they have been examining Tobias Capital is somewhat surprising. The SEC investigates many activities, such as insider trading and improper manipulation of securities. Most of their investigations do not result in prosecutions or even charges being brought. The current interest of the SEC in Phoenix or in Mr. Tobias will be a factor in my recommendation, but it is not necessarily a contra-indication."

"Sure," injected Tanner. "But we all know how this works. You have your inside sources."

Hochstein merely glanced at Tanner. The expression on his face could have conveyed significant meaning—or nothing. Tanner knew the subject was closed.

"Regardless of the actions of the Securities and Exchange Commission," Hochstein continued, we will do an independent analysis of Chequamegon Resource Recovery and determine whether it is an appropriate investment for Whitney Enterprises. Of course, my dear, you realize that any decision we make will no doubt be colored to a degree by the history Whitney has with this area. I daresay there will be members of the investment committee who will argue that even if Chequamegon falls a bit short of our investment standards, we should repay something of the debt."

"Debt? What debt?" said Mary.

"You see, my dear, in the days when the shores of the lake were being logged, there were sometimes questions about exactly who owned what. Boundaries were not always precise. Logging companies vied for stumpage rights and sometimes rightful owners were simply overrun. Then, of course, there are the enduring questions of Native American rights." Hochstein stopped to sip his sherry. "Are you two privy to the logging history of the area?"

Mary and Tanner glanced at each other. Hochstein

was famous for his lectures on any number of subjects, some germane, some not. Now Tanner and Mary seemed unable to find a way to avoid this one.

"Let me elucidate." Hochstein clasped his hand beneath his prominent chin and seemed to look inward to his apparently inexhaustible store of information. "Two centuries ago, that would be the late nineteenth century, these shores were thickly covered with forest. Pine, hemlock, various oaks, maple and birch, as well as other desireable varieties. It was thought to be an inexhaustible supply of valuable hardwoods.

"Asa Whitney and a Milwaukee man named, as I recall, Schroeder, formed a combine which not only endeavored to lease what is called stumpage rights to the best timber tracts their forest cruisers could locate, but they also built one of the largest lumber mills of several that crowded the shore of this bay."

"There's a man named Ted Schroeder who's a vice president at CRR," said Mary.

Hochstein appeared mildly distressed at the interruption. "Yes. He is not a relative, so far as we are able to determine. This Chequamegon Bay is a fine natural harbor, and at one time it was thought it would become an international port.

"But, I digress. The issue before us is whether Chequamegon Resource Recovery is a fit and sturdy investment opportunity for our consideration. I have already called the president, Mr. George Anderson, and arranged to meet at their offices tomorrow morning. Meanwhile, in the time remaining this afternoon, I intend to thoroughly examine the documents that were waiting for me here at the hotel. You will therefore permit me to say good afternoon."

"Where shall we have dinner?" Tanner asked as they left the hotel.

"Mr. Krizyinsky suggested the Platters," responded Mary. "It has a good reputation. He told me it's halfway up the hill on the south end of Ashland. In an old turn-of-the-century house. Apparently one of ill repute. Formerly ill repute."

"What, a Victorian bordello? Another of Molly Cooper's establishments perhaps?"

Mary smiled. "Dunno, sailor, but it's supposed to have a fine chef."

"Okay, the Platters it is," said Tanner. "I'll call Hochstein when we get back to Bayfield and give him directions. Incidentally, I think it's interesting that you and I almost always refer to him as Mr. Hochstein. I also began to wonder just how much influence he has on you."

Mary laughed and turned the car northward on Highway 13 toward Bayfield. "I don't know anyone who calls him by his first name. He's always been a fixture in my life, even as a small child, and after my uncle and my dad died, he became the de facto head of the family. He's very judicious in his use of influence. I don't think I would ever go against his advice."

"You did when you married Tobias," smiled Tanner.

"Yes, that's true, but Mr. Hochstein never came right out and told me not to marry the guy. He said Tobias was an unfortunate choice. But I had to find out for myself just how unfortunate."

Chapter 19

The weather that had been threatening for hours broke just as Tanner and Mary climbed into their car for the 20-mile drive around the bay from Bayfield to the Platters restaurant in Ashland. Rain lashed the windshield, sometimes so hard the Lexus' wipers couldn't keep up. As they made the big curve around the bottom of the bay, the uncertain glow of Ashland bloomed in the water-streaked windows. Wind-driven spume from the lake reduced their vision even more. Mary glanced across Tanner toward the lake. In the darkening evening, she could see the storm-tossed waves, white teeth reaching skyward only to be pounded down by another angry burst of wind and rain. Other fingers of the wind picked at the edges of the Lexus' doors and pushed against its sides.

Mary pulled her flowered silk shawl tighter around her shoulders and shivered.

"Cold?" Tanner asked, reaching for the dashboard. He was carefully piloting the car through frequent pools of standing water on the highway. The damage from being repeatedly rammed by the truck hadn't affected its handling, so they'd chosen not to drive to the Twin Cities to replace the vehicle, the only option offered by the rental agency. Bayfield City police had taken a report of the incident and promised to look for the offending driver.

"Not really cold, just the wind, the rain, and the

damp." Mary glanced over her shoulder as distant headlights behind them registered.

"That's the third time you've checked the rear. I'm going to get you a special mirror."

Tanner's tone was light but he knew why Mary did it. He too was checking the rearview mirror much more frequently since that frightening night before last.

Tanner turned right at the flashing yellow electric arrow with PLATTERS on it. Two blocks up the hill away from the lake, through a screen of storm-lashed trees, they glimpsed a substantial-looking brick building. Beside it was a broad gravel parking lot with several cars already there. They entered the lot through a narrow break in the thick dripping bushes.

"Creepy in all this rain," murmured Mary.

The entrance stairs started from the front corner under a pillared roof and projected down to the parking lot at a right angle. Rain cascaded in sheets from the tiled roof and puddled on the concrete steps. Tanner stopped as close to the steps as he could manage. Mary held a light plastic raincoat over her head and dashed to the meager shelter of the portico. Tanner parked the car and ran through the rain to the entrance. Together they went in.

Like many homes built late in the nineteenth century, this one had a short entryway and a second door that opened into a front hall. Directly ahead of them a narrow stairway rose steeply to a landing, then disappeared in a sharp left turn. Tanner glanced to his left into what must once have been a parlor. It had been converted to a small barroom where four patrons sat at a tiny table and another leaned casually on the heavy oak bar set across one corner of the room. A woman standing behind the bar straightened when she saw Tanner and smiled. She wiped her hands on a towel and came toward them out from behind the bar.

On their right, in a much larger room, several tables of different sizes occupied the space. They were covered with snowy white table cloths. Sparkling glass and silverware were neatly arranged on the surfaces. An ornate crystal chandelier hung over the large center table. The walls were papered in what appeared to be a small flowery Victorian-era pattern. There was a dark carpet underfoot.

The woman from behind the bar smiled broadly. "Good evening," she said. "Welcome to The Platters. I'm Adele Stevens. My husband and I are the owners and your hosts this evening."

Tanner identified himself and Mary and they all shook hands. Adele Stevens led the way into the dining room, a large pleasant room to the right of the entrance, saying, "We've been expecting you. I think this corner table will be satisfactory." A waiter appeared at her side with water for the glasses on the table and three menus.

"Mr. Hochstein will be here any minute," said Tanner. They both ordered cocktails, scotch for Tanner and bourbon for Mary, which arrived several minutes later along with a damp Edmund Hochstein.

"My, my," he said, rubbing his hands briskly. "When it decides to rain in these parts it doesn't hold back, does it?" He ordered a martini from the attentive waiter and glanced around the room. "The Platters, what an interesting name. Have you any idea what the derivation might be?"

Mary shook her head and Hochstein craned his neck to look around. "Certainly an isolated location, even now. I imagine when the house was first built it was even farther out of town," he commented.

"On the other hand, the area had a larger population around 1900 when lumbering, quarrying brownstone, and mining were in full swing," said Mary. "Apparently this building was a bordello at one time. One of many here in

Ashland and throughout the lake shore counties. Are you aware that there used to be a place near Iron River called the 'Palace of Pleasures Among the Pines?'" Tanner smiled and Mary hid her grinning mouth behind her napkin.

"Yes indeed. That was the place supposedly run by a woman known as Muskeg Sally, was it not?" Hochstein responded.

"I'm surprised, Mr. Hochstein," said Tanner in a neutral tone, "at the depth of your research into these matters."

Hochstein gave him a sharp look as if to determine whether Tanner was serious or poking fun at him. "Hmmm, yes. It never hurts to learn some of the history of a place, you know."

"Exactly," said Mary. "While Michael has been dealing with the executives at CRR and setting up a contract, I've been doing a bit of research. Apparently, in the 1890s Ashland alone boasted between three and four hundred working girls." She was unable to completely contain her glee at the look of consternation on Hochstein's face. Apparently he didn't consider research into turn-of-the century prostitution a fit subject for the daughter of one of his old friends and an heir to the Whitney millions.

Tanner, familiar with Mary's sometimes offbeat humor, merely sipped his scotch and retained a bland demeanor.

"But, to be serious for a moment," she went on, "what can you tell us so far, after your examination of CRR's books?"

"I have not completed my examination, and I have found a few omissions. When I ask about them, the response is frowns, and I am referred to the president, George Anderson. He seemed forthcoming, whenever he was available, which was less and less as the day went on.

Curiously, there is no mention of Phoenix or of Edwin Tobias III as an investor. And that is where most of my questions remain. It is apparent to me that the involvement of Tobias and Phoenix has been hidden from everyone at the company except those directly involved. I'll need at least several more hours tomorrow to prepare a list of questions, get the answers, and formulate an opinion for a preliminary report to our board."

The waiter arrived and the trio shelved their discussion. Mary selected a seafood salad of shrimp and Lake Superior whitefish on a bed of mixed greens and diced peppers, after being assured that the shrimp and fish were indeed fresh, with an oil and balsamic vinegar dressing on the side. Tanner decided he owed himself a serious injection of protein and ordered a medium rare slab of prime rib with baked potato while Hochstein selected the house specialty, broiled fillet of walleyed pike.

Mrs. Stevens stopped at their table to take a new drink order and she confirmed that the place had indeed been a bordello for a brief time in the late 1890s. "Guests frequently ask about the history of the building. Several books mention the place. The house was originally built by one of the Schroeder quarry supervisors. Schroeder owned the quarries as well as the mills. They took a lot of brownstone from several of the islands for building in Milwaukee and Chicago and other places. This building stone is from the same quarries. We're expanding off the back of the place to increase the capacity of the dining room." She pointed toward the back wall, behind a large window. Through the rain, construction materials could be seen piled up on the porch.

"We'll move the porch farther out. Eventually I'd like to enclose it for summer dining." Mrs. Stevens went away and their meals arrived. Hochstein smiled and nodded his approval of the presentation, and after his first bite, cautiously declared the pike perfectly broiled. Tanner and Mary Whitney also agreed their meals were excellent and conversation was suspended for several minutes. Rain rattled against the dark window at Tanner's back.

There came a sudden burst of laughter and a loud voice from the direction of the front entrance. Three men appeared. They shook the rain off their coats, and without a glance into the dining room, went immediately up the stairs. Mary frowned at their backs as they disappeared.

Their waiter proffered the dessert menu and an offer of coffee or tea. "Excuse me," Mary said, "but I thought Mrs. Stevens told us they live upstairs."

"That's right, Mr. and Mrs. Stevens, with their two children, do live upstairs. They converted two of the front bedrooms right at the head of those stairs into private meeting rooms. The two rooms are separated by a wall from the rest of the second floor. There's a back stair which the family uses. I've been told there used to be another, a third stairway, leading to an outside door at the back of the building, but it's been bricked up for years. I think it was there for people who didn't want to be seen coming or going in the old days." The waiter smiled and poured cups of coffee.

Mary was still looking at the now empty stairs just outside the dining room entrance.

"My dear?" said Hochstein. "Is something wrong?"

Mary started and then shook her head. "What? No, I just thought—never mind, it's nothing."

Tanner looked at Mary and smiled. He said nothing, but his mind was racing. Whatever it was that caused Mary to get that peculiar, if fleeting look, it wasn't insignificant. But if she chose to dismiss it for the moment, he knew better than to press the issue.

Tanner and Hochstein argued in gentlemanly fashion over who would pay the bill, Tanner eventually winning. The men left together, trotting down the steps into a wet night with now a light mist falling. Hochstein drove out of the parking area with a brief wave, and Tanner maneuvered the Lexus close to the steps. Mary got in and buckled her seat belt.

"So, are you going to tell me?" smiled Tanner.

"What? Oh, my little mental departure at the table? It was kind of a *deja vu* thing. One of those three men who came in late and went upstairs looked a lot like Edwin."

"ET? You only saw him from the back. Are you sure?" Tanner had started to drive out of the lot.

"No, and why would he be here, anyway? It doesn't make any sense. I thought one of the others seemed familiar too. What are you doing?"

Tanner had driven into the street from the graveled lot and now he was turning around at the next intersection. There were no streetlights in this part of Ashland and the mist made everything look darker than usual. Tanner drove back up and into the Platters' lot. Slowly he circled the lot until he was behind a row of cars toward the farthest corner, away from the yellow yard light that illuminated the front of the restaurant and the stairs to the entrance. He switched off the lights and killed the engine. Then he pointed at the two windows over the entrance portico.

"Look," he said. "Those windows must be the two meeting rooms upstairs."

One of the windows was dark, but the other glowed white light. Mary and Tanner watched in silence for a few minutes and then a man came into view, paused and crossed out of sight. Tanner knew instantly from Mary's altered breathing that she had recognized the man.

"It is Edwin! I wonder what that's all about? He never left New York while we were married. He said he hated anywhere else," she said. "Even when they were in the final closing phases of some deal, he'd be in his office on the phone and some flunky would be somewhere in the world doing Edwin's bidding. He hates flying. If he's all the way out here in Wisconsin, something very serious is going on."

After a few minutes more of silent watching, while the damp crawled in, Tanner reached down and twisted the ignition key. As the engine came to life, he glanced up once more at the window to see Stanley Krizyinsky cross their narrow field of view.

Chapter 20

When Tanner walked into the offices of CRR, he was still going over in his mind whether to confront Stanley Krizyinsky about his undercover meeting with Tobias and that unknown third man.

Edmund Hochstein was hard at work running down in meticulous detail answers to his remaining questions. The conference room had been turned over to Mr. Hochstein and his examinations for as long as necessary. Hochstein had always believed that an important part of due diligence included a careful assessment of the people, not just on paper, but through an interview process. When Tanner poked his head into the room that had become Hochstein's temporary office, he found Hochstein almost hidden behind several mounds of files, ledger books, and pads of paper.

"Morning, Mr. Hochstein," said Tanner. "I'm just passing, but I'll be available if you need me." He turned and softly closed the door.

The other offices were noisy and busy.

"You look tired, George," said Tanner when he walked into Anderson's office.

"Yeah, well, I didn't sleep all that much. Kay told me about her conversation with you and Ms. Whitney." He tapped his teeth with a pencil. "Tanner, how come she isn't Mrs. Tanner? Didn't she want your name?" His querulous tone set Tanner's teeth on edge.

"You'll have to ask her, George. I'm glad your connection with Tobias and Phoenix is out in the open. Did Tobias tell you he was once married to Mary?"

"No! That must be why he insisted he remain a silent investor. I wondered how he had got so much information about you two. I suppose that's why he insisted part of the deal included getting you on board to do our marketing."

Tanner nodded and said, "George, did Tobias ever say anything to make you think the arrangement was off-kilter?"

"No, but to tell you the truth, I've talked to a lot of strange investors, and we were desperate right then so I didn't question much except to work out the specific details. Well, it's all out in the open now."

"What's on our agenda this morning?"

"Sheriff Olsen is coming by to discuss their findings on McGregor. He'll be here any time. He says it's just preliminary, of course, but I want us to keep on top of this so we're ready for whatever comes down the pike." George dropped his pencil and swiveled nervously back and forth.

"Any interest from the media?"

George glanced at Tanner and grinned without humor as he waved him to a chair. "Have I been spoutin' off to the reporters again, don't you mean? I learned my lesson. From now on I'm going to leave all that to you and Eddington to handle. I'll be strictly 'no comment' unless you guys give me a heads up. At least until things settle down around here." The telephone on George's cluttered desk buzzed and he punched the speaker button.

"Yeah?"

"Sheriff Olsen is here, Mr. Anderson," was the scratchy response.

The door opened and the Ashland County Sheriff

together with a slender man in civilian clothes entered and took the remaining seats. Sheriff Olsen nodded at Tanner and introduced Cliff Monson from the Wisconsin Bureau of Criminal Affairs. Monson took some papers from a slender brown leather briefcase and began to read. "The deceased died as a result of blunt force trauma. He was struck on the back of the head by a blow that crushed his skull. He died almost instantly." He looked up and said, "There's more work to be done, but nothing thus far indicates anything other than an accident. The only suspicious thing is where the body was found."

Tanner listened to the dry, matter-of-fact recitation, thinking that it must be this way with police everywhere. In order to cope with the violence they too frequently encounter, they depersonalize the situation. Thus, Ted McGregor, active, young, passionately dedicated to his environmental concerns, became "the deceased." Tanner wondered if the young man had a wife or a girlfriend somewhere. Surely he had living relatives who by now had been told that Ted McGregor had died in an obscure warehouse in a small town on the east side of Chequamegon Bay, a stretch of water attached to the south shore of Lake Superior. He watched the BCA man closely. Tanner got an impression that Monson didn't want to be there, talking about an investigation still in progress. The sheriff had apparently applied some pressure of his own. George Anderson and CRR carried weight in the county.

"Have you located McGregor's family?" asked George Anderson.

Sheriff Olsen nodded. "Yes. He wasn't married and his parents are deceased. We found a sister living in Portland, Oregon. She'll claim the body when we're finished."

There was a pause, and the faint noises of office routine from the other side of the wall intruded. None of the four men looked at each other. Finally, the sheriff shifted in his chair and said, "George, is there anything you want to tell me? Do you have any idea why McGregor was in your warehouse?"

Anderson shook his head slowly and stared at his hands, loosely clasped on the desk in front of him. He hunched forward, curving his spine and lowering his head. "I just don't know, Pat—Sheriff. You already know McGregor and I had words. Shouting at each other. He pushed and I pushed back, but I never hit him, and I never figured on something like this." He glanced at Tanner, who nodded encouragingly.

"If McGregor broke into the factory, as seems obvious, he must have been trying to do some damage, sabotage our operation. It would have been a way to at least delay our work."

"I assume McGregor set the fires that caused the propane tanks to explode and he was in the place looking for something that could be used to delay us. Trouble is, he couldn't find anything 'cause there isn't anything," said Anderson.

"Would more delays be a problem?" asked the sheriff.

"Sure. We've already had a couple of years of delay sorting out the state and Native American concerns. And the Feds. A new company like this needs to be moving forward in order to attract new investment. Delays always hurt. Investors who came in at the beginning start to get antsy. You know that. McGregor could have been a real burr under my saddle."

Tanner looked at the others and saw they drew the same inferences. Anderson had given up one possible motive for wanting to be permanently rid of Ted McGregor. Then he wondered if the sheriff might be a local investor.

"Mr. Anderson, do you have any reason to believe McGregor was planning vandalism?" The BCA man was staring intently at George. "We have no evidence that McGregor was violent. We've been in touch with People for the Earth and they're shocked at McGregor's death and the circumstances."

Anderson scrubbed a hand over his seamed face. He appeared more discouraged and apprehensive than Tanner had ever seen him. "Well, all I know is I never invited him here. I'll take that back. I did invite him to tour our operation right after he first came to Ashland. I was trying to persuade him that we aren't environmental bandits. But that was months ago. I haven't seen him at all since we had that shouting match uptown a week or so ago."

Tanner considered suggesting that Anderson might want his lawyer present but then decided it wasn't his place and it could aggravate the situation.

"Did McGregor take you up on that invitation?" asked the sheriff.

Anderson shook his head.

"If he was wandering around the factory floor in the dark, his death must have been accidental." said Tanner.

Sheriff Olsen nodded. "Yep, but finding him in that chair is suspicious." He stood up. "Well, George, we're off to check in with the local gendarmerie. They'll get the same report I just gave you."

And probably a bit more on how the investigation is going to proceed, thought Tanner. "Excuse me, Sheriff? Any further information on the skull from the bay?"

The sheriff shook his head. "No, other than to confirm that it's pretty old and probably been down there a hundred years, give or take. The hole in the back of the skull most likely came from a large-bore pistol, though. So whoever it was was definitely murdered. We've called off the search and lifted restrictions on that part of the bay. I expect we'll see a gathering of ghouls." He and Monson went out.

Anderson returned from ushering the lawmen out and closed the office door. Tanner saw what he interpreted as a question from the expression on Anderson's face. "What do you think?" Anderson asked.

"I think that if the forensic report on McGregor indicates a probable homicide, you're in some difficulty," Tanner responded.

* * *

Preacher Merlin Ames leaned closer to the stove and rubbed his tingling fingers. Outside, the snow continued to fall. It had begun softly at first, just a few random flakes drifting down through the tall trees. It was a little heavier in the stump areas and along the shores where the trees had already been cleared. Loath to slacken the work, the logging company foremen didn't halt the almost ceaseless work of felling the big trees, cutting them into logs, and skidding them to the stream banks there to await the snow melt.

Ames was mightily discouraged. In spite of his efforts, tensions were still high in the camp and no one would say what had happened, other than some admitting they had heard shouting and arguing in the woods. Tompkins' absence from the bunkhouse that night had gone unremarked. The day after the argument, a timber cruiser had stumbled across Tompkins, just like Ames had seen him in the shed, with the hand ax stuck in his chest.

If anyone knew, no one would say whether they recognized the ax. The only other thing Ames had been able to learn was that two other men had gone missing from camp about the time of the unseen argument and the murder of Ed Tompkins.

The sheriff had come and gone, taking the remains with him. A crude travois to cradle the body had been fashioned from lodge pole pines cut near the camp site and a scrap of canvas tied to the poles with rawhide strings. Neither of the two missing men, Jarl Rylston or a man known only as The Finn, had been seen after the discovery of Tompkins' body. Ames decided to travel across country the next morning and make his way to Bayfield, fifteen or so miles up the bay. He'd stop in Washburn to make inquires about both missing men. He informed the sheriff of his plan. Neither Ames nor the sheriff had expectations of finding the missing men anytime soon. Neither had they any illusions about determining who had killed Ed Tompkins.

The next morning, just as the gray light began to filter down through the high canopy of needles, Ames set off on a wandering trail that led him north-northeast toward the road to Washburn. It was many degrees below zero and there wasn't a breath of wind. Clouds of moist, exhaled breath from rider and horse hung in the air for a long time before slowly fading over the trail.

* * *

Mary shivered and took a deep breath. She recalled the cold winters she'd spent in New York, and the raw wind that slashed down the canyons, shoving dirt around, and spitting dirty snow and sand into her face. But it had never been as cold as a February in northern Wisconsin. She couldn't imagine it. What's more, she didn't want to ever experience such cold. She wondered what Edmund Hochstein had learned as his examination wound down. She wondered if Tanner would confront Anderson and Krizyinsky about the mysterious meeting at Platters. And she wondered again why her ex-husband was in Ashland and about the identity of the third man.

The previous night had been a strange mixture of emotion; The pleasant dinner with Tanner and Hochstein, and then the cold shock of seeing her ex-husband for the first time in more than a year. She and Tanner had sat there in the cold car and watched for several minutes more, but the third man in the room had never appeared in the window frame. They'd discussed it all the way back to Bayfield and even longer, over a nightcap.

"I still think we ought to at least talk to George," she said. "Michael, we know Phoenix is investing in CRR anyway, so where's the harm?"

"I'm not sure there is any, Mary." Tanner handed her a balloon of brandy. "But it seems odd to me that late on a rainy night in Ashland, Tobias and Krizyinsky and a third party are meeting in an out-of-the-way restaurant." He shrugged and finished pouring himself a brandy. Then he saluted Mary with the glass and hummed a snatch of the song *Rainy Night in Georgia*.

Mary acknowledged the song with a nod and said, "Well, I'll tell you what else is odd. Krizyinsky knew we'd be there. He's the one who suggested we take Edmund to that restaurant, remember? I didn't mention it to anyone else. Why would I?"

"I do remember, babe. I'm sure I never told anyone, either. Which is one of the reasons I don't want to talk about it with either George or Stanley right now."

"You think Stanley K suggested Platters knowing he'd also be there last night?" She shook her head. "Wheels within wheels. Very complicated, don't you think?"

"I think it's possible he did it deliberately to expose Tobias's link to CRR. It's more likely that since he likes the restaurant and probably recommends it to lots of people, he just forgot he'd recommended it to you, or that we were going to be there last night." He took a sip of brandy. "Tell you what I will do. I'll mention it to Hochstein privately. He can help decide how to handle it."

Now, on the sunny morning after, the questions and the sense of foreboding wouldn't go away. She went to the big window overlooking Bayfield's waterfront. She was beginning to regret her decision to stay in the condo while Tanner went to Ashland.

Chapter 21

Twenty miles away from Chequamegon Bay in Ashland, the morning sun streamed through the tall windows of the CRR conference room and cast sharply defined shadow patterns on the wall. Two men at the big table sat facing each other across one corner. Around them were heaped the papers that gave insight into the vitals of Chequamegon Resource Recovery. Edmund Hochstein, his unwavering gaze fixed on Tanner's face, held his head cocked slightly to one side. He hadn't said a word for several minutes while Tanner told him first of the apparent attempt by a truck driver to run them off the road on their way back to Bayfield from the Moqua roadhouse, and then their discovery last night after dinner, of Edwin Tobias's meeting with the CRR marketing vice president and a third man, as yet unidentified.

When Tanner finished, there was silence for a time while Hochstein digested the information. "This is most serious and somewhat perplexing. Have you considered the possibility that the truck driver was not simply drunk, but was deliberately trying to do away with you and Mary?"

"I have thought about that, but why would he? And if the driver wasn't acting alone, who could possibly be behind such a move? Since we have little hope of identifying the driver, I guess we may never understand."

"I wouldn't be so sure, my boy, that the incident

with the truck is not connected in some way with your mission here. I think the wisest course of action is for you to take your wife back to Seattle immediately and abandon this entire enterprise."

Tanner allowed himself a faint smile. "Mr. Hochstein, you can't be serious. In the first place, Mary would never hear of it."

Hochstein nodded. "You can't persuade her that her life may be in danger?"

"Oh, I think I can remind her of that, although I'm sure she hasn't forgotten our harrowing ride back to Bayfield, but you know her as well as I do. Mary's not going to be scared off. I think she's more likely to go looking for whoever is behind this."

"I expect you're right. Mary has always had a most independent streak. Still, I'd never forgive myself if something happens to her." He leaned forward slightly. "Or to you."

"Nor would I forgive myself, you can be assured of that," agreed Tanner. "I am going to try to reduce our exposure to possible danger. I think I can persuade Mary to stay closer to our condo for the duration."

Both men sat silent for a moment, each knowing the other would take whatever steps seemed prudent to protect themselves and Mary Whitney. At that moment, Tanner began to suspect that Edmund Hochstein was half in love with Mary Whitney himself.

"Now, as to that meeting last night. Since we already know that Phoenix didn't want you to be aware of their connection to CRR, it isn't so surprising for Mr. Krizyinsky to meet in an out-of-the-way place with Mr. Tobias. Moreover, even without your wife's connection to Mr. Tobias, when delicate financial negotiations are going on, such meetings are frequently held in private venues, out of the public eye."

"Do you have any indication of new negotiations?"

"No, however it is not uncommon for a company to receive additional infusions of cash from earlier investors. Chequamegon Resource Recovery may well have turned to Phoenix again. If so, I will discover it, unless what you witnessed was a private and preliminary overture from Mr. Krizyinsky. That would be unusual, but again, not unheard of. I wish you had ascertained the identity of the third person at that meeting." Hochstein paused a moment, tapped his forefinger on his lips several times and then, having arrived at a decision said, "Michael, I'm counting on your discretion. Normally I'd wait and write a report. However, it appears you may need to be forewarned."

"Naturally, I'll be discreet. In my business we are privy to many business secrets of our clients. We'd be out of business very quickly if we revealed those secrets."

"Hmm, yes, I do see. I still have some more documents to examine, but for the most part, the company has been very open and forthcoming. I am largely satisfied, and even to a degree impressed with the quality of the board of Chequamegon Resource Recovery. Particularly those who are working members. I also believe they have been quite prudent and conservative in their operations. Although the venture is somewhat more risky than most, it does meet Whitney Enterprises standards. Unless I find some surprises in the final few documents, I will write a positive report to my board. As you are no doubt aware, it is rare for the board to go against my recommendation."

"Will you tell that to George Anderson?"

"Yes. I have scheduled a termination interview with Mr. Anderson for later today. Of course, in that interview I will include many caveats and escape clauses, stressing that the board has the final decision. One of the more important considerations will be the way in which

CRR has handled the secrecy surrounding the investment of Phoenix. That connection is revealed in the financial records, of course, but I am still disturbed by the manner in which CRR enticed your agency and Mary to come here to Wisconsin. In addition, I'm concerned that Phoenix has not exercised its right to name a person to a seat on the board. It troubles me a bit, but again, it is not unknown."

"That is something that I will pursue, Mr. Hochstein. As you know, I've agreed to a contract with the company. But I can always cancel it if I don't get satisfactory answers."

Tanner left the conference room and went to Anderson's office. The door was closed and Tanner could see that someone was with Anderson. He turned away and almost bumped into Stanley Krizyinsky. Krizyinsky just looked at Tanner, nodded and brushed on by. Tanner was hit with a sudden desire to ask Krizyinsky if he'd enjoyed his dinner at Platters the previous night. He didn't, and went looking for Anderson's secretary and a telephone.

* * *

Preacher Ames stood on the dock in Bayfield, shivering from the wind that blew off the lake. Ice rimmed the shore and stretched most of the way to Madeline Island, the nearest and the largest of the cluster of wooded islands that lay scattered across the water and sheltered the deep bay where commercial enterprises lined the shores. There remained considerable stretches of open water. Citizens of Bayfield had told him that the lake almost never froze over completely and that winter boat travel between Bayfield and Ashland had only been curtailed for a few weeks in February.

There wasn't much activity now, but the coming spring thaw heralded the usual increase in fishing and the hauling of logs to the mills. Ames's inquiries had gleaned information that a few tug boats had been able to haul floating booms of logs down the bay to the hungry mills in Ashland.

Two weeks had passed since Ames had left the Whitney lumbering camp down the peninsula, trying to trace the teamster Jarl Rylston and the other man missing from camp, the one called The Finn. Tompkins and Rylston had fought when Tompkins accused Rylston of seducing his, Tompkins's, daughter. It was a charge Rylston had hotly denied. When fists had been swung, men in camp had pulled the two apart, but the dire threats each had made against the other hung over the camp. Not two days later, according to the beetle-browed foreman, Tompkins had been found near a trail with the hand ax buried in his chest. Ames couldn't remember a more troubled logging operation in his many years of travel through this part of the state. His sermons the three days he stayed were not well attended, and while some of the men had come to him for individual talks, he sensed that his words of peace and of God's grace were not falling on receptive ears.

The mysterious man called The Finn was proving even more elusive than Rylston, and Ames was fast coming to the conclusion that the man had nothing to do with the bad blood between Rylston and Tompkins.

Ames had been able to tentatively trace the missing teamster to Bayfield, but there the trail had died, just like the woodland paths, buried under many feet of silent snow and ice. Even more worrisome, word had come that Tompkins's younger brother, living on the family farm in southern Wisconsin, upon learning of his brother's murder, had sworn terrible oaths of revenge. He'd last been heard of traveling north. Ames didn't know what had happened to the boy since, but in this land of tenuous law, peopled by many individuals who had little regard for the tenets of a

*civilized society, or the word of God, violence was too often
an easy remedy for real or perceived wrongs.*

* * *

Mary marked her place and put the book down
when the telephone rang. It was Tanner. "I had a talk with
Edmund and went over the incident with the truck, and told
him about seeing ET and those other men at Platters."

"What was his reaction?"

"He urged me to take you home forthwith."

"Fat chance."

"So I indicated. He also said that meetings between
principals and investors, even private meetings, weren't
unusual. But he'd really like to know who the third person
was in that room."

"So would I. What does he think about CRR as an
investment opportunity?"

"He's pretty positive, but he still has a few more
things to look at. I get the impression he'd like to get his
examination wrapped up in time to get a late flight out of
Duluth back to Seattle."

Mary looked out the window toward main street. "I
think I see a friend of yours in town. At least the rust
bucket truck you described that took you to Red Cliff has
just parked across from the Sea Store. I'll see you later.
Ask Mr. Hochstein what he wants to do about dinner this
evening. And don't worry about me. I'll watch out."

"Can't help it, babe," came Tanner's voice. "Of
course I'll worry."

Mary smiled at the telephone. "'Bye, sailor."

She hurried out into the sunny day. Intent on
talking to the old Indian, she paid scant attention to others
on the street. When she trotted across the road, Joe was
struggling to get the driver's door latched. The hinges

protested loudly when he leaned his weight against the door to latch it closed.

"Excuse me, sir," called Mary.

The man turned around and touched the frayed rim of his straw hat. "I've been called a lot of things in my time," he smiled, "but never 'sir' in my memory, and never by such a fetching lass." His smile broadened. "Ms. Whitney, it's my pleasure to make your acquaintance."

Knowing she was being gently teased, Mary stopped and put her fists on her hips. Then she cocked her head and said, "Fetching? Lass? Here I thought I was accosting a native of these parts, not some old Scot."

Joe tipped back his head and laughed out loud. "Ma'am, it would give me some pleasure to buy you a cup of coffee. I assume you have the time to indulge this old Indian, since you came racing across the street toward me with some purpose in mind."

"Oh, absolutely. I was planning to drive up to Red Cliff sometime soon, but this works just as well."

They walked along the street toward a small cafe across main street. Just as they stepped off the curb, a truck seemed to abruptly lurch toward them, its engine racing. Joe stuck out a bar-hard arm and grabbed Mary by the shoulder, almost throwing her back toward the sidewalk. The truck, spewing clouds of unburned oil and gas, the angry blast of its horn banging off nearby buildings, screamed by. The wind from its passing tore Joe's straw hat off his head and sent it sailing into the street.

Mary fought to regain her balance, clutching Joe's wrist. The truck skidded around the next corner and tore up the street, its engine whining as the driver clashed through the gears.

"Wallace Zane, that fool," muttered Joe.

"What—what did you say?" said Mary.

Joe looked at Mary and said, "I hope I didn't hurt you." He went into the street and bent to pick up his crushed straw hat. He set it firmly on his head, straightening his ponytail as he did so.

"I think you just saved my life! Any possible bruises thankfully received. Didn't I hear you mention a name? Did you recognize the driver?"

"Not exactly. But I know that truck. It belongs to a fellow who lives hereabouts. I'm not sure exactly where. He's a handy man, a sometime drunk, just someone who gets by." Joe shrugged and they entered the cafe.

"His name is Wallace Zane? Is that what you said?"

"Yup. I'm pretty sure that was him. It certainly was his truck."

"I may have seen that truck recently. It chased us down the highway one night." Mary told Joe about their frightening experience returning to Bayfield from Moqua.

"This here looked to me like an accident. I wasn't paying a whole lot of attention to the street. But if it was Zane both times, it raises interesting questions, doesn't it?"

Mary took a long drink of water and they both asked for coffee and rolls. "I think it's something worth paying attention to but I wanted to ask you about something else entirely. Or at least about somebody else entirely."

Mary proceeded to relate her experience of getting stuck in the woods on that isolated track and the Indian man who came to her aid. As she described him, Indian Joe began to smile and nodded. "That was Matthew. My nephew. He often walks through that part of the reservation. Like a lot of his generation, he's upset, even a little angry, perhaps at the history of our two nations. He's upset with us, the elders of the band. He thinks we should have done more to protect our birthright from you loggers. And of course, he's angry with people like the Weyerhaeusers and with the Whitneys for what he sees as robbery of the land and the forests."

"I'm not so sure he isn't right," said Mary softly.

"I'm sorry if he frightened you. Angry or solemn as he may be, he's not a violent man. I think he and your husband, Tanner, hit it off when I introduced Tanner to our council. We explained where and how our attitudes and beliefs about the timber, whether growing as should be, or sunk in the big lake, come from. I think he understands. Your Michael Tanner. He was careful to articulate both the realities and some ways we may reach accommodations." The old man smiled.

Mary looked at the seamed brown face. A complex man, she considered. His language changed depending on the subject and context. She thought she'd like to know him better.

"What about that other man, McGregor. Did you know him?"

Joe took up his coffee cup in gnarled, weathered fingers. He was silent and Mary could tell he was sorting out the words he would use. "Oh, yes. He came to the reservation right after he got here. A very energetic young man, that one. He wanted to meet with the council immediately and was very impatient when it didn't happen as quickly as he wanted. Indian time, you know."

"Did he go into detail about what his concerns were?"

"Generally, I think he wanted a protest. An uprising."

"An uprising?" Mary frowned.

"Oh, yes. He made some remarks about the incidents along the Minnesota River at the time of your Civil War." A small twitch of a smile passed over the Indian's weather-etched face and his deepset brown eyes seemed to sadden. "We got the feeling he'd like us to go to war with Chequamegon Resources. Mr. McGregor had many hard words. Words like retribution, payback for ancient wrongs. I guess you could call Mr. McGregor something of a hot head. Some of the younger members of the council were a little stirred up." Joe patted Mary's hand on the table in a fatherly way. "But wiser heads prevailed."

"What happened?"

"Nothing. In spite of what some people think, we are not without intelligence. Nor are we unaware of the ways of white law. Instead of going to the mattresses," he smiled again, "our attorney filed claims and took other action. As you must know, the clans will be paid for the harvested timber."

"Are you personally satisfied?"

Joe leaned back and pulled out a red and white bandanna from his hip pocket. He patted his brow. "I don't know. You can't replace the old ones, all those trees that built Chicago and Milwaukee. The world revolves and time goes by. Going back is never an option. We will all do the best we can, in spite of the past, or perhaps because of it. And, perhaps, in spite of agitators like Mr. Ted McGregor. You understand. I am sorry Mr. McGregor is dead, but I'm not sorry he is gone." They were silent for a small time while the activities of the cafe swirled around them. Then, the Indian rose and bowed slightly to Mary.

She rose and smiled, returning his bow. "It has been a pleasure, sir, to make your acquaintance and to speak with you."

Joe nodded. "And with you, daughter," he said, and proceeded out the door of the cafe.

Chapter 22

Tanner put his head around the jamb of Anderson's open door and said, "I'm going to run some errands. I'll be back in an hour or so. Then I'd like to go over some preliminary ideas I have for marketing initiatives."

"Good, I don't have much on the calendar for this afternoon that can't be shifted around."

Tanner went to the Lexus and drove east on Lake Shore Drive to the big neon sign that advertised Platters. There were only two cars in the lot, parked at the very back, but the front door was open.

When he went through the heavy door, a slender dark-haired woman of medium build smiling broadly approached and said, "I'm sorry, sir, we're not open for lunch today."

"Thank, you. It isn't lunch I'm after. I wonder if Mrs. Stevens is in? I'd like to discuss the rental of your private upstairs rooms."

"Of course. If you'll wait in the bar I'll find her."

Tanner seated himself and glanced around. He hadn't had an opportunity to look at this room which must originally have been a front parlor when the house was built. A bar had been added. The back bar was an ornate unit of dark-stained oak shelves, a large oval mirror and a broad, waist-high counter. It was set against the corner of the room nearest the parking lot. In front of the counter, a plain wooden bar left a narrow space for a working bartender behind it. The bar itself had no padding and no foot rail. The whole thing was only long enough for four spindly-legged metal stools. Tanner sat at one of the four small round tables in the room.

He heard a soft rattling noise as the ice maker dropped more cubes into a pan. He cocked his head and detected the faint hum of a refrigerator. Farther away, toward the back of the house, he heard women's voices raised in faint song and footsteps briskly moving back and forth along unseen corridors overhead as workers went about their duties.

He stood up and went to the corner of the bar so he could look at the tidy bins of supplies ready for the evening's customers. The polished wood of the bar glowed in the indirect lighting. Tanner glanced toward the door, then walked behind the bar and down its short length to the wall of the room. Once more he looked toward the door. As he turned and walked back toward the chair where he'd been seated, a figure appeared, silhouetted against the light streaming in through the entrance window.

"Have you completed your inspection? Mr. Tanner, isn't it?"

"Yes, thank you. I'm surprised you remember me."

Mrs. Stevens smiled. "It's the mark of a good restaurateur to remember customers. Besides, we have a small regular clientele and a certain amount of notoriety has become attached to you and your wife."

"Really?"

"Umm. Now, how can I help you? You told Robin you were interested in our private meeting rooms. Now I wonder if that was the truth."

"It is the truth. But I admit to not being entirely open with her—Robin is it? Shall we sit down? That is, if you have a moment."

Adele Stevens said, "Of course," and indicated the table nearest the parlor door.

"I understand you have meeting rooms upstairs that are available for small groups who want privacy. Do you also serve meals upstairs?"

"Yes, we do. A patron can book either or both of the two rooms for a meeting at an hourly charge. We can set up a small bar and either engage a bartender or they serve themselves. They can also order dinner from the regular menu. If the meeting is small, customers often use one room for the meal, and the other for their meeting."

"You have a bartender here most nights, isn't that true?"

"Yes. Usually, the heaviest traffic in the bar occurs at about the same time many patrons arrive for dinner. Since we don't take reservations, we sometimes have a small crowd in the entrance hall and here in the parlor. As you already know, my husband, Paul, is the chef and is quite busy at dinner time. I normally function as the hostess, at least in the evening."

"But the night Mary and I and Mr. Hochstein had dinner, you were here in the parlor when we arrived."

She nodded. "That's correct. Billie Young, our regular bartender was ill that evening and I was doing double duty."

"And, you were here, in the parlor, most of that evening, except to seat patrons. Specifically, you were in the parlor when we left and for some time before that. At least, that's my recollection."

"Your recollection is quite good, Mr. Tanner. May I ask the purpose of all these questions?"

Tanner thought a moment. He very much wanted to know who the third person present in the room with Tobias and Krizyinsky was, but he didn't want to offend Mrs. Stevens, nor did he care to have her alert any of the participants. Finally he sighed and said, "I'm going to be frank with you, Mrs. Stevens, and I'm going to take a chance. I'm doing some work for Chequamegon Resource Recovery."

"I'm quite aware of who you are and your business in Ashland, Mr. Tanner. Most of us hope the company is successful. Because Ashland is a small community, we know a lot about what's going on, although not always all the details."

"Ah, I should have remembered that. Small town or not, I hope I can rely on your discretion. There are some disturbing things going on and I'm trying to sort them out to everyone's satisfaction. Let me get to the point. Last night, three men came in rather late. We had just finished our dessert. You were not in the entrance, and the three men in question just continued up the stairs without pausing or looking around. I presume you were here, in the parlor, tending to drink requests. You would have been in a perfect position to see those men when they came in."

"So, that's why you were behind the bar. You were checking sight lines."

"Exactly."

"Of course, I might have been doing something at the bar with my back turned when those gentlemen arrived."

"Yes, you might have, but I think you would have turned to greet your customers."

Mrs. Stevens smiled again. Tanner was getting the impression that she was enjoying their conversation. "Right again. I was at the bar wiping glasses when I heard the door open. I was expecting the gentlemen and I looked up. I could see all three quite clearly and we acknowledged each other. I didn't know the first man who led the way upstairs, but it was obvious he was the out-of-town guest Mr. Krizyinsky mentioned when he reserved the room."

That, thought Tanner, would have been Tobias.

"He was the second person through the door. The third man was also a stranger."

Tanner's mood sank. He wasn't going to find out what he wanted to know. He thought for a moment, then said. "Can you tell me anything about him? The third one?"

Mrs. Stevens paused to think. "Actually, I can. He was neither a small nor a large man. I suspect he does not frequent establishments such as Platters. I'm certain he has never before been a guest here."

Tanner furrowed his brow. Mrs. Stevens laughed. "I'm not being snooty. It's just an observation. You know from dining here that some of our guests dress up a bit and some don't. Frankly, we'd prefer they did, but the town isn't large enough for us to raise that kind of barrier. It's just that the third man gave me the impression of being a working man. He was wearing heavy boots and he tracked in mud. I remember there were bits of straw in the mud we swept up."

"But you didn't recognize him."

"No, but I'm sure he's a local man."

"Really? Why do you say so?"

"He ordered Arrowhead Beer without looking at a drink list. Arrowhead is a very small local microbrew. I'm told it's an acquired taste and an out-of-towner would probably not have known about it without first seeing the menu. It's sold in only a few places, like Iron Lake or Port Wing. Moqua, probably. We carry a small supply." She smiled again. "And he smoked a brand of small cigars which is also not widely distributed."

"Mrs. Stevens, you could be a detective." Tanner stood up and replaced his chair at the table.

Mrs. Stevens rose gracefully from the table and gave Tanner her hand in a firm but gentle clasp. "In the restaurant business, you learn very early on to utilize your powers of observation. We have to assess our customers very quickly."

Tanner said, "I appreciate your help, but I wonder why you've been so open."

"As I said, I've learned to assess people quickly and I'm seldom wrong. I hope you and your wife are successful in helping Mr. Anderson's enterprise."

Tanner smiled and left. He hoped this conversation wouldn't be all over Ashland before he returned to CRR. The question still in the forefront of his mind was how to identify the local man in that late night meeting.

Chapter 23

When Tanner returned to the Pierce Street offices of CRR, he headed for a side entrance closer to the parking lot. He walked around the back of the Lexus, grimacing at the dents and scratches. Back in Seattle, his Porsche, still in pristine condition, got washed and waxed every week. He bent over and flicked some backwoods Wisconsin mud from a rear fender. For the first time he saw flecks of pinkish-gray paint from the truck that had tried to force them off the road still embedded in the car's body.

From his briefcase on the front seat, he took an unused envelope. Tanner folded his lean six-foot frame into a squat beside the car and using his thumbnail, scraped several flecks of the foreign paint into the envelope. He didn't know if the evidence would make any difference but it seemed a good idea to hold on to it. Carefully, he folded the envelope and sealed it, then dated and initialed it, just like he'd seen on television. Inwardly smiling at his actions, he put the envelope back in the briefcase and relocked the car.

Trotting up the wide stairs to CRR's second-floor offices, he was startled by the unnatural quiet. There was no one at the front reception desk and he could hear murmurs coming from down the hall. When he walked to the conference room, he found the door open and several staff members confronting Edmund Hochstein.

"Michael, I'm glad you've returned," said

Hochstein.

"Here's another of them vultures," boomed a voice. Tanner looked around but couldn't see the speaker.

Jeri Reif turned to Tanner with tears in her eyes. She clutched a white handkerchief in one small fist. "The police came while you were out. They've arrested George for the murder of that Ted McGregor."

Tanner took Jeri's hand and pressed it gently. "Get hold of George's brother. I should talk with Chuck Eddington as well."

She shook her head. "Arne and Mr. Eddington left this morning. They're driving to Milwaukee to meet with a timber buyer. I tried their cell phones but there's no answer. I'm afraid we won't be able to contact them until they get to Milwaukee."

"What are you saying to him?" cried the same booming voice. "We never had any real trouble until George brought in these out-of-town hired guns." The protester was a tall burly youth, unfamiliar to Tanner.

Tanner glanced at Hochstein and shook his head slightly. He ignored the voice and looked back at Jeri. "Then I better talk to Mr. Kemperer and Mr. Krizyinsky. Would you locate them please? I can talk to them here in the conference room. I assume George has called his attorney and Kay?"

Jeri nodded and wiped her eyes again. "I think so. I'll find Richard and Stan right away." She turned and left the room. Tanner looked at the group of frightened employees and raised his voice to be heard over the noise of several conversations.

"Please folks. Could I have your attention for a minute? In spite of what some of you may think about Mr. Hochstein and me, we're not planning a takeover, or anything that would harm you. The opposite is true. I understand that things have been a little uncertain and our presence here has raised questions in your minds.

"I want to assure you that Tanner and Associates was called in by Mr. Anderson to help put together a marketing plan. Since I suspect you all have some stock in CRR, if we can improve profits and make the company more attractive to investors, your stock value will rise, as I'm sure you understand. I've heard there are rumors floating around that George and some of the other early investors have been selling off their stock because CRR is shaky.

"That isn't happening. So far as Mr. Hochstein's presence here is concerned, Mary Whitney, who I know many of you have met, began to see Chequamegon Resource Recovery as a possible investment opportunity. That's why Mr. Hochstein is here. He represents Whitney Enterprises and he's doing the usual investor examination." Tanner glanced at Edmund, hoping he hadn't overstated the case. Hochstein nodded and smiled as much as he ever did.

"Now, it's not really my place, but I'd like to encourage all of you to go back to whatever jobs you were doing when—earlier." The small crowd, some still muttering, began to move toward the door when Tanner stopped them. "One more thing. I know George has always had a very open policy about sharing information with you all—good and bad. But please remember there may be people out there who would try to make mischief or take advantage of this morning's events. Repetition of rumors won't help."

"That's for sure," said a voice from the doorway. George Anderson stood there, a scowl on his face. "I don't know where the information got started that I'd been arrested. I wasn't. The Ashland police just asked me to meet with them and with the sheriff about Mr. McGregor's unfortunate death. That's all. Now, if Tanner and I can have some privacy—"

Anderson's reappearance seemed to abate the tension and the people in the conference room filed out. Several exchanged high-fives as they passed Anderson.

Tanner and Anderson walked to Anderson's office at the other end of the corridor.

"What have you learned, George?"

Anderson grimaced. "They kind of updated me on their progress. Asked a lot of questions. The latest skinny is that McGregor was definitely murdered. There was no smoke in his lungs which means he died from that blow on the heard before the fire was set."

"Couldn't the hit on the head have been accidental?"

"The cops say not. Something about angle, force of the blow. I don't remember all the details. There's more."

Tanner waited.

"Now some of this I infer from the questions they asked. The other thing is they could be deliberately trying to break something loose by giving me hints."

"Hints about what?"

"More like who. It sounds to me as if they're looking at three people as most likely suspects for killing McGregor." Anderson rubbed his chin and suddenly Tanner had a bad feeling about what he was going to hear.

"Their prime suspects are you, me, and your wife."

"What! That's ridiculous."

"Of course it is. There was also mention of a possible conspiracy."

Tanner thought a moment. "I can see where they're going. The authorities figure McGregor was becoming a threat to us if he succeeded in getting you shut down, especially after Mary called in her financial guys. I bet McGregor was killed at a time when none of us has a real good alibi."

Anderson nodded.

"All right. We know we didn't kill McGregor, and we didn't discuss hiring someone to do it, so this is a real distraction for the authorities. Did you get any clue as to why they're thinking that way?"

"Nothing, and as I said, telling us they're looking at us for the murder may be just to try to rattle us into a mistake. I don't know. I really don't need this right now." He rubbed his face.

For a minute the two men sat silently. Tanner examined his emotions. Being suspected of murder wasn't a good feeling. Knowing Mary was also a suspect was even worse. He sighed and said, "Who benefits if CRR goes under?"

"I sure don't. All the stockholders will lose money, of course, and a lot of people will lose their jobs. Then there are some heavy investors who'll also lose out. You'll lose a good contract."

Tanner stared at the table for a long moment. Then he stood up. "George, what if money isn't the point?"

"I don't get you."

"A lot of what's happened around here has been since Mary and I got involved. I'm not sure where this might lead or why I thought of it right now, but suppose this all has less to do with money and more to do with something else?"

George stood also and shook his head, a frown of bewilderment on his face. "What else? I guess I'm dense. I don't see what you're getting at."

Tanner started for the door. "Just think about it. Has anything or anybody made you wonder about the motives of someone connected to this enterprise? I know that sounds pedantic and mysterious, but I don't want to program your thinking. Think about everyone involved, both insiders and those of us on the outer edges. Who have you wondered about? I'm only suggesting that we not limit our vision. I'm going back to Bayfield and I'll call you later here, or at home."

Halfway back Tanner realized he'd been so thrown by the news he and Mary were suspects, he'd forgotten to talk to Krizyinsky and Kemperer.

Chapter 24

Tanner found their condo empty when he arrived. He poked at Mary's cell phone with one finger while he gazed out the window. He decided to look for her in town after first scribbling a note to her, in case he missed her. An hour later, he'd covered the town, looked into most of the shops, and walked the docks. Mary Whitney was nowhere to be found.

"Damn," he muttered aloud. "I should have called." Back in the condo he found a voice mail message from Hochstein saying that he'd finished what he came for in Ashland and was leaving immediately to go to Duluth to catch a flight home. He concluded by urging Tanner to get out of Bayfield and back to Seattle with haste. To Tanner, Hochstein's departure seemed abrupt, but he had other things on his mind. He realized that he hadn't told Edmund that the police were suspicious of Mary and him. And where was Mary? He changed into more casual clothes and was starting to think about calling the police when the door opened and she breezed in, flushed and happy.

"Where in the world did you disappear to?" Tanner closed the gap between them in two strides and gathered her into his arms. "I was beginning to get seriously worried."

"Really? You mean more than just plain worried? Did you think I'd run off with some younger fellah?" She bussed him on the nose. Then, realizing his concern was

deeper, stopped and looked at Tanner more closely.
"What's happened?"

Tanner guided Mary to the big sofa and they settled
side by side. "There's been a development. McGregor was
definitely murdered, according to the Ashland police, and
George says they are looking at three possible suspects.
George and you and me."

Mary's mouth dropped open.

"George told me he got the clear impression that the
police don't believe they have enough evidence to arrest
anybody just yet, but we're their primary suspects. The
problem is that as long as they believe we're responsible,
they aren't likely to go looking for anyone else."

"Maybe we should get a lawyer," said Mary "I
have a funny feeling in my stomach."

"Yeah, I know what you mean. They also told
George they're considering a conspiracy theory as well."

"Oh, right, all three of us hired someone else to kill
McGregor. That's just nuts. I know we didn't do it, and I
just can't believe George would do such a thing."

"That's what I said when he told me." Tanner
paused. "Of course, we don't know that for sure."

"Nuts!" Mary said again. "I don't believe George
could do something like that."

"McGregor was killed sometime late on Monday
night or very early Tuesday. Where were we?"

Mary frowned and said, "That was the day we had
the tour of the plant out on Lakeshore Drive, wasn't it?
That nice man, Antonio Prada, I think his name was—yes,
I remember now. That other executive, Richard Kemperer,
was there at the beginning and at the end."

"That's right. As I recall, you didn't like him
much."

"He came on too strong. Nowhere near as subtle as
Krizyinsky."

"So we left around noon for lunch. Then what? I don't think we did much of anything the rest of the day."

"Dinner at the Rittenhouse, "Mary smiled. "Now that was memorable."

"It certainly was. Then we took another stroll around town. So we're each other's alibi. The police aren't going to like that."

"Well, tough. I can't imagine anyone fingering us for killers. What would we gain from it? Apart from not liking Mr. McGregor, whom I've never even met. I vote for my favorite ex-husband, Edwin Tobias. Incidentally, do we have any new information about that clandestine meeting at Platters?"

"Only a little. I talked to Mrs. Stevens and she told me he was local man."

"How'd she know?"

"Because she said he was smoking an unusual brand of little cigars—Little Badgers—and he ordered a local beer without consulting the menu."

Mary stood up and paced a few steps away from the sofa. "What does Edmund have to say?"

"He's sort of thrown up his hands since we won't abandon ship here. I left him at CRR but he called and left us a message, said he'd finished and decided to beat it back to Redmond. Something about being needed in the office. I expect he's almost to Duluth by now. He did leave me copies of the financial records of the principals."

"Well, why don't we both go through them? Maybe we'll find some leads."

"Leads? Are you thinking about becoming a P.I.?" Tanner grinned.

"Not hardly, sailor, but we might unearth something worth following up."

"O.K., but I'm having a scotch and water while we read. You want something?"

Mary plucked the folder from Tanner's hand. "There's a bottle of pinot grigio cooling in the 'fridge. I'll have a glass of that, if you please." She sat and curled her long legs around each other. Tanner shucked his jacket and went to the kitchen.

* * *

Two hours passed and they leaned back and sighed simultaneously. Mary stretched her arms overhead. "That's a lot more boring than reading a mystery novel, don't you agree?"

"Umm, hmm. And what have we learned?"

"That the board members are pretty ordinary as far as their financial status is concerned."

"Except for two," said Tanner.

"Right." Mary scratched her nose. "Stanley K and Richard K are both in hock up to their eyeballs and if CRR goes belly-up, they'd lose everything and probably have to declare bankruptcy."

"And that's about the only information in the whole file worth thinking about, unless we've missed something. Tobias and Phoenix are already heavily invested and about to get more so if Edmund's interpretation of that mysterious meeting at Platters is right."

"Unless ET and Krizyinsky are planning a separate deal."

Mary shook her head and said, "They stand to lose their original investment if the company goes under. As will George and the rest of the local investors. The environmentalists want the harvesting stopped but this People for the Earth group seems to be one of the more non-confrontational."

"I'm not sure I agree," said Tanner. "You didn't hear McGregor yelling at me. He was practically foaming at the mouth the other morning."

"Yes, but he's dead," Mary objected, "and these groups aren't in the habit of killing their members to make their case." She gnawed a knuckle for a moment. "I kind of wonder if McGregor even had an organization. Where are they?"

"Interesting point. I can't see the local Indian clans doing this either. Even if there are a few hotheads around."

"That reminds me, I had a little chat with Injun Joe this morning."

"You did?"

"Yep. I looked out the window and saw him getting out of his old red truck, so I ran across the street to talk with him." She stopped and frowned. "I had a small incident."

"A what?"

"I'm sure it was nothing. A pickup truck bolted from the curb when we were crossing Main Street. It tore around the corner, missed us by a hair. In fact your Indian's reactions were so good he may have prevented me from getting banged by the truck."

Tanner stared at Mary. In a low voice he said, "Maybe you better tell me a little more about your morning."

"Now don't get all agitated. It was just a near miss. As I said, the old truck started up abruptly when we had just stepped into the street. Joe grabbed me and yanked me back. His old straw hat sailed off and got run over by a car, but that's all." She sipped her wine.

"Nothing, huh? Did the jerk stop?"

Mary shook her head.

"Remember anything else?"

"Nope. Please, Michael, let's not make a big thing out of that. But it reminds me. I got Joe a new straw hat. Could we take a run up to Red Cliff?"

Tanner seized the opportunity. "Sure, how about right now? I have a few more questions I'd like to ask him, anyway."

Mary sent a sharp look at Tanner, but said nothing and they went down to the lot and their dented Lexus.

Thirty minutes later, when they pulled in at the big round red-roofed building that dominated the slopes just above the marina, they found few people about. Tanner realized that he didn't know where the old Indian lived, so he inquired of the woman they finally found in a small office at the back of the building.

"Oh, I'm sorry," she said, after introducing herself as Molly Whitebird Sings. "Grandfather and many of the clans have gone west. There's a Pow Wow at Turtle Mountain. They won't be back for several days."

"I'm sorry to have missed Joe," said Mary. She lifted a white paper box in her hand. "Will you keep this for him? His straw hat was crushed in the street in Bayfield this morning. This is a new one."

Molly nodded and placed the package on a shelf behind her. "He will appreciate the gift, but don't be disappointed if he still wears his old one."

On their way back to Bayfield, Mary said, "You know, I just remembered. Joe muttered something about Wallace Zane when the truck went by. I think he meant he thought Zane was driving, or at least it was Zane's vehicle."

Tanner glanced at Mary. "Yeah, that's what I wanted to ask him about. I'm not inclined to dismiss that incident, as you term it, quite so fast. Can you describe the truck?"

So Mary did. Tanner nodded. "Sounds like it could have been the same truck that tried to run us off the road. I found some paint chips on the fender of this car. I scraped them into an envelope. Let's stop at the Bayfield cop shop down by the harbor and I'll see if I can get them to take a look at it."

* * *

The patrol officer they encountered was just coming off duty and was impatient to get going but he explained what would happen to the envelope of paint scrapings.

"I'll contact the sheriff and he'll send someone up to get it. We don't have the facilities in this county and I bet they don't in Ashland, either, to run any kind of analysis. So they'll send it to the state lab." He sighed and filled in some more blocks on a form he'd found in a drawer.

"Ordinarily, it'd take quite a while, but because you're involved in that murder over in Ashland, they might rush it. 'Course, without something else to compare the paint to, I don't know that this'll be much use." He glanced shrewdly at Tanner and Mary. "You people have caused quite a ruckus up here. More excitement than we've had in years."

Tanner grimaced. "Not our intention, believe me. By the way, have you heard anything more about the skull they found in the bay?"

The officer shook his head. "Nope. And I don't 'spect we will, either. Everybody says it must be over a hundred years old. They haven't found any other bones either."

Outside, in the late afternoon sun, Mary took her companion's arm. "Hey, sailor. Let's dump all this misery for the rest of the night. There's supposed to be a nice restaurant on Madeline Island. Let's take the ferry over."

Tanner glanced toward the dock where the Madeline, largest of the ferry company's three vessels, was just backing out. She was carrying a full load of vehicles and passengers, many of whom waved enthusiastically to people on shore as they passed.

"Sounds like a good idea. I'm really sorry we haven't had much real vacation time on this trip. Guess I should have known better."

"Pooh. Don't give it another thought. I want to change into something much more summery. We can walk on instead of drive. The restaurant is just a half mile or so up the road from the dock. You game?"

An hour later, Tanner and Mary walked aboard the smaller *Nichevo II*. The blue and white ferry was crowded with vacationers as well as a number of local people headed for home. The early evening sun lent a warm glow to the faces of the passengers. Children hung on the stanchions and peered over the high steel sides of the vessel. Tanner and Mary climbed to the top of the cabin that formed an observation deck behind the pilot house. Tanner noted many prominent signs indicating life preservers and other safety equipment. The powerful diesel engines sent the ship through the water at a rapid pace toward the ferry dock at La Pointe at the westernmost end of the island. The ferry path took it across the mouth of the Bayfield marina.

Mary was dressed in a light, silk dress with a full, flowered skirt. Cool wind blew across the deck and the couple nestled together into a corner directly behind the pilot house and out of the wind. Tanner wrapped his arms around Mary and let her hair blow across his face. They watched small motor boats and sailboats darting through the wake of the ferry and the dancing waves of the big lake. Even with the nearby sound of happy children and the throbbing of the big diesels, it was a romantic moment they savored to the fullest.

The town of La Pointe was alive with tourists having a wonderful time. Tanner and Mary made their way slowly up the road to the Retreat, a bed and breakfast in an old mansion. It had once been a religious conference center, and it now served dinners in the evening. They lingered over coffee after a fine meal of fresh broiled lake trout and summer potatoes and fresh mixed greens. Suddenly Mary realized they were in danger of missing the last ferry of the night back to the mainland.

The sun had long since gone and the Madeline was full of vehicles and people. They stepped aboard and a horn sounded. Crew members raised the ramp. The engines increased their revolutions and the big ferry pulled slowly away from the La Pointe dock.

Chapter 25

Tanner leaned against the cold steel side of the ferry and watched twinkling running lights of boats in the North Channel moving between Madeline and Basswood Island. A small three-masted schooner, with a full set of sails drawing in the light evening breeze, slipped behind Madeline Island and headed away into the night. Her cabins were lighted and Tanner saw people on deck waving at the ferry. He listened in agreement to people around him commenting on how pretty the sailboat looked as it sailed serenely up the dark channel. For a few moments he wished himself and Mary on that schooner, heading away from the mainland, into a simpler, cleaner adventure that didn't involve murder and financial dealings.

He squeezed Mary's shoulder and she glanced up at him. "You'd like to be on that schooner, wouldn't you? Going onto the lake, away from all these difficulties?"

Tanner nodded.

Mary sighed. "Me too, sailor. Me too. But now for more practical concerns. I'm going to the ladies' room." She drew her fingers softly across Tanner's cheek and disappeared around the rear corner of the cabin where there was a door. Tanner returned to his silent contemplation of the dark lake and soon he felt the vibrations under his feet change their tempo. The boat began to turn and the lighted mainland of Bayfield slid into view.

The crew lowered the ramp that formed the front of the boat and walkers, backpackers, and bicyclists began to stream off, Tanner among them. He stepped off the ramp onto the mainland. He stopped and scanned the crowd for Mary, who hadn't returned to his side. The question turned quickly to worry and then alarm. Tanner raised his voice.

"Mary? Where are you?"

Nearby walkers glanced at him curiously. By now the foot traffic was almost cleared off the ferry and vehicles were starting their engines and beginning to move off as well. Mary was still nowhere to be seen. Tanner grabbed the nearest crew member by the shoulder and wrenched the heavy-set man around.

"Hey, what's the big idea!"

"My wife! She's disappeared!"

"Did you walk on?"

"Yes."

The deckhand raised his walkie talkie to his mouth. Tanner turned and raced to the ladder leading to the pilot house. Alerted by the deckhand, the captain met Tanner at the top of the ladder.

"We were about halfway across," Tanner yelled, "she went to the lavatory. She didn't come back right away. I didn't think anything of it until we docked."

"You're sure she didn't walk off ahead of you?"

"No! I was right at the front. Besides, she'd have waited for me. We have to go back and search!"

"What's her name? What was she wearing?"

Crew members raced over the *Nichevo*, checking restrooms and every other nook and cranny where a person might be hiding. Except for Tanner and the crew, the boat was empty.

"Does she get motion sickness?" asked the worried captain.

"No, man, she's an experienced sailor. And she

wouldn't have fallen over the side."

The captain frowned. "You think she was pushed? Good God, man! Describe her," he said, spinning on his heel to rush back to the pilot house.

Tanner followed, quickly described Mary and the bright summer dress she was wearing. The ferry captain called the Coast Guard and the local police.

The Coast Guard station was just across the marina and within minutes three inflatables, powered by big outboards and equipped with powerful searchlights, began working their way slowly back and forth across the path the ferry normally traced. Gradually they extended the search pattern out into the lake past the mouth of the Bayfield marina, making a crisscross pattern in the choppy water. As word of the missing woman spread, private boats with flashlights and small searchlights began to appear in the mouth of the marina as civilians joined the search.

A Bayfield patrol car appeared at the dock, and when the officer approached, Captain Taylor immediately asked, "Did anyone check their condo?"

"I just came from there," said the cop. "And we've also checked along the most likely routes she would have walked from here."

Tanner, his entire body trembling, collapsed into a seat in the cabin. "God, this can't be happening," he muttered. "Not again." A hand thrust a cup of steaming coffee under his nose. The thought made his stomach rebel and he waved it away. Tears came and ran down his face.

"Can she swim?" asked a voice.

Tanner glanced up, nodded, and then looked back at his hands clasped between his knees. He had a powerful urge to run and find a boat and join the search, but he knew it wouldn't help.

"Well, it's good she could swim. Problem is, the lake's so damn cold. Especially this early in the spring."

The man shook his head.

Tanner didn't want to hear that. Couldn't get beyond his anguish of the moment. "Not only is she a good swimmer, she's an experienced sailor. If anybody could survive going overboard, it's Mary. What I don't understand is why no one heard her call out." He stood up. I've got to go out there. I can't just sit here. Is there someplace I can get a boat?"

A Coast Guard officer who had arrived unnoticed took Tanner by the shoulder. "We can put you in one of ours, if you wish, but frankly, Mr. Tanner, you're better off waiting right here."

Tanner realized the truth of it and sagged again into a seat. Another cup of coffee was offered and this time he drank. Someone offered a cigarette, and for the first time in three years, his lungs and throat felt the harsh picking fingers of tobacco smoke as he inhaled. After two deep pulls, he dropped the cigarette to the deck and crushed it under his heel.

An hour dragged by and there was still no word. Looking out from the ferry pilot cabin toward the entrance to the marina, Tanner could see that many of the private boats were giving up the search and returning to the marina. The Coast Guard stayed on the job, joined by boats from the water patrol of the Bayfield County sheriff and the Park Service. Like lightning bugs, the small ragged flotilla of searchlights traced their patterns over the waters of Lake Superior, growing smaller and smaller as they moved away from the mainland toward Madeline Island.

Time passed but Tanner had no sense of it. Everything around him was blurred. Tears started and then dried up. His breath whistled and sang in his ears. Voices seemed to come fuzzily from far away. He knew he wasn't answering questions coherently. His fingers balled into tight fists and his nails cut tiny crescents into his palms.

He knew he had to get it together if he was going to help rescue Mary. This could not be happening. He'd lost one wife in his lifetime. It couldn't be that he'd lose another love. He stood up abruptly and thrust himself toward the window of the cabin. The chair fell over on the steel deck with a loud clatter. There was sudden silence. The Coast Guard officer and ferry hands looked at him, then away.

The radio in the ferryboat cabin abruptly crackled to life. "Get somebody to the rocks at the marina entrance. Starboard side. Might be a body."

Tanner snapped around, rejecting the idea, his mind shutting down. He refused to believe it was Mary. The Bayfield officer and the Coast Guardsman grabbed Tanner and hustled him down the ladder and into the squad car. "C'mon, we'll drive down there."

The patrol car, lights flashing, burned rubber off the ramp and careened around toward the commercial dock. Tanner looked out toward the lake and saw some of the small boats turning back toward the marina entrance. Others, farther out on the black water, continued their search. Several boats clustered around the base of the green starboard light marking one side of the entrance to the harbor.

Red flashing lights and a wailing siren signaled the arrival of an ambulance with an EMT crew. Tanner jumped from the squad car before it stopped and bulled his way through a growing crowd as the medics and the Coast Guard crews secured the figure to a stretcher and lifted it away from the icy water and the black rocks. As three men raised the stretcher in the rays of several wobbling searchlights, Tanner caught a glimpse of the sodden skirt the woman was wearing and recognized it instantly.

"Omigod! It's her. It's Mary!" he cried and stopped. The sounds around him faded and he seemed unable to move forward as the paramedics carefully lifted the still figure onto the gurney. Then, like a miracle, he saw the figure's arm raise toward the mask the paramedic was fitting over Mary's face. Her mouth moved and Tanner knew she was alive. He threw his arms around the young Bayfield officer who pounded Tanner on the back and grinned wordlessly into his face.

"Clear a path here!" bellowed the officer. "Coming through." The two officers cleared bystanders aside and Tanner got to the ambulance just as the paramedics struggled back up the sharp, dark rocks and slid Mary Whitney into the back of the ambulance. Quickly they threw blankets over her. She tried to sit up against the restraint of the strap as Tanner climbed into the vehicle and leaned down to look into her eyes.

Tanner's breathing caught for a moment. A tear ran off his cheek and fell onto the oxygen mask. He folded her hands in his. They were cold, icy cold, and Mary shivered without pause. The paramedics busied themselves with tiny flashlights and pressure cuffs. They glanced at each other, smiled, nodded with satisfaction. "Vital signs are all in normal range," one said. "You're gonna be fine once we get you warmed up."

With the drama reaching a satisfactory ending, the crowd rapidly dispersed. Only a few curiosity seekers, wondering, perhaps, how the pretty woman came to be in the cold lake, still stood in a loose knot near the back of the ambulance.

Tanner slid closer and when Mary raised up on the gurney, took her into his arms. Cold lake water from her wet hair dripped onto his shirt, a chill reminder of the power of the unforgiving lake. Mary pulled back from a long, fervent kiss and said. "You've been smoking again, sailor."

Tanner hugged her close again and said to the EMT smiling down at them. "What hospital are we going to?"

"Hold it. I don't need a hospital."

"Look at you, you're trembling so much you couldn't sign your name."

"Don't care. Let's just go home. I can warm up just as quickly in bed."

Tanner looked a question at the paramedics.

"Her vitals are good. I think she'll be okay." He turned to Mary, "You may have an upset stomach for a few days if you swallowed much of the lake. I'll give you some pills."

"What I need," she said firmly, "is a gallon of hot tea, my bed and blankets in that condo over there, and my husband." A wan smile came and went. "Not necessarily in that order."

"One thing more," said the officer. "If you can spare us a few minutes, I'd like to get a statement." Tanner opened his mouth to demur, but Mary nodded, so she and Tanner, followed by the officers of the Coast Guard and the town of Bayfield, moved to the condo where Tanner got Mary into a hot shower and busied himself in meaningless conversation with the officers while he made tea and coffee and poured himself a drink of scotch.

For a long moment, Tanner stared at the rich fluid in the heavy glass. The ice cubes tinkled from the trembling of his fingers. He tipped his head up and took nearly half the scotch in one long swallow. When he pulled his head back down he saw the two officers watching him closely.

"I lost my first wife a few years ago in a boating... accident," he said, and shook his head.

Mary, swathed in a heavy robe with a towel twisted into a turban over her hair, came slowly into the room. The paleness of her face was highlighted by the dark robe. Tanner embraced her and felt her trembling. "I'll take that gallon of tea, now," she whispered.

"Are you sure you want to do this now? It can wait 'til morning."

She shook her head and sat on the sofa, cradling the steaming cup in her hands. Tanner watched the ripples of liquid across the wide-mouthed mug.

"Mrs. Tanner," said the Coast Guard officer. He was older than the policeman and easily took over the questioning. "Just tell us in your own words what happened."

Mary nodded. "It's Mary Whitney," she said in a husky voice. "I prefer to keep my own name."

The officer made a note.

"I had to use the lavatory. I left Michael in the corner of the cabin on the main deck and went inside. After that I walked to the starboard side to look at the lake."

"Were you alone up there?" asked the officer. "Most people watch the shore when the ferry comes in."

"I know," Mary nodded. "I'm fascinated by Lake Superior. I was alone at the stern. At least I thought I was. Everyone else was getting ready to go ashore. I remember I started to turn around. Someone grabbed me from behind. I struggled and opened my mouth to yell. A hand clamped over my mouth. He had tape in it, a wide piece of duct tape, I think it was. Then I believe I smelled something but I'm not sure what it was. It all happened fast so I have no clear recollection. Then, everything went dark and I couldn't seem to move my arms." She took a swallow of tea. Tanner could see that her trembling was lessening.

"What happened next? How'd you get into the water?"

Tanner started to protest, but Mary shook her head and said, "I don't really know. I sort of recall the lights tipping and then I hit the water and it was a terrible shock.

It was so cold!"

She shuddered and Tanner touched her shoulder with gentle pressure. After another sip of tea, she looked up and said, "The shock when I hit in the water must have roused me. I pulled the tape off my mouth and looked around. I remember the water was all roiled up and waves were going every which way. It must have been the wake of the ferry. Or maybe it was another boat passing close by."

Now it was Tanner who shuddered. A powerboat passing behind the ferry would have no chance to spot a person in the lake. If that boat had hit her...

Mary took a deep breath and sucked in more tea. The color was coming back to her cheeks and she looked more alert. "Anyway, I rolled over and located the ferry. It was already too far away and making too much noise so I didn't waste any energy yelling. So I just located the marina entrance by the lights and swam to shore."

She stopped and the Coast Guard officer looked at her like he didn't believe her. "That's it? You just swam to shore? You were over a hundred yards from shore. Lady, that lake is cold! Hypothermia sets in after about fifteen minutes or less."

"I know. I was in it. But even there, where the water is disturbed by passing boats, if you stay flat on the surface, there are pools of warmer water. I found some of those."

"It's lucky you didn't go to the ladies' room until you were most of the way across," said the policeman. "If you'd gone over the side ten minutes out of La Pointe, you wouldn't have made it." Everyone was silent with their own thoughts for a moment.

"I don't understand how you went over the side without anyone seeing you," said the Coast Guard officer.

Tanner stared at the man, not liking the implication

in his words.

The officer raised one hand. "I don't mean to imply your story is wrong."

"I understand. I'm not clear about that either. Whoever jumped me must have drugged me. I didn't go all the way out. Things just got dim and I couldn't seem to function. The lights tipped up on one end. That must have been when he threw me over the side. I was alone on the deck. But I don't know why no one saw me fall."

Tanner interjected, "I was thinking about getting off. Most of the people around me were watching over the bow, or looking at the shore. Whoever is stalking my wife saw his opportunity when people were getting ready to disembark. He grabbed her and threw her over when no one was watching. She couldn't scream and he was lucky no one saw her go over."

"Mrs. Tanner, is there anything else you can tell us about this incident?"

Mary raised her chin. "It's Whitney, Mary Whitney. Tanner's a nice enough name but I like my own..." Her voice trailed off. She took a breath. "You know, it didn't seem to take so long to get to the rocks, but then I couldn't get out. They—the rocks are so steep and slippery—I couldn't seem to get out of the water..." Her voice trailed off.

Tanner realized that Mary's strength and her will to stay awake were rapidly waning. "I think, gentlemen, we better let Mary get some rest. "We can resume in the morning if necessary. If we come up with facts or even reasonable speculation, we'll be sure to tell you."

When they were alone, Mary held up her arms and said, "Bed." Tanner helped her to rise and walked her to their bedroom. As he slid in beside her, Mary murmured, "I couldn't drown you know. I knew you were waiting for me. It would have been too cruel."

Chapter 26

Mary slept fitfully that night and once woke Tanner from his light doze when her hand flailed across his face. "Nightmare?" he whispered, drawing her even closer in his arms. Her answer was an unarticulate murmur. Tanner watched for long moments in the dark. He could see the play of emotion across her sleeping face and he wished he could be there, in her dreams, to support and comfort her.

The sun had long since begun its hot march across the sky when Mary, showered and dressed, appeared from the bedroom to join Tanner in the kitchen of their condo.

"Mmmm. That coffee smells especially good this morning." She leaned over and bussed Tanner affectionately on the cheek.

He put up a hand and smoothed her cheek. "I can't begin to tell you what it felt like when I discovered you'd disappeared off that ferry." His voice quivered with the memory.

"I know, babe. I know. I wish I had a better recollection of what really happened." In a brisker tone she said. "We'll find out, won't we? What a glorious day. What's on the agenda?"

"I'm packing up. We have to talk with the sheriff's people again. But then I'm getting us out of this town. This business is too dangerous. I don't care who's behind it. This contract with CRR isn't worth putting you in jeopardy."

"Whoa. Just hold on a minute. I am so far from letting ET get away with this, I can't express it. I'm *not* going to let him get away with it."

"But Mary—excuse me?"

"Who else? I bet you Tanner & Associates' next month's profits that ET is behind everything that's been going on. Well, maybe not McGregor. ET may not have gotten his own hands dirty, but I'm convinced he's responsible. This isn't about money, Michael, it's about revenge. It's about getting even for what he thinks of as the wrongs I did him."

Tanner looked away, out the window. He took a swallow of coffee and after a moment said quietly, "Is that before or after T&A's profit sharing distribution to employees?" Then he smiled. It was not a nice smile. "You're right, of course. I guess I hoped you'd come to the same conclusion I was reaching, but I didn't want to be the one to say it out loud."

"Really! Why not?"

Tanner shrugged. "It was just the other day you unburdened yourself about that unhappy time in your life, you know. I'm still not sure of your reactions when the guy's name comes up. This is complex emotional stuff."

They were silent, just looking at each other. Then Mary nodded. "It's like if I say something critical about your father. Even if it's repeating what you've said, you have a tendency to jump in with both feet to defend him. And I guess I do the same when you or anybody criticizes one of my family."

"Too true. Nobody criticizes my family but me. But we'll work it out. I'd rather work it out somewhere else. I'm just not at all happy with you in the role of sacrificial goat. I'd rather leave Bayfield and keep us safe."

Mary got up to refresh her coffee. She took a circuitous route so she had to brush by Tanner at the window. As she did so she leaned up and kissed his cheek. "Don't think for a moment I don't appreciate your feelings, but if I'm right, he'd only try again."

Tanner muttered to himself and then said, "At least if he tried something in Seattle, we'd be on home turf. And you know, it's hard for me to believe that you, my love, could do anything so heinous as to rate attempted murder, even from one besotted with love who saw you run from his arms."

Mary snorted. "Besotted with love? Never. I doubt he ever really loved me in any fashion. At all. But I sure ran, from his arms, his bed, his every little thing." Their eyes met across the room and Mary suddenly giggled. She covered her mouth and began to laugh. The coffee in her cup sloshed dangerously.

Tanner sent her an answering grin. "All right. If we agree that ET is responsible for this, what next? We have no proof, just our own instincts, based on some coincidences."

"Let's run this down so we're both clear about the sequence, at least. Let's make a list."

Tanner said, "Good idea." He picked out a pad of ruled paper from his briefcase and sat at the dining table.

Mary took a sip of coffee and said, "First, Anderson calls you, then you get a letter from him, pressuring you to take this promotional job."

"Actually, the letter came first. I just didn't see it until after the call."

"Is the sequence important?"

"I don't think so. It just indicates how impatient Anderson can be. Anyway, the result of those contacts was we decided to come out here. That was based in part on our curiosity about how Anderson developed so much detail about us."

"Right. Funny though. Even with Anderson's offer of a sailing vacation on Lake Superior, I might have declined except for that unfortunate collision with the Hunter during that race."

Tanner looked up and said, "Hey, maybe we should look into the ownership of that other boat. The Hunter? Do you remember the name?"

"What, you think ET planned that too? Nah." Mary waved the thought away with a broad gesture, almost spilling hot coffee as she did so.

"So, we came to Bayfield," resumed Tanner.

"Right. We came, we saw, and we didn't conquer. You start negotiations with CRR and we meet their board at our very first encounter. I get interested in the company as an investment." She stopped. "Wait. Before all that, ET, through Phoenix, invests a chunk of money, setting up the whole thing. Make a note, Michael, me boy. We should find out whether Phoenix got a position on the board."

"I was going to do that, wasn't I? And if so, who be it? It's sure that ET isn't, that would have blown his cover."

"Something we should have checked earlier. My money is on Krizyinsky."

"So then we, the hired guns, arrive in town. We meet and greet and you get interested in the company as an investment and call Seattle."

Mary paced up and down the living room. "I think we can discount the finding of that skull, although I'm getting an inkling as to who it might belong to."

"You are? Just a minute here. This is news to me!" Tanner stared up at Mary, his pencil quiet on the page.

"It's not part of the rest of this, you know. I just ran across this book in the local library. As I say, it's not

connected, but it's an interesting story. I'll tell you about
it later. Let's stick to the main issues for now. A day
passes. You meet with that Ted McGregor."

"Yes, and had a disagreement with him."

"Same day, you meet that Indian elder, Injun Joe?"

"Right again."

"We charter *Spindrift* and while out there in the
islands, somebody, you think, tries to locate us and a
couple of boats make passes that seem out of the ordinary."

Tanner nodded, writing busily. "All very iffy isn't
it? Until last night. There's no question about that. I mean,
even that business with the truck could have been
accidental."

"Well now, let's wait until we're through the whole
sequence before making judgments.   What happened
next?"

"We toured the plant in Ashland."

"Yes, and met that interesting fellow Kemperer,
about whom I have this uneasy feeling."

Tanner wrote some more and said, "The next
morning there is an explosion, or several, and a small fire
at the plant. It's apparently more ordinary sabotage, until
they find the body of that fellow, McGregor."

"Which is either an accident or murder."

"After that we meet with Kay Anderson at that
backwoods place—"

"Baraks," offered Tanner.

"Baraks. And she tells us about Phoenix and my
old flame."

"I can't even think of his name," hums Tanner
softly.

"Don't I wish. And then, when we leave to go
home, some guy in a truck apparently tries to run us off the
road."

"More than once."

"Next day our Edmund Hochstein arrives, and that night we go to dinner at that nice restaurant," Mary adds.

"Platters. Afterward, we happen to see ET in a clandestine meeting with Stanley Krizyinsky and some local guy, still unidentified."

Mary drained her coffee cup and said. "All right, and then Edmund H decides the company is okay and would be a candidate for investment. You go off and I have coffee with that old Indian fellow, who saves me from a near disaster from a rattletrap truck, down there on the street."

"Don't forget, Joe seemed to think this guy, Wallace Zane was the driver. Meanwhile I'm in Ashland where George hears from the police that McGregor was murdered and they suggest a conspiracy by us to kill McGregor."

"Something about that bothered me at the time and now I think I know why." Tanner tapped his pencil on the table. "We're dealing with two police agencies there. The Ashland County Sheriff and the Ashland Police. It wasn't the sheriff who accused us of conspiracy, it was the local cops."

"Meaning?" asked Mary.

"You know police agencies don't always cooperate. I can't get straight in my head who's really in charge of the investigation over there."

Mary nodded. "You think the accusation from Ashland might not be coming from the sheriff?"

"I have a sneaking suspicion that wealthy local investors might have more clout with the city police than with the county sheriff."

"That could account for the accusation against us," agreed Mary. "Money does funny things to people. Let's just suppose for a minute that money is not the prime motivator here. If Whitney invests in CRR, it's possible that ET could ruin the company and still make money. But it isn't my personal money. I think ET has a different purpose. I think he's been after us, and this business with CRR is an elaborate plan to get us out here so we'd be more vulnerable."

"I've had the same thought," said Tanner. "In fact, I wondered to George yesterday if there was any other funny business going on. He didn't tumble. I don't think his mind works in such devious ways."

"So, this is all personal," said Mary. "Very personal, and that Zane character is being used by ET. Which might mean that Zane murdered poor McGregor. I can't see what that accomplished."

"Neither can I," Tanner said. "Maybe it was an accident. Okay, back to our list. That night, last night, you and I go to dinner on Madeline Island."

"And I was damn near murdered coming back." She took a deep breath and shivered, leaning over Tanner to look at his list. They paused to contemplate Mary's close call on the return trip to the mainland. "Okay, that brings us up to date. What have we got here?"

Tanner pressed Mary's fingers where they lay on his shoulder and said, "This does suggest some questions to pursue."

"Umm, such as?"

"Such as McGregor's contacts and movements between the time he and I had that confrontation in the restaurant and when his body was discovered in the factory. Such as who was the third man in the upstairs room that night?"

"Sounds like an Agatha Christie plot."

Tanner frowned thoughtfully at his list. "Such as, who and what is Wallace Zane?"

In turn, Mary frowned. "Wallace Zane. Yes, he definitely needs some close consideration."

"Exactly. His name came up at Barak's road house, remember? Kay Anderson mentioned him in some context. He was there that night. And we saw his truck in the parking lot."

"Oh, right, when we left with Kay. I remember now."

"It was an old, faded pinkish and rust pickup." Tanner nodded, now making more notes on the paper. Mary came around and sat across from him. "True," she said. "And it was an old light-colored truck that tried to run us off the road. What's more, Zane's truck in Barak's parking lot and the truck that almost ran me down looked a lot alike!"

"Dollars to donuts he isn't doing this on his own. Why would he? We'd never set eyes on each other before we came to Bayfield, so he must be in the pay of somebody. And what better candidate than old Edwin Tobias III. By God, I'll dismember that man!"

"Easy, my love," said Mary, "I don't wish to visit you in prison. Maybe we should turn this over to the authorities?"

"Maybe we should. Chasing criminals isn't my true calling, but the Bayfield force is really small and the sheriff has his hands full with McGregor. Besides, a lot of this is supposition and speculation. But if I can find a picture of that rat Zane, I might be able to turn some of these suppositions into facts. The we could go to the authorities with something concrete."

"Meanwhile, I'll—"

"Meanwhile," Tanner interrupted, "how about if you work the phone and see if you can locate your dear ex-husband? He must be staying somewhere fairly close by."

"Thanks for putting it in the form of a question, my dear, but I see through your little ploy. All right. I don't want you worrying about me while you're chasing leads around rural Wisconsin. But you be careful too. I didn't come to Bayfield to become a widow."

"On that score, don't worry. I'll watch my back. And I may be back in no time at all unless I can find a decent picture of Zane."

A call to CRR in Ashland revealed that they had some snapshots of Wallace Zane taken during the brief time he worked at the company. Tanner took Mary in his arms and they embraced for a long minute. Then Tanner went out the door, pausing just long enough to hear Mary set the deadbolt behind him.

Chapter 27

Without explaining to Jeri Reif precisely why he was interested, Tanner had a look at Wallace Zane's thin CRR employment file. It was unhelpful. There was, however, a snapshot that showed Zane in a three-quarter front view with his arm across the shoulders of another worker. The picture had been taken outdoors at a company outing. Both men were holding bottles of beer and grinning hugely. Tanner was not hopeful of obtaining an identification from the snapshot, but he made a copy. His luck improved when he stopped by the Ashland Police Department. They were accommodating. Yes, Zane had been arrested and photographed in the past year. Tanner sensed the police were not entirely pleased with their relationship with the county sheriff at the moment. He made a copy of Zane's mug shot as well. Then he drove to the Platters.

Mrs. Stevens had no hesitation when she saw the two photographs. "Yes, that's the man who was with Mr. Krizyinsky and the other man. I'm quite sure." She smiled at Tanner. "I hope I have helped."

"Thank you very much, Mrs. Stevens. I'm sure you'll get an explanation before very long." Tanner smiled and shook Adele Stevens' hand. Then he hurried down the steps to his car. He experienced a rush of satisfaction mixed with a certain trepidation. Tanner hoped he wasn't pursuing revelations that would damage his relationship with his wife. Little as she cared about her ex-husband, Tanner knew he could be on treacherous ground. As he leaned forward to start the car, he glanced around and then stopped, his fingers just touching the car's ignition slot. Across the Platters' parking lot, sitting at a picnic table in the shade of a big oak tree, a young woman seemed to be staring at him.

Tanner recalled he'd seen her in the restaurant the first time he'd come looking for some answers. Robin, wasn't that her name? Why was she staring at him? Tanner finally shrugged and started the car. The girl didn't move when he pulled out. Well, he thought. Probably nothing, but I better take my own advice and be more aware of what's going on around me. He turned west to drive back to Bayfield.

* * *

Mary hung up the telephone with a frustrated sigh. Using the Internet and local phone directories she found in the condo, she'd made a dozen unsuccessful calls to local motels, trying to locate Tobias. He was either using a false name or staying way out of town. She realized he might have completed his business and flown back to New York. Mary recalled that he'd never seemed comfortable even when driving to the family vacation houses on the Atlantic shore. On the verge of starting to call motels and hotels in Superior and Duluth, she decided to take a break. The Ames story in the book she had from the library beckoned. She only had a few more pages to reach the end and she was anxious to learn whether the itinerant preacher had successfully completed his mission.

* * *

Preacher Ames sighed with great disappointment. It appeared the trail had grown colder than the weather. He gathered his wool coat and scarf tightly about him and turned about to trudge through the snow back to his dark, meager room.

His footsteps dragged a new path through the light snow, but it was an effort to make progress. Night had long since fallen, and most of the small houses he passed were dark, smoke rising peacefully from their crude chimneys.

He came to an intersection with three liquor establishments facing each other across the roads. The dim, quavering light of candles and lanterns struggled to beat back the night and show warm welcome to the passing traveler, be he friend or stranger. Ames glanced at the fourth corner where a large, square, two-story frame building squatted. It was dark and looked unwelcoming around its narrow entrance steps. Many of the upstairs windows appeared to have shades drawn tightly but weak lights made the frames a little lighter. Ames wondered briefly why so many lights were on at this late hour in a place that appeared to be a private dwelling. Then he realized it could be another of the bordellos that seemed to appear and sometimes disappear, though never quickly enough. Ames generally didn't take his soul-saving services into such establishments, where he knew he would know only stubborn resistance. On rare occasions, he was approached by a poor unfortunate woman seeking help in leaving her onerous occupation and he helped wherever he could.

His weary steps took him across the intersection

and to the door of one of the bars. He pushed through the heavy wooden door and stepped into a dim world, one with which he was more than passingly familiar. The place reeked of cheap whisky, unwashed bodies, wet wool, and badly tanned leather. The room was typical of frontier barrooms. A rough plank floor, springy due to too few underlying beams, supported a bar, several shelves with a small selection of bottles of cheap liquor, and a mismatched scattering of chairs and tables. Several men sat talking and drinking.

The proprietor, wrapped in a smudged butcher's apron, looked up from wiping down the counter. Ames nodded and went to the bar, declining the offer of a drink. He stumbled when he caught the heel of his riding boot on the raised edge of a warped floor board. He had been in this barroom before.

Reverend Ames leaned close and explained he was looking for a man, a teamster who had recently worked for one of the Whitney logging crews. Rylston may have been involved in an incident, and he needed to find the man and ask him a few questions. Not to restrain Rylston, Ames carefully explained, that was the sheriff's job if it came to that, but rather to try to save another man's involvement in a nasty business that might turn out to be another murder.

The bartender, closemouthed as most of them were if they valued the continued custom of the inhabitants, cautiously admitted he knew Rylston. Not well, but he had been seen in town occasionally during the off season. Not recently, he emphasized. Not this winter season.

What about young James Tompkins? Ames wanted to know. Had he been around in the past week or two? Yes, the bartender admitted reluctantly. The young man had indeed been in. As it happened, he too had inquired about Rylston.

And what about the man they called the Finn? Now

the bartender was silent, shaking his head. He had not seen nor heard of the Finn in many a week. Ames glanced around the dark room but none of the few patrons hunched over their tankards amid their quiet conversations showed the slightest interest in the tall, gaunt preacher.

* * *

Tanner paced impatiently back and forth across the ferry parking lot. He stepped around cars that drove up and watched the people in them who bought tickets and then parked. They too were waiting for the ferry, Nichevo II, to return from Madeline Island. Company staff watched him surreptitiously. Tanner had already shown them the photographs he carried of Wallace Zane, but none of the three could say they had ever seen the man, much less that he had been a passenger the previous night.

Tanner felt a surge of anticipation and watched the *Nichevo* make the sharp, thrashing turn into the slip. He waited by the side of the slip until the crew lashed the thick mooring lines to the pilings and lowered the ramp. As the passengers and cars began to roll off the ferry, he could wait no longer.

At a brisk walk, he started up the ramp toward a member of the deck crew who raised his head and started to warn Tanner back. When he recognized Tanner he nodded, motioning him forward. At the same time he spoke briefly into his radio handset.

"Hey, man, I hear your lady was rescued okay. How's she doing?" He stuck out a big callused paw and whacked Tanner on the arm.

"She's doing okay. Thanks for asking. I have some pictures here I want you to take a look at." He thrust the pictures of Wallace Zane at the man. "Do you know this guy? Think hard. Could he have been on the ferry last night?"

The other crewman and the ferry captain approached and crowded around. "Hey, I know that guy," said the second deckhand. "Isn't that Zane? Sure, Wally Zane."

The other man frowned and then said. "Guess you're right. Zane does odd jobs around town. Once in a while the ferry company hires him when we need an extra pair of hands. You know?"

Tanner nodded. "Right, Wallace Zane. What I want to know is whether you can recall if he was aboard last night coming back from the island when Mary was thrown into the water."

"It's hard to say, you know? He's around sometimes and I can't really say whether he was on board last night. He does ride across from time to time. Looking for work, I guess."

"Yeah," said another, "he drives that freaky-looking truck. I'm sure I would have noticed if that thing had come aboard, so probably not last night."

"What do you mean, freaky?" queried Tanner.

"Well, you know. It's an old Dodge pickup that's barely hangin' together. And the paint, what there is left, has faded to that awful pinkish color."

The others nodded agreement and then turned to their jobs of finishing the loading of passengers eager to get to Madeline Island for their vacation outing.

"Look, Tanner," said the captain. "Why don't you ride over to La Pointe with us? You can talk to the crew at the other end. It's the same people who were there last night."

"Thanks, Captain. I appreciate the offer."

Minutes later, with a blast of its powerful electric horn, Nichevo II thrashed out of the ferry slip, turned about and sped off across the bay toward La Pointe.

When he got to Madeline Island, Tanner closely questioned the two crew.

"Boy, it's hard to say," said one, scratching his head under his ponytail. "My impression is that he could have walked aboard during the return trip. Last one, wasn't it?

Tanner nodded, hoping the man could be more positive.

"I'd have to say I'm pretty sure I saw him go aboard for that trip, but I couldn't swear to it." He shook his head and gave Tanner a sharp glance. "Not in court."

Tanner nodded and shook the man's hand. "That's okay. I'm just trying to build a scenario. If there's a chance this Zane was on board, it gives me some direction, some questions to ask. And without his truck, it would have been easy to miss recognizing him."

"Well, I hope I helped a little, at least. And I'm sure glad to hear that woman who fell off the boat is okay."

"Thanks," said Tanner and went back aboard for the return trip to Bayfield. He stood at the notch on the car deck, just where he and Mary had stood the previous night. As he watched the lake slide by and felt the thrumming vibration of the powerful engine, he realized that he was unconsciously urging the boat to greater speed. He was impatient to get back to the mainland and continue his search. If he could talk to Zane, several answers would surface.

When the Nichevo II docked in Bayfield, Tanner was one of the first off, waving his thanks to the captain and the crew. He trotted down the street and into the condo.

"Mary," he called. "I think I'm making some real progress." Mary looked up from where she was curled up on the big couch. She marked her place and smiled up at Tanner. He crossed the room, bent down and kissed her soundly.

"Mmm, nice. Me too, but tell me what you've learned."

"I found a man on Madeline at La Pointe who works at the ferry dock. He can't swear to it, but he's pretty sure that Wallace Zane was on that last boat to the mainland. It's not much, and it won't hold up in court, but it might be enough to rattle Mr. Zane."

"If we can ever find him."

"There is that." Tanner leaned over and slid Mary's book around so he could read the title. "*Tales of Lake Superior Country*. Real history or stories?"

Mary smiled. "A little bit of both, I think. Some of the stories are backed up by statistical stuff and contemporary newspaper stories I looked at, but a lot of it would be categorized as oral history. It's great stuff." She looked pensive. "You know, this lake attracts me in an odd way. Maybe the book has something to do with it, but I felt a connection the first time I saw the water."

"I noticed."

"The story I'm reading now is based on the journals of a preacher who traveled to the camps and ministered to the loggers. The Reverend Ames' story may even have a bearing on the present day."

Tanner placed a finger on Mary's nose and leaned closer. "You mentioned that before. This mysterious preacher you're reading about. When will you reveal all?"

"Soon. What's our next move?"

"I'm going to Ashland to talk with people at the company."

Tanner spent most of the twenty-mile drive around Chequamegon Bay thinking about the third man in that upstairs room at Platters. Stanley Krizyinsky. If, as he now suspected, Tobias, Zane, and Krizyinsky were working together, Tanner wanted to have a heart-to-heart with Stanley Krizyinsky very soon.

When he banged into the downtown offices of CRR, there was a look on Tanner's face that sent people scurrying out of his path. He walked into Krizyinsky's office without knocking. "Hang up the phone," he growled.

Krizyinsky muttered a hasty goodbye and complied. "Is something the matter?"

"I'll say something's the matter!"

Unlike most of the people at CRR who usually dressed in casual fashion, Stanley Krizyinsky was wearing a lightweight tan silk suit. His cuffs gleamed with heavy gold links when he leaned forward over his desk. "Really? What is it you think I can do for you, Tanner?"

"It's Mister Tanner to you. For starters you can tell me about your meeting with Edwin Tobias and Wallace Zane at Platters, the other night."

Krizyinsky opened his mouth to say something and then thought better of it. He sat there staring at Tanner. Finally he said, "I hardly think that's any of your concern."

"Really?" Tanner's anger suddenly blossomed and he lunged across the desk and grabbed Krizyinsky wide lapels. He hoisted him out of his chair. "I think you and Tobias and that Zane are planning some kind of takeover. I think you're Phoenix's undercover spy on the board and I think you're paying Zane to harass us, to get us out of Bayfield. Slimy as that may be, it goes way too far when your man tries to run me off the road and when that doesn't work, you had Zane try to murder Mary!"

He grabbed Krizyinsky by the coat and lifted him onto his toes, then slammed him back into the chair, sending chair and man skidding across the office to bang into the wall.

"My meeting that night is none of your business." Krizyinsky choked out, struggling to adjust his coat.

"It is when it involves attacks on my wife!" Tanner

started around the desk, itching to get his hands on the man again Somewhere in his brain he knew he was losing control but he wasn't aware he'd raised his voice until the door behind him banged open and Anderson's secretary cried, "What's happening here?

Chapter 28

The big Ashland cop stood behind Tanner, his massive arms folded across his tight blue uniform shirt. His leather holster and tool belt creaked in rhythm with his slow measured breathing. Tanner sat in a chair leaning forward, his right hand immersed in a pail of cold water. He flexed his fingers tentatively. It appeared he hadn't broken anything when he'd slammed his hand on Krizyinsky's desk.

The big cop's partner came into the conference room. He ushered in a still-flustered Stanley Krizyinsky. "Sit over there," the cop said, pointing at a chair a safe distance and across the table from Tanner. Krizyinsky opened his mouth to protest but the cop gave him a hard look and Krizyinsky remained silent.

The younger cop leaned down and said to Tanner. "You're lucky we showed up when we did. Somebody coulda got hurt. This one," he pointed at Krizyinsky, "had a pistol in his desk."

"I have a permit," Krizyinsky started.

"You just keep quiet," growled the big cop behind Tanner.

"Mr. Tanner," the cop turned his attention away from Krizyinsky. "You mind telling me something?"

"What," muttered Tanner. He was evaluating his actions. He came to the conclusion he'd made a fool of himself and skated very near something tragic. Still, in a small recess of his mind he admitted that grabbing Krizyinsky and throwing him against the wall had felt good.

"What did you expect to gain by blowing into this man's office and committing assault like that?"

"I apologize for the way I acted, officer. I admit, I lost it. My wife and I have been the target of several attempts on our lives since we got here last week. The other night someone threw my wife off the ferry from Madeline Island. I think this man has something to do with everything that's happened since we got here. Including the death of Ted McGregor!" Tanner's voice rose and he started to get up from the chair. The big cop stepped forward and applied pressure to Tanner's shoulder to keep him in the chair.

"Let's all just settle down until the sheriff gets here."

The younger cop glanced at his partner. "I don't get what we're waiting for. Let's just run 'em both in and lock 'em up."

The other cop shook his head and said, "That's not the way things work around here. This town's too small not to cooperate with the county. You know the sheriff's workin' on the McGregor thing and these two are in the picture. He said hold 'em here and that's what we're gonna do."

The other cop shrugged and turned toward the window. Tanner breathed deeply and realized shouting at Krizyinsky wasn't going to help, so he gradually relaxed to a waiting posture. A few minutes later, the sound of heavy tread in the hall outside Krizyinsky's office intruded. Sheriff Pat Olsen came into the room.

Tanner remembered him from their brief encounter at the CRR plant the morning McGregor's body was discovered. He was a big, sandy-haired Swede, over six feet tall, and Tanner figured he weighed well over two hundred pounds. He had the look of an experienced lawman. Today he was wearing a forest-green twill shirt open at the collar and matching twill pants.

The sheriff glanced at the four occupants of the office and nodded.

"Okay, fellas, I appreciate your call. I'm going to take Mr. Tanner here into another office and have a little chat. My deputy will stay with Mr. Krizyinsky."

Tanner slumped into the side chair in Eddington's office. Sheriff Olsen quietly shut the door and looked down at Tanner. "I'm surprised. Everything we've learned about you suggests this is unusual, to say the least."

Tanner nodded and rubbed his face. "You're right. I kept remembering Mary thrown into that cold water while I was coming from Bayfield. I didn't realize how much tension has been building up. God, is it only a week? It seems more like a month."

"Why don't you just take a few minutes to tell me everything that's happened so far?"

"Well, you know most of it. We've reported every incident and most of our suspicions as well."

"Indulge me."

So Tanner did. Toward the end of his narrative, he began to realize that the sheriff had something else on his mind. "Sheriff, if you don't mind my asking, are you one of Anderson's investors? Do you have shares in CRR?"

Pat Olsen smiled and nodded. "Astute question. As a matter of fact, no, but some of my relatives have invested in the company. So have lots of local folks. So you can see there's a lot of interest in the company.

"I have a couple of questions about your wife's ex-husband. Do you seriously believe he's behind the attacks on you and your wife?"

Tanner stood up and paced to the window. "I've never met him. So it's hard for me to say, but I trust Mary's instincts and she says he's the vindictive, get-even sort. Some of the stuff Anderson used to get us to consider a contract with CRR isn't readily available. You can't go on the Internet and find out personal stuff about Mary Whitney. I'm a little more exposed that way, but not much. Anderson knew a whole lot about us before we arrived in Wisconsin. That's what got us here. Now I see that information must have come from Tobias."

Olsen nodded. "I understand that this Edwin Tobias is not big on traveling. So it'd be unusual to encounter him here in Ashland, or in Duluth."

Tanner nodded and then sent a sharp look at the other man. "Duluth, you say. I guess you've been doing some looking of your own."

Olsen smiled. "Mr. Hochstein was able to provide us with several leads, one of which panned out."

"Hochstein? How'd he help? Which reminds me, did he get off all right?"

"Your Mr. Hochstein was very helpful. Turns out he knows a lot about Ms. Whitney's ex. He gave us some ideas where to look. We located a Mr. Edwin Tobias at a bed and breakfast just north of Duluth. Of course, we can't be certain it's the same Edwin Tobias formerly married to Mary Whitney, but this particular B&B is one of Phoenix's smaller investments."

"A B&B? Mary will be amused. That doesn't sound at all like what I've learned about ET."

Olsen smiled. "Well, this is a very private, very upscale B&B. I understand their rates run around a thousand dollars a day."

Tanner blinked.

"Mr. Tobias flew in several days ago on a private jet now housed at the Duluth airport. We don't have enough to lean on the people who run the B&B, but the private jet is still on the ground. If Tobias decides to leave Duluth and go back to New York anytime soon, there isn't much we can do about it. All we have right now are suppositions and suspicions. I'd need something more concrete before I'd even attempt to talk to the man."

Tanner switched subjects. "I take it Mary and I are no longer suspects in the murder of Ted McGregor?"

"Mr. Tanner, you never really were. When it was determined that McGregor was murdered and there were some very wealthy people involved, some folks got a little nervous. We were under enormous pressure to solve the case quickly."

"Politics?"

Olsen smiled. "I won't deny we've had some contacts, cautionary representations, let me say. Sheriffs are elected and police chiefs serve at the whim of an elected city administration. Not everyone in town is a big fan of Anderson and CRR. There's a certain amount of jealousy. Frankly, when George got the idea he and you two were under suspicion, I let it go. I should have squashed the rumor, but it was useful, for a while at least, to have people think you and the Andersons were engaged in an infernal conspiracy."

Tanner nodded. "I appreciate your candor, Sheriff." He turned around and looked down at Eddington's desk. On a small pad of paper he saw the name Kemperer with two black question marks after it. The name had been printed heavily and overwritten several times.

"We have enough to take Stanley in for questioning, and I'm gonna do that. But I seriously doubt he's involved in the attacks on you and your wife, Mr. Tanner. I trust you'll be available as needed, from time to time. Try to stay out of dark alleys until we get this all sorted out. Oh, yes, we've issued a pickup order for Wallace Zane. We'll be in touch." Sheriff Olsen touched the brim of his Smokey Bear hat and quietly went out.

Tanner reached over Eddington's desk and picked up the pad of paper. Then he tore off the page with Kemperer's name on it.

Chapter 29

Mary brewed a fresh pot of coffee, wishing Tanner would call and let her know what was happening, and settled down to read the final pages based on the journals of the Reverend Merlin Ames in the *Tales of Lake Superior Country*.

* * *

Ames took the information from the bartender with him in his mind as he trudged through the dark Bayfield night toward the docks. Just off Main Street he passed a low wooden building with a light from a lantern glowing in the window. He saw the hand-lettered sign over the door that said simply, Police. He turned aside from his path and went into the tiny warm room. Like many other structures in Bayfield, the police station was small and had few amenities. The constable had his mackinaw off and his shirt opened to reveal a mat of black hair curling above his woolen long underwear. His hat sat back on his head and he hunched over a newspaper. Ames figured it must have been difficult to read in the dim and flickering light of a second lantern on the scarred deal table. Opposite the door through which Ames had entered was another door, this one barred with a big padlock hanging from the iron hasp that secured it.

The constable looked up and asked the preacher

*what business he had with the law at this time of night.
Ames explained. The constable, his brushy handlebar
mustache twitching, nodded, and told Ames that he had
heard from the sheriff. He was told to be on the lookout for
the Tompkins boy, son of the murdered man and brother of
the girl that Jarl Rylston was accused of assaulting.*

*No, sir, he told a disappointed Ames, he had seen
neither hide nor hair of either one, although the word was
around that both men were in town. After the two agreed
that this late spring snowfall and cold snap was sure to
delay reopening of the mills at full throttle, Ames departed,
turning toward the lake shore and the docks. The wind was
making up and it howled around Ames's muffler-wrapped
head, plucking at his nose and ears. He ducked his head
and when he rounded the corner of the jail, he ran full tilt
into a man coming the other way.*

*Neither went down, but they clutched at each other
to stay upright. Ames peered at the man he'd walked into
and recognized him from earlier journeys to Bayfield. He
owned two small boats and worked mainly on the docks
and as an occasional extra hand on passing steamers.
After some close questioning, he admitted to Ames that he
had just this minute returned from rowing a man out to a
passing tugboat. The tug had been towing an early load of
logs to mills at the head of the bay, mills desperate for
work. Ames was certain that the passenger he described
was Jarl Rylston, although this man claimed he did not
know Rylston, nor was he aware that Rylston was being
sought by the Bayfield County Sheriff for questioning in
regard to a suspicious death at one of the logging camps.*

*Ames wanted to know if the man knew where
Rylston had come from. The man professed complete
ignorance of anything other than what he'd just related.
Yes, Rylston seemed a little worried, nervous, perhaps. He
had paid well for being ferried out to the passing boat.*

Now, the man was anxious to get home to a warm fire and out of this infernal wind.

* * *

Mary put the book down and went to get more coffee. The telephone rang. It was Tanner.

"How goes your investigation?" she asked.

"I'm embarrassed to admit I lost my temper and put my hands on Stanley Krizyinsky. Rather heavily."

"Really. That's not your style, my love. Did he confess?"

"No, he didn't. Somebody called the cops, and then Sheriff Olsen arrived. The local police and the sheriff have an interesting relationship. The sheriff took Stanley in for questioning, but I'm not as sure as I was earlier that Krizyinsky is the man. They've issued a pickup order for Wallace Zane. I just hope we can find out why Wallace Zane was at that meeting."

"Maybe he can supply some answers. I'm afraid I wasn't able to locate ET."

"The sheriff did that. He's in a very upscale private B&B of some kind outside Duluth. Owned by Phoenix. Sheriff Olsen also told me ET flew in on a private jet that's at the Duluth airport."

"How did the good sheriff come by all this information?"

"Hochstein. Turns out your Mr. Hochstein knows a good deal about Mr. Tobias."

"Are they going to arrest ET?"

"Not now. No evidence. But he did tell me they don't seriously consider us suspects in McGregor's murder. Apparently they never did."

"Really? Then why—"

"Sheriff Olsen said they let that out partly to satisfy

some political pressure they were getting. He didn't exactly apologize, but I could tell he wasn't pleased with having done it. He's enlisting the Ashland police to assist his deputies. They're really looking for this Zane guy. I have one other piece of news. When the Ashland policemen peeled me off Stanley, they put me in the next office, which happened to be Eddington's. While I was talking to the sheriff I noticed a pad of note paper on his desk. Eddington, or somebody, had written Kemperer's name on it several times. Heavily underlined in one case. There are other scribbles which I can't interpret. Kemperer's name is surrounded by several question marks."

"You think that means something significant?"

"Possibly. Kemperer was one of the board members we weren't comfortable with almost from the beginning."

"I remember. The cabinetmaker. I thought he was coming on to me rather crudely the day we toured the factory."

"It's tenuous, but it's worth checking out." Tanner sighed.

"When can I expect you back?"

"Soon, I think. George just told me he and Kay are scheduled to leave later today to catch a flight to the Twin Cities and then New York. They have meetings with some investors who are ready to pump more money into the firm."

"So it looks like CRR is on solid financial footing?"

"Yep. I'll see you soon, babe."

* * *

That afternoon Mary stood on the tiny balcony overlooking the municipal harbor. Directly ahead of her lay the red and green navigation beacons where she had dragged herself, cold, wet, exhausted, out of the lake and heard the rising call when a water-borne searcher had first spotted her clinging to the sharp granite rocks.

The day was cooling from the lake effect and she enjoyed the fingers of light breezes that brushed the back of her neck. The harbor scene was calm and peaceful; a sailboat carefully maneuvered away from the gas dock to make room for another. Elsewhere along the many docks, owners worked at maintaining their boats or getting them ready for a journey onto the lake.

Farther out, in the blue North Channel separating Madeline and Basswood, sailboats sailed their separate courses, some hurrying home for the night, others on headings that might take them across the shipping lanes to the rocky coast of the North Shore, perhaps to Grand Marais or Isle Royale. In spite of the troubles of the past days, Mary smiled with a measure of contentment and then returned to her book.

* * *

Preacher Merlin Ames stood for a long time staring out into the blackness of the night over the cold restless waters of Chequamegon Bay. Somewhere out there, he was now persuaded, Jarl Rylston had been ferried to a shifting platform of timber leading to an uncertain destination. Exactly where the fugitive would end up, Ames knew not. But in his heart he was somehow certain that Bayfield and the big woods of northern Wisconsin would never again know the tread of Jarl Rylston's boots.

* * *

Mary smiled at the florid writing and turned the

page. Then she looked up. The sound of footsteps came to her door and the latch rattled when Tanner inserted his key. She dropped the book and went to greet him.

"Well, sailor, home from the wars, home from the sea." She wound her arms about him and pulled him close. Her pulse surged as she felt his arms come hard around her. "What news?"

"First things first, my love. I'd really like a drink about now. Could I interest you in building us a couple while I wash some of the road dust off?"

She glanced at her watch. "The sun is certainly over the yardarm somewhere in the empire."

Tanner disappeared into their bedroom and Mary went to the kitchen. Moments later, side by side on the divan, they discussed the day's happenings.

"Anyway," Tanner finished, "I need to have a serious talk with Mr. Kemperer. I called his place in Washburn, but there was no answer."

The telephone rang. When Tanner picked up, he heard Eddington on the other end. "Tanner," he said, "we can't locate Kemperer."

"Is that unusual? I saw the note on your desk, by the way. What have you learned?"

"I've just had confirmation that Kemperer has been talking out of turn, revealing private information about the business to outsiders."

"Any specifics?"

"I'm pretty sure Kemperer is an under-the-table representative for Phoenix. We wondered why Phoenix seemed to be in no hurry to name a board representative. Now we know why. It was Kemperer all along. He's been feeding information to Tobias for months. We, the board, would never have agreed to keep him on the staff while he was representing Phoenix. That's unethical. I'm not sure it isn't illegal as well.

"Look, he may know his cover is blown. If so, he could be planning to skip. The only place I can think Kemperer might be is on his boat at Superior Charters."

"He's on this side of the bay? Why would he have a boat way over here?"

"Maybe because that's where George keeps his boat? Anyway, you're closer. Would you run over to the marina in Pike's Bay and look at Kemperer's boat? If you find him give me a call and I'll drive around and we can both talk to him. Try not to tip him off to what I've just told you."

"Well—Oh, hell, why not? I'll run over there right now and call you from the marina office."

Tanner dropped the phone in its cradle and turned to collect his keys and windbreaker, saying, "That was Eddington. He's trying to find Kemperer. Turns out Kemperer has a boat at the marina on Pike's Bay, where we chartered *Spindrift*."

"Sure," said Mary, "same place George and Kay berth their yacht."

"I'm going to take a quick run down there and see if I can find Mr. Kemperer."

"Not by yourself, you're not," said Mary rising off the couch. "I'm going along."

"Okay. I'll tell you the rest on the way," Tanner said.

A few minutes later Tanner and Mary Whitney parked next to the building that housed Superior Charters, the restaurant, and the condo sales office.

Tanner stuck his head into the marina office. "Excuse me," he said. "I'm looking for Dick Kemperer's boat. We're meeting him there."

The deeply tanned girl behind the high counter who looked like she'd just returned from weeks in the Caribbean flipped through a loose-leaf binder. "Right," she said. "He has that new Crealock 44. It's in slip E14."

"Has he shown up this evening yet?"

The girl shrugged. "I haven't seen him. Unless he needs something, he wouldn't necessarily stop in the office."

"Okay, thanks."

Tanner and Mary turned to the docks and walked through the sunset down the wooden jetty toward E14. They could see the slip was empty.

"Damn," muttered Tanner.

A marina employee came up behind them. "You looking for Mr. Kemperer? 'Fraid you're outa luck. His boat's been gone a while."

"How long?" asked Tanner turning to the boy.

"Slip's been empty all day. I think he took her out yesterday sometime."

Tanner and Mary looked at each other.

The boy was halfway back to the shore when Mary called, "Just a minute, please."

The boy stopped and looked back. "Where's George Anderson's boat? The *Merry Kay*?"

He pointed. "That's her, behind the red cigarette boat."

The *Merry Kay* was moored along the shoreside jetty. Two fat yellow power cables ran through a hawsehole, along the dock and into a big blue junction box nearby. Tanner and Mary stood close together and stared at the big yacht.

"What are you thinking?" Tanner murmured.

"Suppose you had a warning that things were coming apart and you wanted a quick way out."

Tanner considered it. "I don't know. A boat? Why not just drive out of town?"

"Suppose you're are a yachtsman and you own a big expensive sloop."

"A 44-foot, year-old Crealock certainly qualifies," Tanner agreed.

"You could claim to be off cruising while things are happening and it would be difficult to prove otherwise. And if you had to run, a sloop that size could take you through the St. Lawrence to almost anywhere."

Tanner nodded. "And if you wanted to be ready to leave suddenly, you might just move your own boat away from its regular mooring to someplace where you could get to it relatively easily and almost anonymously."

"If I were doing this," said Mary, "I think I'd move my boat from here to the transient docks on Madeline Island. Then I could either take the ferry or hitch a ride over when I was ready to run."

"Sure, and if I didn't want to be found, I'd hide out somewhere that I didn't usually frequent."

"Such as on a friend's boat."

"Good thinking. Kemperer probably even has a key to the hatch." Tanner continued to stare at the *Merry Kay*. "Kemperer would know the Andersons are in New York for a few days. So he'd know the boat is unoccupied. He could be staying right there until he's ready to go."

"I don't see any lights," said Mary.

"No, but the air conditioner is running. Hear it? It's unseasonably warm tonight, but not that warm. If you were George Anderson, out of town for a few days, would you leave that on to suck up all that electricity?"

Mary smiled in the gathering darkness. "George doesn't strike me as the wasteful kind."

"Maybe I'll have to check out the *Merry Kay*,"

"Maybe I'll go with you."

They turned slowly and walked back along the pier toward the shore.

Headlights pierced the night and a light-colored dented pickup appeared from beside the marina office building. It stopped, engine coughing and sputtering. It reversed into a corner of the gravel near the *Merry Kay*. Its headlights swept across Tanner and Mary Whitney for an instant.

"Zane!" exclaimed Mary and Tanner simultaneously.

A dark figure exited the cab and slammed the door. The figure went directly to the boarding ladder at the rear of the *Merry Kay*.

"Huh," said Tanner. "Let's get closer."

Before they had taken three steps along the pier, they saw shadowy movement at the stern of the boat. There was a sudden sputtering sound and an aluminum fishing boat with a big outboard hung on the back nosed out from behind the *Merry Kay* and, quickly gathering speed, rushed along the backsides of the boats moored in the farthest slips and roared out into Pike's Bay. The motorboat showed no running lights.

Chapter 30

Tanner gripped Mary's hand and they went along the jetty toward the *Merry Kay*. Wake from the departing motor boat slapped noisily against the docks. The yacht was dark and silent. When Tanner slipped aboard he tried the sliding door that lead from the open rear cockpit to the main cabin. It was locked. He climbed the ladder to the flying bridge as quietly as he could. The *Merry Kay* shifted slightly against her mooring lines and the fenders sighed quietly. Tanner knew there was no way to keep his movements from being detected if anyone aboard was awake. He was unable to find an open porthole or hatch. The murmur of a well-dampened air conditioner continued to hum, somewhere below deck.

"What now?" asked Mary when Tanner had returned to the dock. She stood, hands on hips, staring at the dark yacht.

"Blessed if I know. Kemperer could be hiding aboard, but as long as he keeps quiet and doesn't turn any lights on, we'll never know. I'm not about to break in."

"We could mount a watch all night. If he's here, he'll have to come ashore sooner or later. Or we can get a cop to open up the boat. Who do you suppose is in that motor boat?"

In answer, Tanner turned toward the parking area and tugged Mary's hand. Together they went to the pale truck the stranger had left. As they walked closer, Tanner heard the ticking sounds of contracting metal as the engine cooled off. He put a hand on the hood and felt the heat of the engine.

"Does this thing look familiar?"

Mary peered through the dark and said, "Well, I can't be sure in this light but it sure looks like the one in Bayfield, the one I saw a couple of days ago. The one that almost ran me down. Hang on a minute."

She walked to the rear of the truck and bent down, peering at the license plate. When she returned to Tanner's side she murmured, "The plate holder and the brake light seem to have the damage I remember. I'd bet money this is the same truck."

"That means the guy who tore off in that motor boat was probably Walter Zane. C'mon, let's go to the office."

In the welcome light of the marina office, Tanner called the Bayfield police station, but only an answering machine responded. He left his name and their location at Superior Marina.

"Guys," said the girl behind the desk. "It's after ten and I'm gonna close up now. The restaurant upstairs is open for another hour or so. You could wait there, if you want. The patrol car will be around before eleven and you can talk to Duane."

Tanner nodded. "Thanks." He turned to Mary and said, "I wish we knew what kind of car Kemperer drove. At least we could look around the lot and see if his car is here while we are waiting."

"Let's talk to Duane and then go home and get a decent night's sleep. Tomorrow we'll find Kemperer and ask him some questions." Mary tugged at Tanner's sleeve and they went out into the warm darkness to wait for the Bayfield officer to arrive.

Once he arrived, Tanner leaned down to talk to the officer through his car window. His radio, tuned to the local law enforcement frequency muttered sporadically. Duane Beckwith was the same officer Tanner had met earlier during his frantic search for Mary the night she'd been thrown off the ferry.

"How ya doin' Mr. Tanner?" Officer Beckwith offered his hand through the window. He smiled at Mary, plucked the mike off the dashboard and called in his location. Then he stepped out of the squad and stretched.

"We still haven't located Richard Kemperer. I guess you know the sheriff has a request to detain him for questioning," Tanner said. "I checked his slip and his boat isn't here where it's usually docked."

"So, I guess he's probably out in the islands somewhere, don't you figure?"

"Under other circumstances I would," Tanner agreed, "but the timing's wrong. According to the people here, Kemperer's boat has been gone for a couple of days. But he's been around. He was seen in his office in Ashland this morning."

"Do you know his car?"

"No, I'm afraid not."

"Well, hang on here. I may have the license plate from the Sheriff."

Beckwith opened the door of his squad and leaned in.

From her position closer to the water, Mary suddenly asked, "Officer, can you swing the headlights over to the left?"

Beckwith shrugged and slid into the front seat. When he turned the car slightly to the left, his headlights swept over the dock and centered the *Merry Kay* in its beams.

"The power lines are uncoupled!" Her voice crackled with urgency. "And the bow mooring line is gone."

"What?" Tanner and the police officer stared at the big yacht. There was an explosion of sound as her powerful engines roared instantly into life. Simultaneously, they saw a dark figure scrambling up the ladder to the flying bridge. The engines wound up and with a cracking sound, the starboard side toe rail splintered off the yacht as the boat turned too sharply left and started moving away from the dock. There was a great frothing of water at her stern as the props thrashed against the water.

Tanner flung himself down the jetty and ran into the dark.

"Michael!" Mary's despairing voice floated after him.

Tanner pounded down the planks and reached an empty slip near the end of the long dock barely ahead of the escaping yacht. Whoever was driving her wasn't paying any attention to the niceties of marina protocol. The *Merry Kay* was fast gathering speed. Tanner turned at a finger beside the empty slip and launched himself off the end. It was a last desperate attempt to reach the fleeing boat. The driver at the helm saw him coming and steered the *Merry Kay* toward the shore and away from the docks. The gap was too wide.

Tanner slammed into the side of the yacht, his fingers barely clutching the broken toe rail that ran around the perimeter of the boat. Winded, the breath knocked out of him, he was able to hang on for only long enough to pull his knees up. Then, as his fingers slipped off, he pushed himself away from the side of the boat and fell into the lake. When he surfaced, he blew out a stream of water and air and looked around. The shadowy figures of Mary and the cop leaning from the finger dock stood outlined against the starry sky.

"Michael! Are you all right?"

"This water is really cold."

"Don't I know it. What were you thinking? My God, Michael! You're not some Hollywood stunt man. There's a ladder of sorts right here." Her voice was a mixture of shaky concern and relief that Tanner was apparently unharmed. In the background the sound of the escaping *Merry Kay's* engines fell away to a murmur.

Tanner struggled up the short ladder, lake water streaming from his clothes. "Officer Beckwith, can you contact the Coast Guard on that radio? We need to get them out looking for that boat."

"Yeah, I'll call 'em, but the helicopter is an hour away and unless we get real lucky, even with the Sheriff's water patrol, and the park service boats all on the lookout, nobody'll find that cruiser until after sunup. Come on. I think I've got a blanket and some towels, in the squad." Beckwith turned and trotted back toward his car, followed more slowly by a shivering Tanner and Mary Whitney. Several late diners had come out into the parking lot to see what all the excitement was. Tanner and Mary shook their heads and ignored the questions.

Beckwith approached and said, "Kemperer drives a late model blue Caddy. I've got the license number. There aren't many cars left out here so it shouldn't take more'n a few minutes to see if it's here." He was carrying his flashlight and returned shortly shaking his head. It's not in the main lot, but there are some wide spots back in the trees. You two hang on and I'll be right back."

The squad did a tight U-turn and disappeared down the graveled driveway. Wrapped in a blanket, Tanner sat slumped in the front seat of their car while Mary rubbed the damp towel over his head.

"Phooey! He exclaimed in disgust. "Zane runs off in a motor boat. Kemperer steals Anderson's yacht and here we are. Of course we're not sure that's who's on those boats, but who else could it be? Even if we're right and the cops grab those two, we don't know exactly what they'll say. Maybe they won't implicate Tobias."

"Huh. Fat chance," said Mary. "I think we ought to go back to Bayfield for the rest of the night and start fresh in the morning."

Officer Beckwith's squad rolled back into the lot and he said, "I found Kemperer's Caddy back there behind some bushes in a little cul de sac. Why don't you folks go home? Somebody will call you if there are any developments. It's a big dark lake and it's not likely anyone will spot either of them before morning. I gotta get back on patrol." He waved and drove away.

* * *

The telephone rang at eight. Tanner picked it up and talked with a deputy at the Bayfield County Sheriff's office in Washburn. When he hung up, he rolled over and saw Mary looking at him through sleep-slitted eyes.

"The Coast Guard and the Park Service rangers have been alerted but there's been no sighting. Look out the window."

Mary did. Their usual view of the tree-covered Chautauqua hill called Mt. Ashtwaby was completely obscured by thick gray clouds.

"Fog came down about two this morning. It's making the search almost impossible. Weather radio says it ought to clear by noon."

"Both those boats will be miles away by then." Mary shook her head and rolled out from under the sheet. "So, what now?"

"Breakfast. Then we'll check in with the Coast Guard and the water patrol guys again. The people at the marina here are being very accommodating and making periodic radio checks for us."

After a quick cold breakfast, Tanner and Mary Whitney walked over to the marina office. By now, word had spread throughout the boating community and a number of people with little else to do were hanging around the office listening to the radio chatter. When Mary and Tanner pushed through the small crowd and entered the office, a college-aged woman at the desk grinned at them.

"Gee, this is the most excitement we've had in a coon's age," she said.

"Just remember, we haven't any proof the missing people are guilty of anything," said Tanner.

"Huh. Maybe not, but that Zane guy, he's a real creep."

"You know him?" asked Mary.

"Sure. He hangs around here a lot."

The radio crackled to life. "Bayfield marina, this is *Rose Marie*. Over."

The girl swung around and grabbed the mike. "This is Bayfield. Go ahead *Rose Marie*." She glanced up and said. "*Rose Marie* is a fishing boat. She's out somewhere east of Madeline, checking her nets."

"Bayfield, be advised we've spotted the *Merry Kay*. She's beached at the south end of Big Bay. I didn't see anyone aboard. Over."

"Copy that. Thanks, *Rose Marie*. Will you notify the Coast Guard? Over."

"Already did that, Bayfield. *Rose Marie* out."

Tanner considered the news. Then, he reached for the telephone. "What's the Sheriff's number in Washburn?"

Without saying, the girl punched in the numbers and handed Tanner the handset.

"This is Tanner," he said. "They've found the *Merry Kay*. You know. Good. Kemperer is supposed to be a pretty good boater so if the *Merry Kay* is on the beach, he put it there deliberately. Yes, he sure could hide out on Madeline for weeks. But I bet he's heading for another boat. Somebody should check the harbor at La Pointe and anywhere else he might have his own launch stashed."

He listened.

"No, I have no idea what his boat looks like or what it's called. I just know it's been gone from its regular berth at Pike's Bay for several days." He listened some more, told the deputy thanks, and hung up.

"The sheriff is sending their water patrol boat to La Pointe and asking the Park Service boat that's here in the marina to ferry us across."

A voice from outside called, "Mr. Tanner? Ms. Whitney?" The man in the dark green Park Service uniform shook Tanner's hand and smiled at Mary. "My partner is bringing the boat to the gas dock. We'll board her there and get you over to La Pointe right now."

The white and green runabout with the big outboard engine idled up to the gas dock and the three stepped aboard. Mary and Tanner donned bright orange flotation vests while the driver wheeled the boat about and set off for the harbor mouth. Once into the lake, she cranked up the engine until they were skimming across the cold water through rapidly thinning vestiges of the morning fog.

"What's your intention?" shouted the Park Service ranger over the roar of the big motor.

Tanner shrugged elaborately and leaned closer to the ranger. "I need to talk with Kemperer, learn what he knows. Maybe I can confirm what we suspect, that the man behind the financing of CRR is also responsible for these attempts on Mary's life."

"So, you think there's a plot to kill you and your wife?"

"Absolutely."

"If it turns out to be true, will it damage CRR?"

Tanner smiled inwardly. Was this ranger another CRR investor? He shook his head. "Not likely. In fact, the irony is, because my wife is now interested in the company as an investment possibility, the whole thing could turn out profitable for everyone."

The Park Service boat traversed the channel to the marina and smoothly tied up at the dock beside the club house.

A Bayfield County deputy sheriff was waiting for them. "I've just asked the marina people to check their transient boats for Kemperer."

"He may have registered under a false name," said Mary.

"True, but he won't have had time to change the name of his boat. We have a pretty good description. Are either of you familiar with his sloop?"

"No. We've never even seen it. You're here promptly."

"I live here on the island. I just happened to call in this morning. My shift doesn't start until four this afternoon. Our water patrol zodiac oughta be here soon."

Tanner, the deputy, and Mary Whitney, went into the office where the harbor master was leaning over the counter talking in low tones with the woman behind the desk.

He turned to the deputy and said, "We've eliminated all but four possibles."

"Eliminated, how?" said Tanner.

"Between us, Bobbie and I personally know everybody who has a boat here." He pointed at the chart of marina slips. These two are out on the lake now but have reserved spots for tonight. They've been here several days. This one," he pointed at a numbered rectangle on the chart, "is a forty-four Crealock." The owner singlehanded it here Thursday. He paid for five nights. He said he's repairing the name plate so there's no state license number or name on the hull. He said it was the Golly Gee."

"Isn't that a violation? Not to have the license number displayed?" Asked Mary.

"Yes, but if he has it readily available on board, they'll let him slide for a while." The harbormaster raised his bushy eyebrows in the deputy's direction. The young man nodded.

"Is that the yacht? The dark wooden-hulled sloop against the jetty?" asked Tanner. He'd walked to the large plate window that looked out on the quiet marina.

"Yessir," said the harbormaster.

"Well, there's somebody aboard her and it looks like he's getting ready to leave."

Two deputies just coming in from the jetty met them at the door as Tanner led Mary and the deputy in a rush out of the marina club office. They all ran down the dock toward the Crealock. In the aft cockpit they could see a dark figure bent over the wheel. There was a bang and a puff of smoke, then water spurted from a pipe low at the stern of the boat. The figure straightened and turned toward the sound of running feet. For a moment it looked as if he would go over the rail, then he reached down and killed the engine. His shoulders slumped and he raised both hand in a gesture of futility.

"Well, Mr. Tanner," said Richard Kemperer in a resigned voice. "You've anticipated my moves, I see. You might as well come aboard."

Two of the deputies retied the mooring lines while Tanner and Mary Whitney and the third deputy clambered over the lifelines and surrounded Kemperer.

"I was hoping to get away for a few days, just until things quieted down. I really don't believe I've done anything illegal."

"I think you better answer some questions first."

"Do I need a lawyer?"

Tanner looked at Kemperer. "I really don't know. You tell me."

Kemperer stared at Tanner, then the fight seemed to dissipate as he slumped down on the cockpit bench. "Ah, hell. Let me just try to explain the circumstances."

"That's a start."

"I had met Edwin Tobias years ago at some conference, or meeting or something, in New York. He's the kind of guy who keeps track of people he thinks might be useful to him."

"That's for sure," said Mary.

"The day that George met with Phoenix, I got a call from Tobias. So I knew, even before George got home, that Tobias was going to invest. Tobias knew I was in debt and he said George had agreed to placing someone on the CRR board. Someone Tobias would name."

"That's fairly common practice. Usually it would be a principal from Phoenix," Mary explained, "but ET doesn't like to fly and he doesn't ever leave New York if he can help it."

Kemperer agreed. "So he said he'd pay me a bonus on the side if I'd be his eyes and ears on the CRR board. That way he wouldn't have to come out here to the sticks, as he put it. I agreed. Apparently, whenever Anderson asked about the appointment, Tobias just put him off. It didn't matter much to George."

"How often did you pass inside information to Tobias?"

"I don't remember, but it can't have been more than a half dozen times. But then Tobias called and said he needed a gopher, somebody to run errands. He intimated that he wanted someone who wouldn't be too choosy about the things he was asked to do. I thought of Wally Zane, partly because he'd just been fired from CRR."

"Did you recruit this Zane?" asked a deputy.

Kemperer nodded. "Yes. I found him and talked to him. Told him that Tobias would call him. But I didn't tell Zane who Tobias was, or what the deal was. I didn't know what the deal was. A few days later, I ran into Zane on the street in Washburn. He told me he had this new job with 'my principal.' That's what Zane called him. 'My Principal.' He wanted to know who it was. What his name was. I wouldn't tell him. Then I asked Zane what the man wanted him to do. He wouldn't tell me. Just grinned and sauntered away. Said, I'm keeping an eye out." Kemperer waved one hand and sighed with frustration.

"I thought the whole thing was nuts. It was like a game of spies, everybody watching everybody else."

"You took Zane's comment to mean he was watching you?"

"Sure. Wouldn't you? Tobias had told me to keep an eye on Zane."

"Ah," said Tanner. "When was all this going on?"

"In the two weeks before you showed up. I got a call one night from New York. It was Tobias. He said he and George were arranging for a new PR firm to handle CRR's work. That you'd be flying in from Seattle any day."

"Did he name names?" asked a deputy.

"No, but he described you and Ms. Whitney. Said you were avid sailors and that Ms. Whitney was a real sexy lady and I'd enjoy getting next to her...and some other things."

"That son of a bitch!" Mary muttered behind Tanner.

"What do you know about McGregor's death?" Tanner shifted the subject.

"I was there. I saw Zane club him."

The deputies leaned forward, their gaze intent on Kemperer.

"Tell us what happened," said the older deputy.

"Tobias told me he was going to arrange a little trouble, as he put it, just to keep Tanner's interest up. He told me to get in contact with McGregor and arrange to let him into the factory. I did it anonymously. I called McGregor and told him I was a supporter and I worked at CRR. If he wanted to get into the plant, I'd leave a door open for him. I did that and I was supposed to just leave, but I hung around to see what was going on. Zane showed up first and hid somewhere on the factory floor. Then McGregor arrived and Zane killed him. God, I didn't know what to do.

"After Zane slugged McGregor, I slipped out. I didn't know McGregor was dead. I was just as surprised as everyone else when the fire occurred." He sighed and shook his head, looked down at his shoes.

"Mr. Kemperer. How'd you come to get involved in this way?"

Kemperer looked up at the deputy as if the answer was plain. "Why for the money, of course. Mr. Tobias was paying me a lot as his sub-rosa representative. And he'd promised me the presidency when he took over control.

Mary shook her head and said, "Boy does that sound familiar. I have to tell you it never would have happened. That's a favorite gambit I watched ET employ several times."

Kemperer opened his mouth to protest and then apparently thought better of it.

"What else?" pressed Tanner. "Was it your idea to sic that Wally Zane on us?"

"No. No. I had nothing to do with that. I don't know anything about that. Apparently Zane was talking directly to Tobias. You can't pin those attacks on me."

"We'll see what Zane has to say when we find him." Tanner turned away in disgust.

Chapter 31

"Kemperer seemed to give it all up pretty easily," said Mary as they walked up the hill toward their condo.

"A weak man, I guess. He wanted what appeared to be easy money and a shot at the top spot without working for it. He didn't bargain for the violence. I suspect after the fire and McGregor's murder he was almost looking for someone to confess to.

"You know, there are still a lot of loose ends to pick up." Tanner mused. "George has some responsibility here, Zane is still missing. We only have Kemperer's word he killed McGregor. Where's Tobias?"

"What's going to happen to George?" Mary sipped her coffee.

"I don't think he'll even be arrested. He's cooperating fully and he really didn't do anything wrong. He had no way of knowing Phoenix had a hidden agenda. I've agreed to take them on as a client, by the way."

"So, you'll be coming back here from time to time, then."

Tanner smiled at Mary. "Yes, and I suspect, because of your interest in your family history, you'll be joining me."

The couple went into their rented condo.

* * *

Mary looked up from the pages of the book. She had been reading it to Tanner who stood at the window looking out on a gray lake that surged restlessly beneath a gray bank of clouds.

"It must have frustrated the poor preacher, not being able to find Rylston," said Tanner. "I wonder is the Sheriff of Bayfield County has a file of old unsolved murders. Maybe he'll have to add poor Rylston to the list."

"You're using unsolved as in, no one brought to justice, right?"

"Yup."

"Poor Ted McGregor too, if Zane gets away. But I think we know what happened to Rylston."

"We do?"

"Yes—"

The telephone rang. Tanner picked it up.

Mary watched and listened but could detect little of the content. Tanner nodded, grunted a few assents and finally thanked the caller and hung up.

"Well, I guess that's that."

"That's what?"

"ET and his private jet are gone. They left Duluth late last night."

"Have they located Zane?"

Tanner looked thoughtful and then said, "Not exactly. They only have the boat he stole from Pike's Bay. It was out in the South Channel." Tanner pointed out the window. "Southeast of Madeline Island. Empty, just running in a big slow circle. The Coast Guard heard about it from a passing yacht. Said the gas tank was still a quarter full. It could have been out there ever since Zane left Pike's Bay. Probably was."

"And no sign of Zane?"

"None. He could have been picked up by somebody, but why leave the motorboat out there? Coast

Guard and the sheriff think he went over the side. Maybe he made a sudden maneuver to avoid another boat and nobody noticed. He couldn't have swum to shore, that's for sure." Tanner glanced down and then back at Mary. For a long moment they just looked into each other's eyes.

"I want to read you something." Mary turned out from under Tanner's arm and picked up *Tales of Lake Superior Country*. Think about the story I've been telling you about. There's a kind of epilogue in Reverend Ames own words, apparently."

* * *

"My own feelings are mixed. After much reflection and prayer I have come to one inescapable conclusion. It is most probable that the teamster, Jarl Rylston, did murder the unfortunate logger, Tompkins. The mysterious man called the Finn has no place in this sad tale. Jarl Rylston fled to Bayfield and somehow was able to persuade an acquaintance to ferry him to a passing log boom from whence he, Rylston, hoped to escape to Ashland. I know now he was never seen in that town. I do know that Tompkins brother was briefly in Bayfield at the time these incidents took place. It is my belief he followed Rylston to the log boom and there, murdered that desperate man in misplaced vengeance for the death of his brother, and the despoiling of his niece. Of Tompkins' brother, I know nothing more, but may God have mercy on all their souls."

* * *

"Mary closed the book and looked at Tanner.

"So, you think the skull the diver found is Jarl Rylston. Interesting. No proof, of course. And the lake did give it up, didn't it?" said Tanner.

"That's right, said Mary.

"I know you," Tanner said softly. "You believe Rylston's story is connected to this present business, don't you."

"Yes. Harvesting the timber on the bottom of the bay was the reason those divers found Rylston's skull and brought it up. There is something about this lake." Mary took Tanner's hand. "It's different from the ocean is so many ways. Experienced ocean sailors often get seasick on the lake. It sometimes makes its own weather. Did you know legend says Lake Superior doesn't give up its dead?"

"It gave up that skull, didn't it?" said Tanner, putting an arm around Mary's shoulder and drawing her to his side at the window.

"Yes it did and now there's probably another body in the lake not far from the first. It's a body also connected to CRR and the harvesting of that old timber, just like Rylston was. It has a kind of symmetry, doesn't it?"